eight goodbyes

Other Books By Christine Brae

The Light in the Wound
His Wounded Light
Insipid
In this Life

Forthcoming From Christine Brae

The Year I Left (Vesuvian Books, 2019)

eight goodbyes

CHRISTINE BRAE

Eight Goodbyes

ISBN: 978-1-944109-65-3

VESUVIAN BOOKS

Published by Vesuvian Books
www.vesuvianbooks.com

Printed in the United States

10 9 8 7 6 5 4 3 2 1

Dedicated to those who never got to say goodbye.
Because the living is left to them.

CB 2017

PART I:

When They Remember

the first goodbye

one

The only benefit of traveling a gazillion miles a year is the braided cord separating those with preferred airline status from the rest of the passengers.

The day she met him, Tessa was second in the priority lane for the Boeing 777 bound for La Guardia from Boston.

He was third.

After boarding the plane, Tessa found her place—7C—then hopped onto the aisle seat to place her bags in the storage space above. She quickly tucked her purse far into the corner to prevent it from being smashed by the larger carry-ons, completely unaware that she was holding up the line.

"I think this is me," said a man as he pointed his boarding pass toward her heavy black boots squashing the edge of his seat. It took her a few seconds to decipher his words. He had a heavy accent, certainly foreign. British, she decided. He had a distinct lilt to his tone.

"Oh! I am so sorry!" Tessa exclaimed, hopping off and backing into another passenger who had tried to squeeze past them. She shrugged and smiled in embarrassment before brushing her hand over his chair. She scampered across the middle seat and settled in next to the window. Before she could turn back to address the man, an elderly gentleman sat beside her with a glass of orange juice in one hand and a torn-up paperback in the other. Tessa couldn't help her curiosity; she wanted a better look at the man who sat by the aisle. He didn't fit the mold of the typical businessmen who normally took this midday flight. If only her view wasn't blocked by the man who separated them.

Without turning her head, she tried her best to assess him. Long, lean legs, slim jeans and those vintage Converse sneakers. Through the corner of her eye, she strained to see his face. He had just put on some reading glasses. She noted his sandy brown hair, side swept and thicker on top, dense eyebrows and prominent nose. It suited his face perfectly, that well-appointed nose. It was also the only thing she could see past the older man, who had now removed his shoes.

When the guy in 7A stood up to retrieve something from the overhead compartment, Tessa noticed some serious abs hiding under his shirt. "One, two, three, four," she counted in her head, disappointed when its folded edges fell back into place. She was sure there were six of them. The way he leaned back in his seat, his lean, lanky limbs, his form, his glasses, the way his fingers leafed through a pile of papers—he looked like an intellectual dressed as a cool dude.

Tessa was a writer. A keen observer of people, events and places. She was obsessed with stories, lived and breathed with a passionate imagination, always finding love in the daily trivialities of life. The characters in her books were a combination of the stories she made up about the people she met in real life, muddled with memories that turned themselves into fiction. Her inspirations started out as feelings and emotions. In time, they would blossom into words that seized control of her every waking moment.

She began to write on the back of her boarding pass.

Hot guy on the aisle seat meets girl on plane to where? Leaves key chain on seat. He searches for her everywhere. Write about that journey. Elderly gentleman. Mentor? Cupid?

God, he's cute.

The whirlwind of book signings and private fan functions left her constantly exhausted. This was all new to her, and the past year had been too hectic. New York was the last stop in this year's spring tour. *Smile, laugh, get your A-game on.* There was nothing more exhausting than sitting at a table, four hours a day, for three days straight. But the satisfaction of seeing her words come to life in the hearts and minds of complete strangers kept her going. There was nothing better than meeting new people from all walks of life and from every place in the world. People who shared your feelings and understood your messages, who ceased becoming strangers and turned into friends.

"You say you hate it, but you do it every single time," her best friend had said. Riley with the flowing black hair, shiny olive skin and the perfect collection of make-up. The same Riley who had the heart of Tessa's older brother Jacob wrapped around her finger.

"I know," Tessa had said while sitting on a bench outside the Soul Cycle on Wacker Drive just two weeks before. "My agent insists I do at least four this year. It's all so unexpected. I don't think we know how to deal with it yet."

"What? Hitting the bestseller list?"

Tessa had nodded. "I think she's in shock and wants to make sure I take full advantage of it. It wouldn't be so bad if I didn't have to sit through these things by myself. You know, it gets lonely sometimes, there's no one to share these interesting times with," Tessa hinted, winking.

"Hmm." Riley had cocked her head and placed her finger on her lips. "New York does sound inviting. I'll tell you what. I'll assist you at the signing if you let us extend for two more days to attend Fashion Week! I'm sure Gaby will be able to score us some tickets to the McQueen show."

And that's how this trip came to be.

The rest of the flight was uneventful. The older man coughed incessantly, and Tessa faced away. Soon, she fell into a deep sleep, periodically woken up by the bobbing of her head from side to side, threatening to fall into the old man's lap.

Tessa jolted upright when the plane skidded to a stop two hours later. She reached for her phone to turn it on. It began vibrating with message after message. Riley would be coming in from Los Angeles about two hours after her flight. Tessa could unpack her stuff at the hotel and walk around Manhattan, indulge in some street food and kill some time before Riley arrived. She was so busy checking her messages, oblivious to the loud ding and the subsequent unbuckling of seatbelts all around her. The young man in 7A shot up like an arrow facing in her direction. And for a brief second, she caught his gaze. He smiled at her, a lopsided kind of smile. Unsure. Maybe even embarrassed.

As the aisle began to fill, Tessa stood, leaned on the headrest and waited for the line to move. All this time, she felt him watching her, the heat of his stare causing her ears to burn. He made small talk with a woman who asked him what he was doing in NY. She overheard the word "convention" but the rest of it got drowned in the melody of his voice. She perked up her ears to listen, but it was soon lost amidst the hum of the other exchanges. She boldly watched as the interesting man unlatched the overhead bin, removed a black leather bag and placed it on his seat. And then to her surprise, he gently handed her bag over.

"Thank you." Tessa smiled as she reached for her burgundy purse.

"You're welcome," he answered. And then he was gone.

two

Simon ran out of the plane, confused and mad as hell. He should have made conversation, said something, asked for her number. He didn't even know what she was going to be doing in New York.

Talk about playing it cool. He had gone overboard and was kicking himself for it. It's not like he hadn't had plenty of opportunity. Back at O'Hare, he'd noticed her as soon as she got to the gate. Of course, extremely punctual as he was, he'd been sitting for a while, zoned out on Spotify and a copy of *Newsweek*. He'd heard her first—apologizing to strangers she had just whacked with a long cylindrical object slung across her shoulder. She sat right next to the counter, and there'd been a seat open right across from her. Slowly, he'd found his way to the open seat, smitten by her looks alone. When she hadn't been sipping on coffee or checking her phone, she'd had her nose buried in a book. Simon was on overload, his mind taking him places no one should visit in the middle of the day. She had on a pair of black leggings, an off-the-shoulder sweater and some bad motorcycle boots. Her eyes were shaped like almonds, lifted at the corners in a permanent smile. And her face. Every feature balanced in perfect harmony with one another. Her nose, her lips. That flawless skin.

At first, he thought she was a fashion model, but she didn't have that air about her. She seemed unsure of herself, self-conscious almost. She kept her head down, like she was always deep in thought. And then one… two… four… seven people approached her, and although she was gracious, the way she checked her watch every second gave her discomfort away.

Minutes before boarding was announced, she gathered her things and walked toward a sweet little woman standing in line at the far end of the gate. He watched them interact, saw them walking hand in hand towards the counter. The elderly lady beamed, her steps slow and deliberate as the woman patiently guided her through the throngs of waiting passengers.

Oops. Another casualty. The object hanging from her shoulder just took a man out, hitting him squarely on the forehead.

Simon followed her as she waited to board the plane. He was struck by the way she glided down the jetway, moving as if she were skating on ice. The strides of her tiny feet, the back of her head with the short and clean eye-catching hairstyle only women with perfect faces could carry. He acted on impulse. Maybe he'd been working too much lately, but her beauty bowled him over. Nice to know he wasn't immune to the allure of a pretty girl.

She stopped at row 7 and stepped on his seat, and he thought it was his lucky day.

When she lifted her bag, she took his breath away. He uttered the first thing on his mind and told her she had just planted her boots on his seat. And before he could salvage his blooper, they had a seat mate. An elderly man who couldn't wait to remove his shoes.

When she nodded off, he gave himself permission to look past the old man and admire her as she slept. It was a welcome departure from his other uneventful flights, especially since all this traveling had been getting to him. Same routine no matter what airline, no matter what airport. Same type of people, day in and day out.

She was different. Everything about her looked uncomplicated. Her face epitomized symmetry and refinement. Yet she was totally oblivious to it. She had melancholy in her eyes, subtlety in her movements. The designer purse, the red and green strip on the side of her boots, and the world-renowned stainless-steel watch she wore, showed her success. He couldn't quite figure it out—this tumultuous feeling brewing in his chest, the deep breaths he had to take to calm himself down. What he saw was a myriad of contradictions. Beautiful yet shy, accomplished yet unsure, friendly yet sad. While she slept, her hands remained tucked under her legs, so he couldn't see whether she already belonged to someone else.

Regardless, he knew they had to meet.

Earlier while sitting at the gate, he had wanted to know what she was reading, whose message she was waiting for, and that frothy bubble on her top lip—was that a cappuccino she was drinking?

Functional.

If someone asked him, that would be how he'd describe the ugly, ungainly hallways of La Guardia, surely one of the dingiest airports in the Western world. But he did appreciate how it took five minutes flat to get from the gate to baggage claim. Normally, he made a quick stop at Auntie Anne's to pick up a pretzel dog, despite his doctor's warnings against consuming processed meats. Instead, he ran down the escalator, two steps at a time.

Baggage claim, if she even had any luggage, would be his last opportunity to meet her. But his brother waved furiously at him from the end of carousel 10.

"Hey bro!" Adrian walked over as Simon stood at the very end of the baggage ramp. "We pretty much landed at the same time."

The two men clasped hands and pulled each other into a loose embrace. Simon was happy to have his brother fly all the way from Essex to support him at the event he was to be speaking at, although he was a little bit distracted at the moment.

"My flight was delayed for two hours!"

"Oh? That's too bad," Simon said. He was too busy scanning the area, waiting for the brown-haired girl to stand in line for her luggage. His suitcase rolled toward him on the conveyor belt. He made no move to pick it up.

In the middle of an approaching group of passengers, he spotted the elderly gentleman who'd sat next to him. He wondered how she was doing with that ridiculous tube swiping every living thing in its way. Damn, he could have offered to help her with it, maybe even shared a cab with her. But who shared cabs these days?

"How long are you staying? I took an extra day to tour the city, you know. Empire State and all."

When Simon turned to respond, there she was, appearing out of nowhere, her shoulders slightly hunched under the weight of the long pole she had slung across her body.

He saw the surprise in Adrian's face when he walked away to slide up next to her.

"Hi," Simon said, resembling a giddy schoolboy but feeling every bit like a man on a quest. He fully realized how idiotic he must look. Why did this have to be a whole production? It's not like he hadn't done this before. It'd been a while, he got that. But this time—the adrenaline rush, the total blackout—felt like nothing he'd ever experienced. The sounds around the normally bustling airport faded—it was the two of them and nothing else.

Surely, he must have pursued Maxine in some sort of way. Well, on second thought, maybe he hadn't. They'd met at a convention, seen each other when they returned home to Boston, and things just fell into place.

He scratched his chin a few times, and then pulled on his ear.

"Hi," she said, her gaze fixed on the moving beltway.

"Have you checked your purse yet?" Simon asked.

Her head snapped toward him and she clutched her purse tight against her body. "Excuse me?" Her brown eyes glinted gold under the fluorescent lights.

She had misunderstood his question. He scrambled for a way to explain so she wouldn't think he was some sort of weird stalker.

She glanced at the conveyor and took a step closer grabbing a mid-sized black Samsonite with a bright-red name tag from the belt and setting it on the ground.

Simon couldn't make the name out for shit.

"Your purse." He tried to put on an American accent, afraid of being misunderstood. A twang here, a twang there. Although careful not to overdo it.

"Sorry, I have to get going," she said as she pulled out the suitcase's handle and transferred the long black pole to her shoulder. She started for the exit but halted after a few steps and turned to him. "Thanks again," she said, this time with a warm smile and a wave.

He saw hope in her smile.

Feeling like he had flopped in front of his brother, Simon tried to mask his blunder by pushing his shoulders way too far back and adopting a swagger. He didn't really know what all that effort was for, this desperate attempt to get her attention. A number, perhaps? A sign of interest? Clearly none of those had materialized.

"What was that about?" Adrian asked.

"A girl I met on the plane. Just wanted to ask if she needed any help with her luggage."

Adrian shot him a look that said he wasn't buying it. "Simon Fremont making a pass at a woman—I never thought I'd live to see this day," he teased. "You finally looked up from those science journals in time to notice a chick?"

Simon pulled his luggage out from underneath Adrian's nose. They were the last ones there, his bag just about to make another round of the airport. He wondered why he was so jittery. It was merely one encounter. A failed one, that is. He had much more important things to think about on this trip.

Like the speech he was going to be giving in a few hours. Or how about the news he just received about his wellbeing.

"Shut up and grab your bag. The hotel shuttle leaves in five minutes."

three

She wondered why the guy at the airport had asked her to check her purse. Not that she was alarmed or anything. After all, she was still trying to get used to the spotlight, strangers coming up to her, giving her letters and gifts. It was a day in the life, sadly. Mostly impersonal, but oddly comforting at times. To know she was making a difference with her words soothed her.

She laughed when a silly thought crossed her mind. Was he trying to get an autograph for his mom or something?

While standing in the taxi line, she was preoccupied with listening to phone messages and forgot all about meeting the stranger.

Attempting to simplify her life, Tessa dated casually. It was a conscious decision, made to ensure she never tied herself down to one place. She often wondered about this, and asked Riley why settling down never appealed to her. Riley always told her it was because love hadn't found her quite yet.

After checking into the hotel, Tessa headed up 53rd street to 5th Avenue where she shopped at Saks Fifth for well over an hour. She walked back to the hotel thirty minutes after Riley texted that she had landed. Tessa was busily searching through her shopping bags when light footsteps on the carpet floor outside her door announced Riley's arrival.

"Hey!" Riley shrieked as Tessa held the door open. In she traipsed, her makeup bag bigger than her luggage. Riley dropped them both on the ground and ran into Tessa's open arms. After giving Tessa a tight hug, she skipped toward the bed by the window.

"Sorry, all they had was a king."

"No biggie," Riley answered, climbing under the covers, coats, shoes and all. "You look great! Did you get your hair cut again?"

"Rye, what are you doing?"

"Ahh." She exhaled loudly, burrowing her head deeper and deeper in between the pillows. "Give me a second. It's the Heavenly Bed."

"Yup. New haircut." An awkward silence briefly followed. They both knew that Tessa's haircuts were controlled by her emotions. Whenever she felt stagnant, whenever she wanted a change, Tessa took it out on her hair.

"It's beautiful!" Riley said. "Short hair suits you so well. You've got that rare face that can do any hair. I'm more worried about why you did it. This book thing. Too much?"

"I was just bored the other day and needed a new look." Tessa climbed over the mound of bags strewn on the ground. She searched through the piles until she found the package that held her new purse.

Riley sighed loudly. "Bored already, huh."

Tessa nodded. Riley knew how she was. There was no point in arguing. They'd been friends since high school, had their share of adventures and misadventures in college. Until her brother Jacob began seeing her friend in a different light. Riley and Jacob had been a couple for the last two years.

Tessa untied the intricately wound ribbon around the silver box that held her new purse. "Look!" She pointed excitedly. "I think I'll wear it tonight." She held her new purse in the air.

"Gorge."

"Where are we going?"

"What about The Standard?" Riley kicked her shoes off the bed but remained buried under the comforter. "Hi-line Fling?" she asked.

It would be good to have a night out. They'd both been in this city often enough to know their way around.

"Sure," she answered without looking up. Tessa turned the bag upside down and watched as each item fell on the bed. She gathered them with one hand and placed them into the new purse.

Riley busily eyed the room service menu. Tessa didn't know how Riley stayed so lean and fit when all she did was eat.

She raised her head as Tessa sprang off the bed. "You forgot something," she said, pointing at an object that fluttered to the floor.

"Oh, the receipt," Tessa guessed, bending down to pick it up.

It wasn't the receipt. Tessa giggled.

"What?" Riley asked.

"He must have slipped it in when he took it down for me on the plane," Tessa mused, holding up a business card. "He asked me to check my purse when I saw him at baggage claim."

> Simon Fremont, Research and Development
> Nanoproducts Licensing
> Gladtech Corporation

Riley whooped. "Oh lord. Seriously? Some guy hit on you on the plane?"

"No, it wasn't like that. He helped me with my bags. We hardly said a word to each other." Tessa sat on the bed next to Riley. She slowly reclined and slid her legs under the covers.

"What a weirdo. Slipping his card in your purse." Riley moved over to give Tessa some room. "Looks like a nerd. A pretty desperate nerd."

"He didn't look like a nerd. He was cute. Had an accent. Definitely not from here." Now it was Tessa's turn to bask in the softness of the mattress. "You're right about this bed. It's making me want to take a nap. Would you mind if I took one? I'm still so exhausted from the signing in Boston."

Riley turned to face her just as she yawned. "Who'd he look like? Describe."

"Stu."

"Stu who?"

"The British model. The guy I showed you months ago, the one on every teaser and book cover on Facebook."

"Another one of your book boyfriends? He must not be too hot if I don't remember him."

"No one but Jake looks hot to you," Tessa teased.

"Well then, look how lucky you are! You look just like your

brother," Riley shot back, laughing. "Same hair color, same eyes. Except his hair is a wee bit longer than yours!"

"Funny," Tessa answered.

Riley and Jacob had the picture-perfect kind of love. The kind that Tessa couldn't even write about because it was so simple and straight forward. He and Tessa came from an unconventional family, and Riley had all the love and support she would ever need. Riley had waited patiently while he drifted in and out of his rebellious years. And when he decided he'd had enough, he straightened up, went to med school, scooped her up and never let go. She was his family now, and he held on to her like he had finally found his home.

Tessa and her brother had been orphaned at an early age, shuttled to and from uncles and aunts and cousins and grandparents. They lived in different houses, changed schools at least every two years. They had love, but it came and went with the tide. Relatives, friends, family members—it was like a game of hot potato. Whose turn, which house and for how long?

"Don't hold your breath for this one. I'm not calling him."

"You complain about being alone, yet you can have your pick of almost anyone," Riley objected. "And all the guys you go out with— you leave them just as they're beginning to grow on me—"

"I'm still trying to figure myself out," Tessa said with a yawn. "And we've talked about this so many times! I'm just starting out and can't be tied down. These guys, they need a wife, someone to start having babies with, which definitely isn't me."

Riley poked her shoulder as Tessa turned to face away, pulling the comforter up to her chin. "You can't be Wonder Woman forever. At some point, she gets Steve Trevor to sweep her off her feet."

"Nonsense. Now, leave me to my nap so I can get back some energy for our night on the town!"

four

Simon surveyed the mass of people in the large glass enclosed ballroom. He scanned the thirty tables of ten, desperate to find a familiar face. Adrian was seated toward the front, next to strangers in ill-fitted suits and oversized name badges. There were other people around him—men and women who were here more for the fancy buffet than anything else. He never seemed to find comfort in such venues; crowds bothered him, and useless chatter annoyed him. But it was part and parcel of who he was and the career path that he had chosen.

Simon was an academe, a mentor and a trainer. All the years of schooling, of research and learning made him an expert in his field. With the most recent economic recession and the unpredicted upswing of the pharmaceuticals market, everyone was interested in what Simon had to say. But Simon had no interest whatsoever in what people had to say to him. A few months after he had been awarded for his discovery, many of his older colleagues began distancing themselves. Some had hinted that his status as a young, ambitious upstart, a millennial with charismatic good looks to boot, and not his intellectual capabilities were responsible for this recognition. He was determined to prove them all wrong. If it took a lifetime, he wanted nothing more than to show them he had substance.

He gazed through the glass doors that led to the hotel lobby. People bustled around and about, different types of people. Just off the side entrance, women holding books pushed carts filled with cardboard boxes and shuttled back and forth to the elevators. There must have been numerous conventions going on at the same time in this hotel.

Glancing at his watch, he noted that the session was about to start in fifteen minutes. There was time to walk around the lobby, ease the nerves that plagued him before every public event. As he walked out of the ballroom, he noticed a commotion in the far corner of the corridor. There were shrieks and screams as a long line began to form. Simon moved along with the line, curiously looking over people's heads to see who was waiting for them at the end of the thread. And, as luck would have it, there she was. A genuine smile pasted on her lovely face, the corners of her eyes lifting as high as the ends of her mouth. She moved her head slowly as she listened intently to a group of women vying for her attention. He angled for a better view, gently pushing through a couple and their three children, who stood surrounded by carts and boxes in the middle of the floor. Simon watched as she began to take the books handed to her and proceeded to sign them. She shared a level of intimacy with these strangers—a touch, an embrace, holding them close as they exchanged laughs and posed for pictures.

Who was she? Was she famous?

Once again, time wasn't on his side. Simon had to take a piss before delivering that dreaded speech. He turned around and headed in the other direction.

Simon made it back to the lobby in two minutes.

"So, you really think I would have called you?"

Simon heard the sweetest sound in the whole world. He snapped his head back; she must have found his card. Time stood still. He forgot where he was and what he was there to do.

"No, not really," Simon answered. It was then he noticed that she had two rings on each hand, none of them on the finger that mattered.

She laughed. He could have sworn there were flecks of sunlight in her eyes.

"Then why..." She pulled his card out of her purse. "The card?"

"Desperate times call for desperate measures." A light chiming of a bell signified the start of the session.

"Oh no. That's my curtain call. I have to run."

She nodded and began to glide away. Her posture statuesque, juxtaposed by her torn up jeans and a sexy cropped sweater. How did she manage to look so poised in those high, high heels?

There's a term for those kinds of heels.

Simon exerted great effort to pull his mind out of the gutter.

"Wait!" Simon yelled, a bit too loudly. "What's your name?"

"Tessa. Tessa Talman," she yelled back, while taking even strides away from him.

"Tessa Talman!" Simon cried. "Meet me tomorrow at 10 a.m. Hayden Planetarium!"

The lecture lasted longer than expected. There ensued a lively discussion with many questions and comments. The reception dragged on like there was no end in sight. Simon and Adrian booted it to the bar as soon as they had the chance to escape.

An Irish Pub called Three Brothers situated right across from the hotel was the closest bar they could find. March Madness and a few beers were all they had on the agenda. It was a jewel of a dive in the middle of 54th Street, loud music, TV screens and a solid oak bar that extended from one end of the room to the other. They sat facing the bartender and were surrounded by women who just happened to be there.

"No way, you're not brothers!" exclaimed the woman with dark hair holding a shot of tequila.

"Way," Adrian answered smugly.

"You have the same hair color, but your eyes," she said.

"Our mum always said his eyes were like the sea and the sky," Adrian answered.

"And his were like the rich earth and the barks of trees!" Simon added with a laugh.

As if reminded by something, Simon saw a shift in his brother's facial expression. He turned to face away from the women and looked directly at him.

"Hey, before anything else, Mum wants to know if you're okay."

"I'm fine. It's not like I haven't known all my life," Simon answered, saddened by the worry in Adrian's face. "I just have to hurry things up a bit. I only have one year before I turn thirty after all."

"Oh, I think you're going fast enough," Adrian said, eyes wide, tone reprimanding.

"I'm extremely annoyed by the fact that I'm wasting all this time traveling when I can be working to get closer to my goal. I know I keep repeating myself, but..."

Adrian shrugged. "The company has asked for another year, right?"

"Yeah, and it's getting old. I signed up to discover things, foster imaginative thinking and new theories, not travel the world and give speeches," he complained. "There are days when I ask myself whether this is all worth it."

Adrian sighed.

Simon sensed his brother's exasperation with his "thirty years old" obsession. Ever since secondary school, he'd mapped out a plan, let his family know what he planned to accomplish before turning thirty. And to everyone else, he'd done just that. Simon had been promoted three times in the last three years. For someone who'd chosen a career that was systematic and predictable, he was uncharacteristically restless. His career was on the upswing—a young trailblazer who had a patent pending on a groundbreaking invention. And yet, he was always in a hurry. Like he had a limited amount of time and limitless untapped opportunities.

"Actually, you should be embracing this new life of yours! Look at yourself, man. The only one in the family who has left Essex, widening your horizons and seeing the world!"

Adrian was getting his goat. Simon just wanted to get back to his apartment in Chelmsford—some peace and quiet was what he really needed. Life had been going full speed lately.

And no, Simon wasn't getting engaged anytime soon. Sure, he went out on dates, had started seeing a woman named Maxine quite regularly. But he wasn't ready to settle down. Thank god Adrian had fulfilled his parents' longing for a grandchild.

He'd been in love once, during his brief internship at a firm in New Zealand. But like all young relationships, it had ended once he returned to Europe. He'd begged her to come home with him, willing to marry her right there and then, but she'd refused to leave her family and her life. It had hurt immensely—the fact that she professed to love him despite her refusal to move home with him. When you love someone, isn't it an all or nothing deal? He had been willing to take the all; why had she been willing to risk the nothing?

After that, he seemed to float in and out of relationships in slow motion. There was never a shortage of women in his life, only an abundance of caution and cynicism.

His parents had been married for over thirty-three years and Simon, being the youngest at twenty-nine, was used to permanence and stability. While he pursued his career with great flexibility, he demanded everything else in his life to stay static.

"My world"—Simon made an air quote with an exaggerated twitch of his fingers—"is staying in one place, thank you very much."

He stared into his glass of Old Fashioned, stirring the plastic sword around and around, stabbing the ice. "Turns out that woman is well known for something. She has fans, like legit fans," he said.

"Which woman?"

"The one at the airport. I saw her again here at the hotel. Tessa Talman."

"Dude, Tessa Talman? That was her at the airport? I thought Tessa Talman was an old chunk who only did radio appearances!" Adrian exclaimed.

Simon looked at him with his eyes crossed. The unmanly shriek that had escaped Adrian's lips somewhat freaked him out.

"Why? Is she a huge deal?"

"Dude, are you blind? Did you not notice how hot she was?"

"I know that, you duffer. Why is she a huge deal, is what I meant!" Simon laughed.

"Apparently, she's some sort of a breakout author. Ashleigh's mom was talking about her once—they're nuts about her. They're making plans to see her at some book signing event."

It was then that Simon decided this girl might not be someone he wanted to get to know after all. Being in all that limelight and shit. He just wasn't into those things. Besides, he should be focusing on looking for a new job, one that wouldn't have him traveling as much.

"I kind of invited her to meet me tomorrow morning," he admitted.

"What time?"

"10 a.m. at the planetarium."

Adrian laughed. "As if she would take you seriously. Besides, we're going to close down this joint, so you won't be up until tomorrow afternoon. I bet it's no biggie that you don't show up. Drink up, man! I never get to just hang with my bro! First time in months I don't have to worry about Ash and the baby!"

five

"Note to self. Get rid of this old piece of junk!"

Tessa shook her wrist in the direction of an imaginary satellite, hoping that her watch would track her speed a little bit better. She had looped around Central Park for more than four miles, but the numbers on the screen were flashing on and off and she had no idea where she was.

She should really stop skimping on things like this. Running was a part of her life and a new watch would be put to good use. It was way past her normal running hour—in fact, it was almost 11 a.m. She had yet to see Riley, who left her at the Standard with an old friend for more drinks the night before. Martin was a TV producer and sometimes friend-with-benefits who always had a suite at the Dream.

She'd drank a little too much, stayed a little too long and now, this late in the morning, she was paying for it. Good thing her event was hours away. She had enough time to get her exercise in and try for a quick nap to sober up.

Tessa ran sluggishly along the path on West Drive, feet pounding on the dried-up leaves and shredding them into pieces. As she glanced up toward the Museum of Natural History, a thought jolted her out of her zone. *Oh shit.* She spotted the man from the plane flying down the narrow steps to catch up with her. She gasped, remembering his invitation from the night before.

He looked frazzled, his facial hair grown out more than she'd originally noticed. He wore a red and black plaid shirt untucked and creased up at the ends. He had a full smile this time, perfect teeth flashing in the light. She couldn't help but smile back.

Tessa kept up her normal pace, holding one hand up to shield her eyes from the sun as he approached. Had he really thought she was going to accept his invitation and show up that morning?

"Hi," he said, hands in pockets.

She slowed to a halt, gazed into his deep blue eyes and thought of Santorini. Her mom and dad had met in Santorini, and she really wanted to go there someday.

"Hey." She untied the jacket that was wrapped around her waist and slipped her arms into it. "Did you—"

"Nah," Simon piped in before she could finish. "I knew you wouldn't show up."

"Then what were you doing there?" she prodded.

"I needed the exercise," he answered. "Right now, I'm on a restricted health regimen and walking is good for me."

"Oh?" she asked. They started toward the museum.

"I was born with a hole in my heart."

"Oh," she said again, not sure whether he meant it literally.

"It's not that bad, really. Most of the time, I can lead a normal life. Occasionally, I go overboard, and it gets cheesed off at me."

"Define *overboard*," she quizzed, intrigued.

"I ran a marathon a month ago, and it wasn't too happy about that." He nodded toward the museum steps. "Do you have time to wander around?"

She heard the tension in his voice. He wasn't like the overconfident schmucks she'd been dealing with lately. And so she decided she wasn't in any hurry. She could use the company. Kill some time before she had to meet more people.

There was something about him that felt familiar. Riley always teased her about falling in love with everyone she met. It wasn't that, really. It was more about a sad, lifelong search for connections. She seemed to have so much trouble in that department. She'd been tired of playing third wheel to Rye and Jacob lately, and she didn't really have many friends.

Clarification: she had many acquaintances. *Followers* might have been a better definition. And that was all they were.

"It's too nice out to be inside a museum," she countered. "I'm dying for a Starbucks. I think there's one on Columbus not far from here. Wanna take a walk?"

"Sure!" he answered a little too eagerly.

Tessa led the way. She knew exactly where to go; the winding sidewalk that led to the main road. They walked in silence, her thoughts overtaken with questions she wasn't willing to ask just yet. The silence between them was masked by the sounds of traffic and sirens and blaring street music.

Tessa turned onto a concrete pathway that led to the Starbucks she had in mind. Simon followed, pausing to allow her to steer clear of the revolving door before pushing his way through. He swiped his phone at the counter even before she could place her order. So, he was one of those vanishing gallant, chivalrous males, and she liked it. The romance book world was full of those types; unfortunately, the real world wasn't.

With coffee in hand, Tessa pointed to a set of wooden benches across the street from the Museum of Modern Art. They sat surrounded by a group of Japanese tourists waving a selfie stick and posing for pictures with lips pursed, fingers up in peace signs.

They sipped their drinks in silence until Tessa's phone began to ding.

"Sorry," she said, pulling it out and switching it to silent. "They just don't stop coming."

"Messages?"

"Messages. Facebook comments. Tweets."

"I'm not on Facebook," Simon declared. "The more my mom tells me to get on it, the more I resist. More of a rebellion, really."

"No way!" Tessa exclaimed. "Don't you feel disconnected? How do you communicate with the world?"

Simon spread his arms, gesturing at the Japanese tourists and the street behind them. "Just like this," he said. "In real time."

She rolled her eyes. "Real time is just that. Social media allows you to live in someone else's head. To walk in someone else's shoes."

"By reliving their perfect lives as evidenced by their perfect pictures?"

She frowned. "Shut up and change the subject."

"Okay," he laughed. "I take it you're here for a book signing of some sort?" He glanced at pigeons encircling their feet.

Tessa cringed and drew her foot back. "I don't like birds." She stomped her foot, but they didn't care. They smelled her fear. "My new book just came out. I'm doing a press tour."

"Ah. And all that beeping on your phone has to do with what?"

Tessa looked at him skeptically. "Are you sure you want to know?" she asked.

Simon gave her a rakish grin. "Educate me."

She wasn't going to lie. That sounded extremely saucy. And how his eyes drilled into hers when he said it, charming and immoral at the same time. This guy didn't know that her mind could turn the most innocent of words into unscrupulous suggestions.

Tessa slipped her phone out and angled it so he could see the screen. "See here?" she said. A picture of her running shoes against the pavement brought 7k likes. "I posted my run on Instagram. People are commenting."

"Ah. I don't really understand how Instagram works."

His ignorance sounded sincere.

"Seriously?" she laughed. She swiped through posts from the past, explaining how the app worked.

"My agent, Revete, advises me to upload at least one picture a day," she said. "Most book lovers use social media as their daily platform, so it's a great way to connect with my readers. People expect it. Personalities these days need to make themselves more accessible." She paused to allow him to comment. He said nothing. "In fact, I pay someone to post for me, in addition to what I generate myself. It's that important as a marketing tool—hashtags, endorsements and followers."

"What do you keep to yourself then, if you're all out for people to see?" he asked.

"A lot," she said, her tone clipped. Pictures don't show what's in one's heart. Pictures don't show the depth, the breadth, the magnitude of your feelings. "I give them what they like to see. But there's a lot more to me than that, buddy." She stabbed one finger to his chest.

"Ouch."

Meanwhile, the birds at their feet had multiplied. Tessa stood up abruptly.

Simon led her away from the wooden benches and toward the sidewalk. "There's a place to sit over at MOMA," he said. "It's indoors."

She was glad he wanted to extend their time together. "In my defense, they've been known to eat people, you know."

He turned to her and replied with a slow, articulate drawl. "And that's why I'm here to save you. From those vicious, flesh-eating pigeons."

When they laughed at the same time, Simon reached out and gently grasped her fingers.

Tessa let him lead her, aware of his touch. She had a good feeling about the rest of her day.

six

He'd lied. He had stationed himself at the planetarium behind the Museum of Natural History, at 10 a.m. in the hopes of seeing her. Not that he'd expected her to show. On the contrary, he'd agreed with Adrian's contention that she didn't seem like the type that needed invitations to a meet up from strangers.

"Nothing is ever coincidence," Simon's father always told him. Feelings, actions, even situations. They all happen for a reason. And how crazy was that? She was there! The flight, the hotel and now this. He wanted time to slow down, hoping that she would give up whatever day she had planned for him.

What a wuss.

His pragmatism just flew out the door. He didn't want to overthink things just yet. He wanted to do something so unlike him—go with the flow. That day, he was going to do just that.

Although, he still wasn't on board with her reasoning about social media. Simon never understood how all that worked, often wondered why people felt the need to share their lives with the world. Especially because there wasn't anything particularly interesting about an uber nerd who loved chemistry. And physics. They seemed like light years apart in personality, but because of that and because he knew nothing about her world, she intrigued him.

25

They rode up the elevator, standing stiffly side by side, and flanked by a group of teenagers who were posing for pictures and yelling at the same time. There was barely room for two at a table close to the window.

Tessa glanced around MOMA's Café 2, taking in the view as if it was the most exotic place in the world.

"I just love being in New York," she said. "It's so alive, bustling with activity."

She took a sip of her coffee while admiring the communal typesetting with long wooden tables facing a large clear view of cherry blossoms bursting into bloom.

"The packs of people are a bit overwhelming," he countered. "I like peace and quiet most of the time."

"Ah," she laughed. "I can only write when there's activity around me. I can't stand quiet."

"I would've thought that writers enjoy solitude," he answered.

"To a certain extent. But writers need stories, and the people around you, all have a story to tell. You can see it in their movements, read it in their faces, imagine it through their actions."

As she spoke, she raised her hand, faltering in a half-wave, smiling and nodding to a young lady in the corner of the restaurant who had covertly lifted her phone in the air.

"Is that lady taking our picture?" he said.

Tessa shrugged. "I'm trying to get used to it."

Simon saw her shift in focus, her head turned to the side, eyes fixed on a group of people. "But you, you don't need this," she said. "I'd understand if it totally makes you uncomfortable."

He didn't disagree. It wasn't the discomfort, per se. He just wanted her full attention. And he knew he didn't have much time.

"Listen. I've got one hour before I have to do a meet and greet. Plug your number into my phone. I'll walk out first and text you where to go."

She handed him her phone, and he typed his name and number into her contacts list. He sucked in a breath before congratulating himself for winning the lottery.

She stood and walked down the aisle and out into the main hallway.

Simon felt slightly stunned. It happened too quickly. What if she decided to ditch him? Then his phone vibrated. It was a text from a number he didn't recognize, and he still didn't trust it until he read her message:

Second floor, art exhibition sign, veer to the left and find the farthest corner of the room to the right.

He found her sitting against a sea of white, pristine, colorless walls. Eight large concrete blocks were piled on top of each other in the middle of the room. There was no one there.

"Richard Serra," she said, pointing at the blocks in front of them. "He believes that the virtual age has taken away our ability to feel our physical presence in relation to objects. That actually being here, feeling, seeing and touching is crucial to the way one understands art."

"Interesting analogy," he answered, as he sat next to her.

"Do you believe it?" she asked.

"Well, in the scientific field, that's all we know."

"What exactly do you do…" She glanced down at the screen of her phone where, Simon assumed, his contact info was still displayed. She giggled when she saw what he had typed in. When she stretched her legs out in front of her, he noticed a tiny tattoo of a seahorse nestled above her ankle.

Simon didn't care for body art. And yet, there was something enticing about the way this one called attention to her smooth, silky skin.

"Nanotechnology. I'm in R&D."

She blinked once, twice. Looked away, disinterested. "Yeah, that's what your business card says, but what does that mean exactly?"

He paused for a moment. He rarely was asked to explain his profession in layman's terms. Nor did he particularly have the desire to do so. But that day, perhaps not surprisingly, he wanted to.

"I have a doctorate in molecular biology. For practical purposes, I'm in research and development for pharmaceuticals."

She gave him a blank look. He tried again.

"Nanotechnology is the science of working with atoms and molecules to build devices that are very small or create substances that are used in medication. We use those tiny devices to manipulate materials in equipment and in medicine."

"And you were in New York to give a lecture? You must be pretty

27

important. What'd you do, discover the cure for cancer or something?" she teased.

Little did she know that he kind of had. He decided to tell her. He had no intention of making this their last time together.

"Well," he said quietly, "as a matter of fact, I was lucky enough to discover a way to polymerize cancer beating drugs into nanoparticles—" He stopped, worried that he would overwhelm her.

"Go on."

"Nanoparticles that are not water soluble so that they retain their effect when they enter the bloodstream." He gauged her reaction. He found it cute that she scrunched her brows when she processed her thoughts. "I discovered a way to break drugs into nanoparticles that can reach their target more effectively."

"As in chemo? Like IV drugs?"

"Very good, Ms. Talman. You got it!" Seriously. Not many non-academics were this quick to understand.

She nodded and smiled. "Ah. You're some kind of a hero, Mr. Fremont. Impressive."

Enough about him. He wanted to suck up the air she occupied, immerse himself in who she was and why she had such an impact on him. "And you, Tessa Talman. What do you do, exactly?"

"Definitely nothing as interesting as you."

"Where are you from? Do you write full time?"

"Chicago. And, yes."

"Family? Originally from there?"

"Extended family. And a brother. My parents died when I was very young."

"I'm sorry to hear that." Simon had a sudden appreciation for the large, crazy family he had back in England.

As they continued their conversation, he couldn't keep his eyes away from her face. She smiled, and he noticed a tiny nick above her left cheek. He wanted to brush his finger against it, feel the dent that marred her porcelain skin. When her face crumpled, he realized he had stopped listening to the words, letting the melody of her voice wash over him while he watched her every movement. He made an effort to listen to her words, but when she waved her delicate hands through the air, he was lost again.

Her dark hair against the white walls and her tiny frame made him think of an angel sitting among the clouds. She radiated like a light in the dimly lit room.

She asked about his family and his work, pressed him to tell her about his latest project.

"If I tell you, I'd have to kill you," he teased. "I'm working on a government project at the moment. The convention I'm attending has the FBI and Homeland Security suits interested in what my company can offer."

"It seems like we operate on the opposite ends of a spectrum. I delve into feelings and emotions, while you live among the tangible and tactical," she declared.

"You could say that, I guess. But as you said, we do it all for betterment. For progress, for convenience, to reach out to people who need it."

"I don't know," she said, sitting up and glancing around the empty room before leaning back against the wall. "It's intriguing. This super-duper secret agent stuff. But don't go all out on my account. I'll stop being so nosy if you can't really tell me."

When she smiled, and the tip of her mouth curved upward, a tiny dimple formed on her right cheek.

Jesus. It must have been the lighting. He wasn't this observant, normally.

"Well, to be honest, that's something I work very hard to do. But not today." He smiled. "Besides, I'm trying to make you like me, so if it makes me look cool, well then…"

She laughed. Their eyes met. And then she glanced at her watch and let out a heavy sigh.

"I have to go. My friend Riley has probably called a search party on me." She laughed. "I haven't seen her since last night."

"Oh?" he asked. "And where were you last night, Ms. Talman?"

"Just out with my friend, Martin." She pushed up off the floor. "I enjoyed talking to you," she said, her tone flat and formal.

"Can I see you again?" he asked, hands in pockets, feeling quite nervous yet bold. "Maybe after tonight's event?"

"No, no," she promptly answered. "My friend and I have plans tonight, and then we head to the airport first thing in the morning."

He didn't blame her. He wondered what she was thinking. One hour. That's all the time he'd spent with her. One hour, and yet he knew that his life had been forever changed. Never in his life had he been this desperate to maintain contact with a stranger. There was time to figure out later why he was acting so out of character. Right there and then, he just had to buy more time.

She reached out to shake his hand. "It was nice to meet you, Simon."

"No, wait," he exclaimed, clasping her hand at the same time. "If not tonight, another time?"

She withdrew her hand and turned around. "Maybe!" she teased, starting to walk away.

He followed her. "How?"

They left the empty room and walked right into a group of tourists, who weaved in between, separating them.

"Get on Twitter. Or WhatsApp!" she yelled.

"What what?" he yelled back, confused.

"It's an app called WhatsApp. Install it. You have my number now, Simon. Technology. Use it to find me!" And then she disappeared into the crowd.

seven

There were times Tessa thought of the man she'd met in New York three months ago. There were even times when she was excited about messaging him back. At first, his notes had come sporadically. Most often, they were single sentences as if he wanted to keep reminding her that he existed.

It took a week after the trip to New York for him to send her a message on WhatsApp.

Downloaded! He'd followed his message with a smiley face. He asked her how to use it, told her that he'd also set up a Twitter account. It amused her to see an imageless egg with no followers. She congratulated him when his followers increased to three. And his name—Disconnected. How apt, his humor aimed at poking fun at himself.

Riley called him "the creeper." Tessa argued that he probably just needed some excitement in his life. Besides, Simon was grounded, worked at a place that gave him stability, a stark contrast to what her life had become.

Over the weeks that followed she began to receive a message from him every Thursday, and from the same location—Boston—where he was fulfilling his subcontract with the government, though he warned her that he'd soon be headed back to his home in Essex, England. They

31

mastered an easy banter. Nothing too deep, superficial conversation that was the basis of every new friendship.

Where are you?

At the lab.

Again?

That's my job.

How are those nanoparticles doing? Are they on to you yet? I'm bored and one of my fans just squeezed my butt.

Lucky.

Tessa's life was exploding at that very same time during those three months. She'd moved into a bigger apartment, obsessed about getting a dog but decided against it shortly after. She traveled around too much. She flitted from one guy to the next, most of them members of the prestigious creative circle she belonged to, but by every third date, she was ready to move on.

Riley was sure that Tessa's aversion to permanence stemmed from the only life she had known. She urged Tessa to speak to a therapist to find out why staying put was such a difficult task to accomplish.

Of course, this made Tessa even more adamant about disproving her case.

Tessa's book had been an overnight success, landing on all bestselling lists to her genuine surprise. Now a company in LA was seriously considering the purchase of its film rights. Three more tours were added to her schedule, and she was preparing to leave for an extended period of time. Her days were filled with interviews and blog entries and ideas for her new book.

"Jesus, did you buy the entire shoe department?" Riley asked as she joined Tessa at an outdoor table which looked out into Rush Street on Chicago's West Loop. Carmine's was a busy Italian restaurant decorated with cherry wood tables and velvety cushioned chairs. Shopping bags lined the perimeter where their table stood. Riley could hardly pull out the chair to seat herself.

"I had to get a few outfits for next week's signing," Tessa said. She waved her arm to get the server's attention, who came over and sputtered out the day's specials.

After they told him what they wanted, Riley began in an admonishing tone, "Jake says he's been wanting to get you to accompany him to your parent's executor. He may have some suggestions for investments you can check out. He's worried about all this." Riley pointed to the hapless pile of shopping bags, as if holding them responsible. "You'll run out if you're not careful."

"Jake always worries," Tessa said. "I get that he believes it's his role in my life. But I know what I'm doing. All of this is from the book sales, not from the funds that Mom and Dad left us. That's still intact."

Riley reached out to stroke her arm. "He's just like that. He loves you."

"I know. And I also know that he thinks I should've settled down by now. He gets attached to everyone I go out with, that's his problem," Tessa answered with a stiff upper lip.

"I did tell him about creeper, by the way," Riley teased.

"Oh, Rye. I'm never going to hear the end of it from him!"

"Actually, Jake thinks it's funny. He said that you had a pen pal from Saudi Arabia in grade school who actually wanted to come to the US to meet you."

"Adir," Tessa answered. "He was kinda cute. He loved to salsa dance, according to one of his letters."

"And what happened to Adir?" Riley asked, leaning on her elbows.

"I don't know. He just disappeared. We just stopped writing. Thanks for changing the subject, by the way."

Tessa grinned. Her friend knew her well. She'd adroitly switched gears just as Tessa was drawn into a foul mood about her brother and his tendency to try to nanny-state her life. Maybe Simon would be like that pen pal. He would just fall off the face of the earth.

"It's Thursday," Riley said. "Have you heard from him?"

They leaned back to give way to the server, who appeared with a large tray of food. Both ladies waited until their glasses were refilled and their silverware arrived. Riley took a bite of her meatball. They had a habit of ordering too many items from the menu and the table was now filled with plates of all sizes.

"He messages after work," Tessa explained.

"Oh, so you know his schedule now?"

"Shut up."

"Are you going to see him sometime?" Riley pressed. "I mean, you're not going to live off each other's messages on Twitter, are you?" She fluttered her eyes and licked her lips. "Talk to me baby, in that sexy English accent of yours."

"Funny."

Tessa reached her fork over to take the last piece of brussels sprout buried under a mountain of bacon.

"It's been nice," Tessa said, "just talking to someone completely oblivious to my world."

"He's not in your world. Period," Riley said. "You see? This is what I'm trying to point out! You shop because you're lonely, but it's self-imposed. This guy's been sticking around on social media, which he doesn't like, for what, three months? As you say, he's outside of your world so it's not like it's your fame that draws him. Or is it?"

"It's not," Tessa said with a stern face, her eyes set on Riley. "Besides, I have no fame. I'm a little two-bit author who just got lucky."

Tessa just had to laugh. She loved her life, her career, her freedom. There wasn't anything she would change. Sure, sometimes all that moving around was exhausting, but she enjoyed it, too. There was always something to look forward to.

The traveling may have been temporary, but her avoidance of permanence was just part and parcel of who she was.

It was time to change the subject. Tessa reached over to one of the bags on the ground and pulled out a pair of jeans. "Fashion week find! Fringed denim!"

"Oh. My. God. You found it! Where?" Riley gently ran her fingers through the frayed bits of thread along its edges.

"3X1. Last one."

"So worth it! You can wear it at your next signing!" Riley exclaimed.

"Totally," Tessa answered. "I—"

The table shook as her phone vibrated. Tessa turned it over and a smile crossed her face.

"What?" Riley asked.

"It's him. He sent a Tweet," Tessa said as she scrolled through her phone.

"Give that to me!" Riley squealed, grabbing the phone. Tessa watched helplessly as Riley began typing.

"There," she said a few seconds later, handing the phone back to Tessa.

"My God, Rye. What did you just do?"

"What I always do. I took care of it for you," Riley answered with a twitch of her eyebrows and an innocent smile.

Disconnected: *What you up to, Girl in 7C?*
Tessa: *Nothing much, getting ready to leave for my next event.*
Disconnected: *Been thinking of you.*
Tessa: *Then #MeetMe #Vegas*

the second goodbye

# eight

If the airport was any indication of this trip, Simon thought, it was bound to be a disaster. Screaming kids, nerve wracked parents, feather clad showgirls, dogs and cats everywhere. The sea of humanity seemed to have gathered in one location that day.

This was karma, Simon thought, for lying to Maxine and telling her that he was going on a business trip. He recalled their conversation while bouncing around on the shuttle bus from the airport. She'd hovered around him as he'd neatly folded his clothes and began packing them in his suitcase. While she'd spoken, she'd stared at the mirror and picked at something in her eye. He'd stopped to look at what she was doing, her back to him, long lustrous blond hair over her shoulders.

"This new mascara is bothering me," she said.

That was Maxine. Beautiful, well made, but also vain.

"Huh. Don't use it again," he answered, dodging past her toward the bathroom.

"When did you say you were coming back?" One eye was shut, and her mouth was wide open as she pulled on her eyelash.

"Two days."

"Funny," she said. "You normally know about these trips way in advance. How are you not freaking out that this is so last minute?"

"Yeah, about this trip." He moved closer to her, gently placing his hands on her shoulders. "We need to talk."

When in fact, he had taken two days off work in response to Tessa's Tweet a week ago.

What was he doing there? This was crazy! For the most part, life had gone on after he met Tessa in New York three months ago. His reluctant introduction to social media had occurred three days after he'd seen her. It took him hours to set those apps up on his phone, hours to learn how to navigate through the settings. He was a pro now, proud of himself for boldly entering a world he knew nothing about. He couldn't tell Adrian, couldn't ask for his advice, lest it raised suspicion. But he was amazed at the following Tessa had and the day to day interaction she maintained with her fans.

As he rode to the hotel, he felt a pang of guilt, remembering that Maxine had always wanted to take him to Vegas. He had no complaints about his life with her in Boston. He hadn't traveled since New York, was happy to stay put in one place. To try new things.

And yet... once in a while, in the heat of the moment, he'd find himself imagining it was Tessa and not Maxine writhing in pleasure underneath him.

It was insane.

Every day, he would swear never to send her another message. And yet, every Thursday after work, he picked up his phone and opened one of the social media apps. He'd consciously chosen that day of the week because Tessa's book tours were always on weekends. Thursday was her travel day—a good day to check in to see where she was heading off to. He decided to see where all this would take him. And lord knows, he wasn't one to date two women at the same time. Even if technically, he wasn't dating Tessa.

And so, he broke things off with Maxine the day before he left for Vegas. Told her he was simply too focused on his work to consider staying in Boston after his assignment.

Why? What was he so excited about? He couldn't even tell Adrian for fear he'd ask that question. He'd been with pretty women before.

Maxine was gorgeous. But there was something about Tessa. Maybe it was because she was so unassuming, so laid back. Nothing seemed to faze her. Her detachment intrigued him, challenged him. He couldn't wait to see her.

With no game plan and an itinerary based on just her Tweets and Instagram posts, he knew what and where her activities would be for the weekend. From the looks of it, she didn't have any other obligation than the four-hour book signing occurring in the afternoon. He made a conscious effort not to arrange to meet, not to pin her down on a schedule. He didn't want to scare her away with so much organization.

Besides, it might be fun, this on-a-whim kind of life. Except that this bus ride had just quelled his anticipation and transformed it into dread. Sweat-soaked fabrics stuck its occupants together like glue. It was standing room only, skin to skin in an enclosed space with nothing but bad odor and perspiration exacerbated by a busted air conditioner.

By the time he reached his destination, he was the last one on the bus. As he stepped down, he was caught off guard by a burst of hot air. He'd never been to Vegas before and was unprepared for the sudden change in climate. He clutched at his laptop bag, making sure his medication was close by.

Back to the present.

There he was, weaving through the insane crowd at the Vegas airport unable to contain the feeling of excitement that had overtaken him.

His concern was overridden by the sight in front of him. The entrance of the hotel was just as bad as the hellhole he'd just been in. Too many people were converged in the middle of the lobby, banners hoisted everywhere, and the place just overflowing with women.

The influx of people overwhelmed him more than the palatial surroundings. Imposing stone columns and marble floors as well as the massive gold statues were hardly visible—all he noticed was a sign saying, "Welcome: Hot in Vegas Signing Event."

Two women, a blond in a ponytail and yoga pants and a redhead in torn up jeans sashayed up to him, their faces painted, their lips in a permanent pucker.

"So, which author are you here with?" asked the blond one.

"Excuse me?" Simon asked.

"You're a model, right? Which cover are you on?" the redhead repeated, her hand now on his arm.

"Oh." He laughed. "No, I'm just a guest."

He circled around them to get to the reception desk.

"Well," the blond giggled. "You should be one."

The women followed him as he stood in line. He grappled with his laptop bag, strapped it onto his overnight bag then turned to them and asked, "Are you here for a book event?"

Might as well engage them in conversation. He had nowhere to go, nothing to do. He began to notice his surroundings. It amazed him to see such extravagance laid out so publicly, everything in gold. It reminded him of an album cover his dad had displayed in the living room when he was a child. He laughed when he turned around to see the same golden grand piano in the flesh, on a giant pedestal peeking from behind a roped velvet curtain. It belonged to the famous pianist Liberace.

"Yeah. We're here for her," the redhead answered, pointing in the direction of a group of shirtless men. One of the male models stepped aside, and he saw her in their midst.

Her hair was still short, but this time she wore a black and white mini dress with her signature high heels. She laughed, her head thrown back as one of the models gripped her around the waist and whispered something in her ear.

Simon forgot what he'd lined up for and started across the lobby.

Tessa looked up and smiled when she saw him. She said a few words, disengaged from the model, and met Simon halfway across the floor, away from the expectant crowd.

"Hi," she said. "You came."

"Hi," he answered. He smiled so hard his cheeks began to hurt. "You look—"

"Cleaned up?" She laughed. "You've got this social media thing figured out, Mr. Fremont."

"Ha!" He guffawed. "The next trick was to find out how to actually find you. I was going to worry about that this afternoon."

He noticed he was rocking on his toes and tried to stop. He didn't quite know how to deal with his excitement. He was acting like one of her fans.

"I wasn't expecting you to come. Riley, she was the one who—"

"Me neither," he said, nervously. "But here I am."

"Here you are."

An awkward silence followed. A few seconds later, the same model appeared by her side. He placed an arm around her, firmly grasping her shoulder. "Tess, we have to go," he said, puffing his hairless chest in Simon's face.

"One minute," she told him. "I'll be right there."

She gripped Simon's arm and led him away. "Sorry. Andrew and I have to take our place in the signing room." She'd explained this to him some time ago. Andrew was the guy who had hit it big after appearing on her book cover. Now a full-fledged model, it became quite a treat for readers to be able to interact with him during these tours.

Simon nodded.

"Meet you later?" Tess said.

"Yes. When?"

"I'll text you."

Her response wasn't good enough. He needed a plan. That was just the way he was. He needed to know what time and where and what did she want to do? At that point, he didn't care about going against his previous intention to just roll with the flow. He was here for her. "What time?" he asked.

She was already a few feet away from him. "I don't know. I'll text you!" she repeated.

Simon had checked out the shops, worked out and even taken a nap to fill the time. Still, he hadn't heard from her. Based on the poster in the lobby, her event had ended earlier at 8 p.m. Bored and feeling off-balance, he walked down to the casino to check out the poker tables. Women in evening gowns roamed the floor, some holding tightly to their men as they took their place at the table, and some sidling up to complete strangers, hoping, he assumed, to find company for the night.

Simon repeatedly glanced at his phone while the dealer began to shuffle the cards. As the minutes passed, he lost all hope of seeing her that night. The clock ticked, the night wore on, and still no sign of a text.

It was almost midnight when he caught a glimpse of Tessa crossing the room arm in arm with the model he had seen her with earlier. He looked at his phone, hoping he had simply missed a text. Nothing. She wore the same outfit he'd seen her in earlier, her hair a bit disheveled, her cheeks ruddied, most probably from drinking a little too much. The way the model held her was grossly inappropriate.

They were sleeping together.

He stood, and she saw him, a look of realization and maybe even guilt crossing her face. Before Simon could do anything, she continued toward the elevator without another glance.

It was then he realized that she'd had no intention of seeing him that day. Her promise to text had been empty. She had appeased him, just like one of her fans. A condescension to those who traveled to this city to see her.

He was one of them, and nothing more.

nine

*T*his is exactly what Jake means when he tells me to grow up, Tessa thought as she woke up the next morning in Andrew's bed.

This is what her brother tried to protect her from. Same story, same reasons. She'd had too much to drink, gotten high on love and the prospect of it, swooned over some momentary professions of adoration, and afterward, never felt more alone in her life.

They hadn't even bothered to draw the curtains. For a few minutes, she lay in bed, thinking of what she'd done the night before. She should have handled it differently, shouldn't have stood him up like that. She had fully intended to see him after the book signing. But the reaction she'd had upon seeing Simon earlier in the day had terrified her. At the signing, she couldn't think straight, wrote the wrong names on the books handed to her, checked her phone a million times, called Riley to tell her how she felt.

I can't do it, Rye. I'm too excited to see him. It's not right.

What's not right? You're being silly.

No, I'm not. This has never happened to me before. I can't see him.

Sunlight streamed in through the fine fabric, illuminating the beautiful face of the man who slept next to her.

"Andrew," she whispered, nudging his leg with her foot.

"Hmmm." He lifted his arm and slung it across her chest.

"I have to go," she said, sliding toward the edge of the bed. "I'll text you, okay?"

"Hmmm," he said again.

She knocked on Simon's door thirty minutes after she left Andrew's room, showered and dressed and feeling contrite.

Simon opened the door with sleep-laden eyes, his dark hair tousled and mussed, his chest bare, his black basketball shorts sitting on his lower hips.

The speech she had planned was lost in the blueness of his eyes. "Sorry," was all she could manage. There he stood, one hand on the door handle, head protruding out the door, hesitant. "Can we talk?" she asked, still standing outside the imaginary line between him and the door.

He pulled it wide open and stepped aside while she strode in. "Let me explain," she started out.

"Explain." He remained standing by the door.

He was pissed. On the one hand, that was a good sign. He'd waited. For a while this morning, she'd consoled herself by imagining him with some girl he'd picked up at the casino last night. Apparently, that hadn't happened.

Now, on the other hand, she felt worse about it.

Tessa looked around. The room was immaculately clean. Simon's shoes were parked right next to an open suitcase, shirts neatly piled on top of one another, ready to be packed. A room service tray had been methodically stacked with plate covers. A napkin lay folded and tucked in neatly between the ice bucket and two bottles of wine.

She allowed her mind to wander for a moment, creating scenarios in her head. So, he was extremely organized and a little intense. It's not like she wasn't either. Just without the organization part.

"I'm waiting," he said.

His irritation was evident. Why was she even here? She could have just let it go, slept in with Andrew and avoided Simon for the rest of the weekend. That would have been the end of this story.

But that's just it.

She didn't want it to be.

She took a seat on the edge of his bed.

"Simon, I'm sorry about yesterday. Everything ran late, and I couldn't get out early enough."

"I saw you, don't you remember?"

"Yes, but…" She paused. "I guess what I mean is." She tucked her hands under her thighs. And then scooted back and crossed her legs instead. "By the time you saw me, it was a few hours after I'd decided not to meet you."

He surprised her by taking a seat beside her. She noticed how long his legs were, his knees reaching up to his abdomen. These had all the makings of a book. Brooding, shirtless guy on the bed with a confused bitch.

"Decided. What does that mean?"

"It means I thought it best not to come," she responded.

"Listen, I understand I can't come barging into your event and expect you to drop everything for me. I'm going to be taking a flight back tonight. My plane leaves early evening."

She turned to face him. "No, no. I'm here now. I'm really sorry. Last night wasn't planned. I didn't mean to upset you! I just saw no point."

She thought his eyeballs would pop out of their sockets, he was glaring at her so hard.

"I traveled across the country to wait for you," he said.

"Yeah. I'm a little weirded out by that, actually."

"Then why are you here?" he mocked her. "In my room."

"Good question. I really don't know." She exhaled loudly. Honest to God. She didn't know. He wasn't joking around. She felt the chill in his eyes. They turned into winter, an icy lake, a frozen river, a dead tree.

"Try," he said.

"It was the next step. Next steps scare me."

"Tessa, we've been texting each other for three and a half months. At least a few times a week."

"I know. But—"

"But nothing. You're talking rubbish," he argued.

There they were, side by side on the edge of his bed. He reached down to the floor, grabbed his shirt and quickly placed it over his head.

In a way, he was right. Why overthink it? She really wanted to make it up to him. What if she forgot for a moment there were even any next steps, would that help?

She tugged at his sleeve and with the sweetest smile she could muster, said, "Please don't be mad. I mean it, I am truly sorry for standing you up."

He stayed still, eyes now focused on his hands, which rested on his lap.

"Simon?" she repeated.

"Apology accepted," Simon said, his head turned toward her, body still facing forward. "I get that you don't really know me, that's why I'm here."

"Thank you," she answered, looking away. She began thinking of words to describe his eyes. Crystalline, turquoise, deep.

"I understand how out of kilter this looks. But I'm hoping this day doesn't all go to pot."

"All to what?" she asked, confused.

"I'm hoping we can still do something today."

"Okay." She smiled. When he remained silent, she continued. "Get dressed, and I'll see you downstairs in what, half an hour?"

"Half an hour," he agreed. "In front of the big arse fountain."

They were both smiling now, the easing tension had brought back their banter.

Tessa went directly down to the lobby to wait for him—she wasn't going to risk somehow standing him up again—which proved to be a mistake. When Simon emerged from the elevators twenty minutes later, a flock of women had gathered around her.

The look of anxiety on Simon's face—and why wouldn't he be worried she'd stand him up again, her track record thus far had been atrocious—was quickly replaced by relief when he saw her. She waved at him and smiled. He stood outside the circle until she excused herself and plowed through the crowd to get to him. Tessa felt a twinge of excitement when she grabbed his hand and led him away from everyone else. It was a gesture reserved for old friends, for people who have known each other for ages. The way he clasped her fingers in his were words that didn't have to be spoken. He followed her through the twisted archway, past stores and restaurants until they reached the outdoor theme park.

"I'm happy you're here," she said, plagued with true remorse. Now she wished she had seen him last night. Standing next to him then, wading in those eyes, made her long for more time with him. But with this elation, Tessa felt fear. She wondered if she'd have to decide sooner or later whether these next steps would be worthwhile. Lord, she hoped not.

"And I as well."

They made their way to the cotton candy stand. They stood and watched as the old man wove pink streams of sugar around a paper cone. "Hmmff." She chomped loudly, offering it to him. "Love strawberry."

He tore off a piece and placed it in his mouth.

"Oh, look, let's do the giant Ferris wheel!" she exclaimed while waving the sticky cardboard in his face. An imposing spherical structure extending hundreds of feet into the sky towered in front of them. The rim of the giant wheel held passenger cabins that looked like pods. She didn't wait for him to respond, leaving him behind and running to the ticket booth.

"Tessa!" He chased after her. "Can we wait a bit? Me and high places, we don't see eye to eye."

"Who says you have to see? Just close your eyes and let's get on!"

Tessa grabbed two tickets, pulled him toward the gate and into one of the glass enclosed cabins. Other passengers followed suit. A shrill, loud siren went off, announcing the start of the ride. Tessa tugged him by the arm until he had no choice but to hop in. And then she pulled him toward a bench facing the northern section of the city. Flat screen TVs were mounted on each side, giving riders a view of the city from every angle.

The operator checked their seatbelts and placed the latch on the metal gate. Simon had apprehension written all over his face. He continuously shook his head at her, his lips tight, stressed.

"Don't worry, little boo boo," she teased as she gently took his hand in hers. "I'll protect you."

ten

Simon wondered whether he should pretend to play with this phone as a distraction to the car rising hundreds of feet in the air. Five hundred eighty, to be exact. As the car climbed farther and farther from the ground, he tried to focus on her shoes.

He would have much rather focused on her face, but doing so would mean looking past the glass enclosure and toward the view below. She looked so... Simon couldn't describe it. Such the guy thing to notice a woman's outside appearance, first and foremost. Her short hair fell neatly in place. She wore torn up jeans and Toms sneakers, her face resplendent with not a trace of makeup. Her lips were a natural bright pink; if you stared at her from different angles, it almost looked as if they were too big for her face.

But it wasn't even that. She was beautiful yes, but the girl on the texts and the messages turned out to be the same girl sitting next to him that day. She was just as he imagined her to be. There was no disappointing revelation, no turn-off point. In fact, it was the opposite.

"Why did we stop?" he asked as the car began to rotate ever so slightly.

"They're just picking up passengers," she answered. "It's a thirty-minute ride. We have lots of time to chitchat." A slight pause. "Give me your phone."

"What?"

She never waited for answers. She took the phone from his hand but handed it back immediately.

"The code," she ordered.

He typed it in and gave it back to her.

"Where are the pictures?" she asked, swiping back and forth.

"Tessa, what are you doing?"

"I want to see pictures. Get to know who you are."

She pressed on the camera and started swiping to the right. He first looked away, embarrassed. And then he watched for a reaction as images of test tubes, hand scribbled formulas, manual pages and clippings appeared.

"Who's this?" she asked as a picture of Maxine came into view. "She's beautiful."

"Someone I dated. Maxine."

"Ah. You have a girlfriend," Tessa acknowledged without batting an eye.

"Long before I met you," he said defensively. Her reaction disheartened him. But why? What did he expect her to do? Did he expect her to fly into a jealous rage?

Simon wondered why he was taking everything so seriously.

She smiled at him and swiped left instead. "It's okay. Guys with girlfriends can still have girl-friends," she said. "Tell me about her?"

The car moved forward a few feet. He began to calculate the radius of a circle in his head.

"She's an accountant. Works for one of the big four in London but assigned locally like me." He was aware of boasting a little; he was proud of Maxine. Her intellect had always turned him on.

But Tessa... Something in him craved the spontaneity that this woman brought into his life. He realized that even after being stood up last night—her unpredictability made him more attracted to her. It was like unwrapping a Kinder Egg. You never know what you'll get.

"Big four of what?" she asked, perplexed.

Thank goodness! There was actually someone who didn't know about nanotechnology, who the big four companies were, and why guys with girlfriends couldn't have girl-friends.

He smiled at her. "Accounting firms."

"Hmm." She didn't try to dig deeper.

"Now, your turn."

She handed her phone to him after punching in her code. He opened her photos app and started swiping.

"These are all dogs," he said. "How many dogs do you have? Are you one of those spinsters with a house full of animals?"

"I wanted a dog."

"Which one is yours?"

"I don't have one. I'm still trying to decide."

The way she said it so matter-of-factly endeared him. She didn't seem to want to impress him, wasn't embarrassed at all about appearing flighty. She possessed confidence in her uncertainty.

"And I'm hardly a spinster," she said. "I just turned twenty-six, for your information."

"When's your birthday?" he said, handing back her phone. But not before noticing a picture of a handsome man and a beautiful dark-haired girl.

"My brother Jacob and his girlfriend, Riley," she answered his thoughts. "May 1st. You?"

"September 2nd."

They leaned against the glass and faced inward.

"Virgo and Taurus," she said. "Both dedicated. You're practical, I'm stubborn. We're both cautious. I'm romantic, and you're overly communicative."

He laughed. "What else?"

"That's all I know," she answered.

A crying baby. Two giggling teenagers. A man and a woman arguing. They all attempted to pull his attention in different directions with little success. Life was there, laid out in front of him, in a glass enclosed pod hundreds of feet in the air. And he watched her lean forward to listen to a mother read a book to a toddler while he fished cheerios out of a cup. Simon observed the lively exchange between two young women with pierced noses and beautiful black tattoos on their arms. He caught them in a kiss as the Ferris wheel descended.

He imagined what it would be like to kiss her.

Amid the noise, they sat in silence. He reached for her hand and held it. And she let him.

They walked along a bridge over a man-made lake. The air felt thick to Simon, despite the pleasant temperatures. He tried to mask his labored steps, pausing a few times to catch his breath. She didn't seem to notice.

Although it had been three hours since they'd met by the fountain, it felt like only minutes. He tried to delay his departure as much as he could. But his car would be there in a half hour to take him to the airport. She asked him to sit with her for a few minutes, on stone steps in the middle of a rose garden. He was at a loss for words, afraid they wouldn't see each other again after this. What should he say, to make her want to see him again? What would it take, when he knew he was going back to England in a month?

Suddenly, the normalcy he had craved was a distant wish. He didn't want to leave her. And yet, it was too soon to tell her how he felt. It was too early to know. He focused his attention on the objects around them. Like the lover-inscribed names and messages carelessly carved on the bench where they sat. Or the stones beneath their feet that were so perfectly shaped, he was sure they were man made, synthetic. Or the approaching bird she didn't seem to notice. It flew away right as she ducked her head.

"So, no next steps, huh?" He glanced at his watch. He needed to know before he left.

"None, unless it involves getting a dog," she said with a smile.

"Even a dog would need time with you."

"True! Scrap that idea then!" she laughed.

He considered himself an intelligent man, but at that moment, he knew nothing. He held on to the lifeline he imagined she held out to him.

"Will I see you again?"

"Yes," she said without hesitation. "I can schedule a signing on your side of the world."

"I'd love that," he said, pacified.

"Tell me, Simon. Why did you come all the way out here to see me?"

The moment turned solemn. She hugged her knees to her chest and tilted her head to look at him.

"Because I haven't stopped thinking about you since the day we met at the airport."

His honesty scared him. What was he doing?

"Just curious, Mr. Fremont. Was that the most out of character thing you've ever done? Follow me to baggage claim?"

"Definitely. That was it, for sure."

"Well, then promise me you'll keep in touch, okay?"

He saw sadness in her face. He wasn't sure she felt the same way, but her words gave him hope.

"WhatsApp." He laughed.

"Yeah. Perfect."

"I have to go," he said, standing.

"Okay." She remained seated, this time slipping both hands under her legs.

He wanted to reach out and touch her one last time, but he was afraid he would scare her away. She was a no next-step kind of girl, and he was enamored with who she was and what she represented.

"It was nice seeing you, Tessa. I'll call when I get back to Boston."

"Bye, Simon."

And with that, he turned around and walked away.

She was sure she'd never see him again.

People say things in the heat of the moment and then they walk away and forget. Connections, affinities—they're hard to come by. Sometimes they never happen at all. She spent a few more minutes in the garden by herself, thinking about how lonely she was, and how much she appreciated his visit. No one had ever done that just for her. Her. Not her book. Not her popularity nor success. Just her. She sat on the bench, immobilized by her sadness, running her fingers along the letters etched on the wood, absorbed in one particular inscription.

Go for it, Taurus!

And that was her sign to get on her feet and run.

She didn't care that there were people waiting for her as she ran back into the hotel lobby. There he was at the end of the hall, right before the elevator bank, his bag at his side, his eyes fixed on no one else but her.

"Tessa! Tessa!" Strangers called to her, books in hand, excitement in their faces. She waved at them and blew them a kiss but kept on walking; she only had eyes for the man with his back against the wall. He was waiting for her. Standing patiently and waiting.

When she reached him, when they came face to face, they were again all alone.

"Don't go, Simon," she blurted in between a deep breath. "I don't want you to say goodbye."

"I wasn't going to," he answered, a smile slowly building. "Say goodbye."

She held out both hands as they stepped into her room and he pulled her close to him. The delicate way he cradled her face in his hands, the soft touch of his thumbs across her cheeks, surprised her. Somehow, she thought they'd be tearing at each other's clothes in a frenzy.

"You're perfect," he whispered, before gently brushing his lips against hers. She kissed him back while tugging at his collar, unbuttoning his shirt and slipping it off his body.

And then she drew her head back and gasped as he lifted her up and pressed himself against her. She was sure he could tell how ready she was for him. He carried her to the bed and laid her gently at the edge, watching as she hurriedly slipped out of her dress and her underwear. He grabbed them from her and threw them on the floor, licked his lips and tore the belt off his jeans as she held out both arms to him.

"Tessa," he growled. "I want to be inside you."

"Simon," she answered, pointing towards the night table directly above his head. "If you want to use—"

He silenced her with his mouth, wrapped her legs around him, made love to her with his lips, his hands, his body. He fit her so perfectly, seemed to know when to pick up the pace and when to slow down. She came twice before he did—something she hadn't experienced in years. The way he held her after that first time, smoothing her hair away from her face and nestling her head against his chest, confirmed her connection to him as well.

Many more times that night, they discovered each other, forming a bond and an intimacy that they didn't dare to speak of. They'd both been there before. Like a one-night stand, nothing was implied, nothing was promised. And even though it was the most tender one-night stand she'd ever had, she berated herself for thinking it could ever happen again.

the third goodbye

eleven

#MeetMeSanFrancisco

Tessa knew she was being ridiculous when she paused to compose herself at the entrance of The Cliff House before walking in. She fidgeted with the straps of her top, making sure they sat neatly on her shoulders before brushing her clammy palms against her hips. Tessa was keen on picking up where they'd left off. In fact, she'd been having trouble thinking of anything else after they'd made plans to meet again.

She sucked in a breath as she approached the hostess, who quickly placed a caller on hold.

"I'm here to meet a friend," she said, squinting against the glare of the sun shining through the glass.

"Is that him?" The hostess tilted her head toward the corner table at the far end of the room. Despite having been separated for weeks, he stood out to her.

Simon didn't look like every other man her age, with the typical J Crew or Ralph Lauren style of dressing. He was European, classic and streamlined. Everything he wore seemed sized to taper him perfectly, from his slim-fitting jeans to his leather lace up shoes. Even his plaid shirts fell tight against his body.

He'd trimmed his beard and his hair looked shorter. He was a handsome man, and she was immensely attracted to him.

We're just having fun, she'd repeatedly assured Riley, who kept wanting to know why Tessa had to meet him.

Correction, she'd argued. He's meeting me. Besides, that's the point, isn't it? I want to get to know him. He's leaving for England soon and I want to see him at least one last time.

One last time, my ass, Riley had said.

Simon looked deep in thought as he folded and unfolded his napkin and laid it neatly on the plate.

"Hi," she said. "Simon?"

He lurched out of his seat, hitting his knee on the table.

She smiled. It wasn't like him to be so rattled.

He pulled her into an awkward embrace, one hand on her shoulder, the other loosely touching her back "Hi," he said. Remarkable how familiar his touch was.

"Hi."

It felt good to see him in person once again. She turned and sat across from him, facing the wide expanse of sun and sea. It was a windy day, the waves crashing wildly along the shore. A sole surfer sat on his board and swished and swashed with the force of the water.

"You look great," he said, his smile shy, demure.

"Considering I just flew in this morning," she responded self-consciously, wishing she could check herself in a mirror. She was there for a book signing, and he was there for her. The texts and messages between then had increased in frequency after they'd seen each other in Vegas. What had been once a week on Thursday was now at least once a day.

She missed him, late at night when she was all alone, when the apartment was quiet and the stillness of everything blared in her head.

"Riley still giving you grief about meeting me?" he asked, taking the menu and looking it over.

"I kinda like it." She waved at the server to let her know they needed more time before ordering. "Driving her crazy, I mean."

"Ha!" he answered with a chuckle. "How's the new book going? Any luck with the writing?"

"Nope. Still muddling through. I've finally figured out that my brain can only handle one thing at a time."

He smiled. "Not true. I think they're just coming at you from so many directions, you can't keep up."

"Maybe."

They both shook their heads while studying the menu. Disoriented by his presence, all she saw were words that made no sense. The server approached again. This time, Simon was the one who waved her off. "I think she wants to take our order."

"I'm not really hungry." She caught his gaze before he licked his lips and smiled back at her. She wished he could read her mind.

There was hope, after all. Maybe he could read hers.

"Me, neither," he answered. "At least not for food."

Tessa shifted nervously in her seat. "We can go for a walk. It's a bit windy, but the beach looks pretty empty."

He slid over to the seat next to her, laid his hand on her lap and slowly trailed his fingers on the hemline of her skirt.

Her breath caught in her throat and her face felt hot.

"Or… we can stay indoors and continue where we left off…"

"I'm starved."

Tessa sat on the floor with her legs crossed, surrounded by two large trays of finger foods and fresh fruit. Simon lay splayed out on the bed, a sheet draped over his legs. He reminded her of the Calvin Klein model on a huge billboard in the middle of Times Square.

He shot his head up, eyes squinted, lips parted. "What?"

She ignored his jibe, knowing exactly what he meant. She wasn't sure she'd had enough of that—to be honest.

"Mmm. Did you try this one? It's got brie baked into the crust. Oh, and here's the one with the gross olives you ordered," she said lightheartedly. "Want me to fix you a plate?"

She popped a strawberry in her mouth, and then threw a piece at him. He jerked his head upwards and caught it with his teeth.

"One of your many amazing skills!" she teased.

"Are you done devouring that yet?" Simon sat up and watched her chomp hungrily on a croissant. "Jesus, where do you put it all?"

"Why? Did you want to go and do something? It's midnight. I wonder what the nightlife is here in this place."

Tessa dusted the crumbs off her and lifted herself off the floor, her robe untied and undone, giving him a clear view of her body. She saw the shift in his face as he stared at her, his eyes like burning sapphires.

Feeling shy all of a sudden, she pulled it closed, her fingers hastily tying a knot as she approached him.

"You know what I want. I want you to come here," he motioned, offering her his right hand.

She bolted on the bed and landed on his lap, facing him.

"Seriously? We're not going out?" she teased, grinding on him at the same time.

"No. I'm more than fine," he growled, "staying in."

He brought his lips to her neck and traced a trail of wet kisses down toward her shoulder. Their coupling had the energy of the first time—the sparks, the butterflies, the overwhelming stimulation, in equal parts with the stumbling, the faltering, and the ardent desire not to over commit.

"Okay." She pulled away from him and slid toward the end of the bed, still holding on to his hand. He let her lead him to the tall window by the corner of the room. She wriggled her shoulders until the robe slipped off and pressed herself against the glass. She could see Alcatraz in the distance, seagulls circling the island and then dipping down into the trees.

Yes, she was still as alone and independent as she was before she met him. But Simon could become her refuge from the craziness of her career. He could be the break she needed every so often—no pressure, no timeline, just a meeting whenever they were able to pull it off.

"I have to make it worth your trip to come see me." She turned her head sideways to address him.

"It was worth it three hours ago." He stepped in to wrap his arms around her, trying to protect her from the cold, hard surface.

"Here?" he whispered in her ear.

His body felt hot against her skin.

"Here."

"Why?" he asked, his nose buried in her neck. "Because I hate heights?"

He used both knees to push her legs apart.

"Precisely."

twelve

Simon stared at the horizon as Tessa walked along the shoreline, dipping her toes in and out with the tide. He'd never been this close to the ocean before. A blue and yellow buoy bobbed in the distance, spraying fine mists of water as the waves lapped against it.

He felt unsettled about leaving for the airport in a few hours, but he had never deviated from his plans. Except that one night in Vegas, when his gut had told him he couldn't leave her just yet. When she'd asked him to stay with her, he hadn't needed to think twice.

The woman he watched on the beach was a constant mystery. She laughed easily, never gave too much of herself away, was worldly, well-traveled, and extremely well spoken. They never ran out of things to talk about, there was never an awkward moment between them.

Add that to a smoking hot body, with curves in the right places and breasts that would put any supermodel to shame.

Two more weeks in Boston and then back home to England he would go. He was chasing a deadline, should have been working this weekend instead of flying out to San Francisco to see her. But all he'd been doing for weeks was working, and this trip was his prize for all those grueling hours.

Testing and retesting, documenting his hypotheses and results. His brain was always in overdrive. In fact, before he'd met her, life to him was all about his career. It still was, but she was his obscurity—a break from the clarity he'd lived in all his life. Outside of this explanation, he needed to admit that he was fixated with her.

"Are you going to check out the Sutro baths with me?" Tessa called from the pile of rubble leading to an uphill path filled with gravel. They had just had breakfast at the Cliff House on Ocean Beach. Adjacent to the restaurant was the historic site that housed the baths—public saltwater swimming pools that had burned down in 1966.

"You're climbing that thing?" he yelled back. "I think we can get to the same place through the restaurant." He looked down at his feet, felt the sensation of soft powdery sugar between his toes. He kinda liked it.

"What's the fun in that?" she asked, pausing at the bottom to gather her sandals while holding her hand out to him. "Don't worry, I'll protect you."

Slowly, he stood and walked toward her, mumbling. "Why do you always have to say that?"

The path was wide enough for only one person. Tessa walked in front of him, still barefoot, maneuvering herself through the stones and climbing up with one leg at a time.

"Don't ask me why I wore white today," she said, poking fun at herself. The last few levels were higher than she could manage with an upward step, and so she landed on her knee and scraped her pants on a sharp ridge.

"You sure you want to keep your sandals off? You've got sand all over you." Simon held on to her as she lost her balance.

She nodded and kept on. "It's only sand, Simon. Believe it or not, it washes off."

Soon, they were walking along the walls of the baths—the narrow foundation filled with stone and cement. Simon couldn't get down quickly enough; he didn't enjoy the feeling of walking on a tightrope. The walls were quite high, about five feet above the muddy path. As soon as he was able to get off the wall, he did so.

Tessa continued tracing the walls, one foot in front of the other, arms stretched to the side. She stopped to take in the view from where she stood before pulling out her phone and snapping a few photos. The blue sea, the dark colored sand, the baths in all their majesty, the cloudless sky—Simon observed this from the ground while she towered above him, twisting her body to maintain her balance.

"Kind of looks like the Roman ruins, doesn't it?" she yelled.

Simon grabbed her hand and gently pulled until she hopped down from the walls. He led her down a path to a small cave.

"I've been wanting to do this all morning," he whispered as he pushed her against the wall and brought his lips to hers. He bit into that softness. She tasted sweet like the cotton candy they'd shared that time in Vegas.

"Why didn't you just say so?" She kissed him back. Last night, this morning—it didn't matter, Simon wanted her again, right now. He loved that her arms, her kisses, her touches were for him anywhere and everywhere he needed them.

"We can go if you want to," she whispered, rubbing her nose against his chin and then nuzzling his neck.

He wanted to. He needed to. The blouse she wore had been driving him crazy all morning. Its crocheted material left much to the imagination. Tessa had tastefully lined it with a tank top, but her cleavage just couldn't stay concealed no matter what she wore.

But first things first. He needed a plan for the next time. It bothered him that she never brought up anything having to do with tomorrow. Or the next hour. Or the next day. They lived in the moment, enjoyed themselves and when it came time to say goodbye, she never had a plan. Maybe that was his role in her life. To give her a plan. Because he wanted to see more of her, more often.

"Okay, but can we sit for a few minutes to talk? You know once we get to the hotel room, there's not going to be much talking."

"Oh baby, if you want me to talk, I can talk," she teased, kissing his nose.

He laughed. "That too. How about over there," he said, pointing to some picnic tables outside the cave.

There they sat, across from each other, Simon with his right leg crossed over his left and Tessa with her head resting on her elbows.

"Look at that couple over there," she said. He turned to see a woman wagging her finger at a man who slapped it away from his face. He couldn't make out what they were saying, but their voices were raised, and she was crying. "Don't they look like they're about to get a divorce? The woman has been nit picking at him for this whole time. I heard them arguing. Obviously, she's upset about something. And he's not saying anything, like he's given up. I wonder if they have kids. Maybe they—"

"Tess."

She looked up at him, her eyes searching his.

"I'm only going to be in the US for two more weeks."

"I know." She reached for his hand.

"Can we talk about when we can see each other again?"

"I can't see you," she blurted out. "I've got commitments in Miami and LA next week. Very important marketing people. Some actor wants to meet me, loved my book."

Way to remind him of her priorities. What did he really expect? "I know. I'm not asking you to do anything." He wasn't disappointed. He was going to be tied up. He just wanted to know there would be time in the future.

"We'll figure it out," she reassured him. "Let's just fulfill these obligations and figure it out."

"Obligations?"

"Revete—my agent. She doesn't know about us. For one, I'm not ready to tell her yet. I've committed to a year of extensive touring. My books are about single women living the single life, finding love—and this is happening way too fast." Her phone rang right on cue. "Speaking of." She held up her finger before swinging her legs and turning around to take the call.

"Yes, Revete, I know. I'll be on time," Tessa said.

Simon's phone began to vibrate. He picked it up. It was Adrian.

Simon triggered the call. "It's not an issue," he said. "I'm taking the redeye. I'll be back by 5 a.m. tomorrow."

They faced each other while streaming in different conversations.

"What? Yes. I mean no! He doesn't have to come and get me. I'll meet him at the event!" Tessa ranted.

"Dude, it will be completed by then. I'm taking the weekend off. Goodbye." Simon turned his phone off completely.

"No one is here, Revete! I decided to spend the day at Ocean Beach. Talk later, bye."

Tessa put down her phone. "Now, where were we?" she cooed, taking his hand in hers.

"Obligations."

"Yeah, those," she joked, pointing to her phone. "Leave it to the phones to go off as we discuss this."

Simon smiled weakly, wondering for a second whether he should even say anything to her. And then he decided that no matter how disaffected Tessa seemed to be, it should count for something. "I stopped seeing Max before I saw you in Vegas."

His gaze fell to his hands. What did he want to accomplish by telling her this? They never discussed any of their personal lives outside of their time together. Even when he would call, it was always about him. Or her. Nothing of the outside world.

She blinked. "Max?"

"My girlfriend, remember?"

"Oh." And then. "Whoa!" as she drew her hand back.

He sat, immobilized, his chest beginning to feel tight.

"Why did you have to do that?" she continued. "I'm not ready for that kind of responsibility."

How dare she think that he would carry on a relationship when he was fucking someone on the side? Phone fucking, imaginary fucking, weekend fucking. He'd never done anything of that sort before this situation. At least he was honest about it. "I'm not a cheater," he ended up saying.

"But you were when you started this," she reminded him.

"Well, that's why I ended it. She deserved more. She was wasting her time with me."

"We're just having fun," she said and threw her hands in the air.

It was his turn to reach for her hand. It calmed them both down. They sat still facing each other, hands clasped and flat on the table.

"It had nothing to do with you," he explained.

Of course, it did. In fact, he was hooked on the crash and burn of their meeting and their parting. Exhilarating and exhausting. At least to him. They were great together, but he wasn't so sure about where he stood when they were apart. "Why are you getting all worked up about something that's not even your issue?" he asked.

"It's too much pressure on me, on us, Simon," she responded. "I just know things never work out quite as you expect them to. I don't want you to give up a good thing for this!"

She looked terrified, her eyes wide.

She stared at him and he stared right back.

"I didn't feel for her. I did it for me."

"Good!" She tilted her head back and exhaled loudly while bringing her hands to her face. "Because we live in different time zones. Your career is just taking off and so is mine. More importantly, we have something good here. Let's not muddle it up for now, okay?"

"Now why would we do that?" he asked with a tinge of sarcasm. "Looks like you're about to set some ground rules."

"No ground rules. We're adults," she said, lowering her voice.

He felt unsure of what she was trying to say. Did she not want to continue to see him? Was she pushing him toward Max? What did she mean, exactly?

"How about this: Game of truth," he said.

"What?"

He took her hand back and she began to rub her thumb on his wrist. It gave him tingles. "We should divulge one truth every time we see each other," he said.

"Where'd that come from? One of your corporate team training sessions?" she teased.

He laughed. "Yeah, for sure."

He circled the bench, then took a seat next to her and placed a hand on her thigh. He aimed for her nearness. And maybe a touch.

"Okay, want me to start?" she asked.

He nodded.

"I am really enjoying these times we have together, Simon."

"But you hate next steps."

She leaned into him before playfully swatting his shoulder. "Oh, come on. You're so serious. Isn't this where the fun is? Figuring each other out, determining what's true and what's not. And not worrying about next steps!"

"I guess," he answered, disenchanted.

"I don't have to know, Simon. I don't have to know what you do when I'm not with you."

"And I don't have to know either," he confirmed.

She nodded her head. "I promise I won't ask. We both know what we're doing, what we're getting into." She pressed her leg against his. "When it's us, it's us. No one else. We'll keep our world safe."

"Roger that," he said, managing a smile. He liked their world. Their sacred space. And she was absolutely right. You never place all your eggs in one basket. For now, it gave him permission to help himself to what was right there in front of him. That morning, that afternoon. Those moments they had left together. Fun with a capital F.

the fourth
goodbye

thirteen

#MeetMeHongKong

Tessa peered out excitedly as the Rolls Royce Phantom pulled into the driveway of the Peninsula Hotel in Hong Kong. Jetlagged and exhausted, with not a wink of sleep, she was just happy to finally be on the ground for a few days.

It'd been over two weeks since she'd last seen Simon. Her trips to Miami and LA had been fruitful but frazzled, with press tours and meetings and appearances over booked and hastily scheduled.

On the way from the airport, she savored the familiar sights she'd seen as a child. The narrow freeways, unlined and without any lanes, flanked on the outskirts of the city by makeshift homes, dilapidated buildings and hundreds of clotheslines with a rainbow of fabric swinging in the wind. The views contrasted as you moved in closer to mainland. Homes gave way to buildings and towers, large malls and beautiful greenery as far as the eye could see.

The check-in process was quick. In less than ten minutes, Tessa explored her suite, creating piles of clothing in different parts of the room and taking short breaks to sift through the books and magazines scattered around the living area. She took the time to admire the tastefully decorated surroundings; beige walls and furniture, streamlined and modern. An Asian inspired mural of cherry blossoms reminded her of the trips to Japan as a child. Chinese wooden screens engraved with gold dragons and warriors took her to another time and place, when heroes saved their heroines and gave up their lives for love.

Where was her hero?

Was he her hero?

The view of the Victoria Harbor was beautiful, old Chinese junk boats with colorful sails skittered across the dark blue ocean alongside yachts and speed boats. Skyscrapers rose out of the water and nestled themselves between the clouds.

It was hard to believe her entire stay was fully financed by her publisher. She was in Hong Kong to host a workshop on creative writing. All because of her first book. Her debut novel. The one she'd written and thought she would never publish. Three query letters and she had an agent. Two months of pitches and she had a publisher. Things had happened too quickly, and now she was on the road, enjoying the life of a world-class traveler.

It was times like these when she missed her parents. They would have been proud of her. Her father, a prominent doctor, had always encouraged her to do what she loved. No one would have been happier for her than him. She'd shared with him her love for poetry and song, made up stories about his patients as she sat in his office all day on weekends. He would listen, he would laugh and then he'd encourage her to sing them to her mother.

Once, when she was five, she'd taken a pick-up stick and punctured a hole in her older brother's head. Her father had stitched him up right there on the kitchen table. She'd watched in awe as his deft fingers lightly pierced through Jacob's skin, her mother gently holding her brother down as he clutched his sister's hand.

They'd been a close-knit family. If there was one word she could use to describe her childhood, it would be *peace*. Her family had been normal. But the universe punishes complacency and security by turning your world upside down. One tragic accident and normal becomes two children with no parents. Was that why she kept running from normal these days?

As a diss to her past, she'd shed everything about herself and taken her life in an entirely different direction. She'd studied business instead of medicine, hoping to parlay what her parents had left them into more than just their legacy.

She failed in that sense. But she'd succeeded in everything else.

Jake had become her father. He had her father's career and her father's heart.

Hong Kong had been a vacation spot for their family. Shopping trips with her mother, conferences with her father. She hadn't had a home for so long. This place brought back too much nostalgia. Even the car, something her father had obsessed about when he'd turned forty and was at the peak of his career.

Impulsively, she picked up her phone and dialed her brother. From her window, she could make out the layers of foam that formed on the tips of the waves crashing into the pier in front of her.

"Sis. You made it." Jake's voice never failed to soothe her.

"Yeah, it's so beautiful here. I'm kind of sorry I discouraged Riley from coming along."

"Well, it works out for me. We're trying to catch a weekend concert at Ravinia. Talking Heads."

"Eww. Poor Rye." She laughed. "All that noise."

She heard footsteps and people in the background.

"Right. Screaming with background music, as you say," he teased.

"Where are you?"

"Making my rounds before calling it a day," Jake answered. "On call all weekend. What are you doing over there? Taking some tours at all?"

"Playing it by ear," she answered a little bit too quickly. "Adjusting to the time change, I guess."

"Hmm. Okay. Well, be careful if you plan to tour on your own. Call when you're back in town."

"K." Tessa stopped short of hanging up. "Jake?"

"Yup."

More voices. She pictured him at the nurses' desk, maybe writing down some notes. She could hear him flipping some papers.

"I'm sorry I put a hole in your head."

Soaking in the luxurious sunken tub with music piping through the walled-in speakers, Tessa thought through her upcoming workshop. She'd meant to draft something during the long flight to Asia, but in between the meals and the movies, her mind had been a total blank.

What did she know about creative writing, anyway? She had a business degree, wrote superfluous words because they bombarded her brain, but she had no formal training, no other familiarity with the art other than this one book.

Her agent had told her to do what she did best—look good, live the life because she could, and channel her manic ways into riling up a discussion.

That, she agreed, she could do. She reached for her phone and began to type.

Creativity is not learned, it comes from within

Manifests in many ways, shapes and forms

Even the way you dress, the way you carry yourself is creativity, individuality

Don't be afraid to think your thoughts, write them out

Darn it, she thought. Seriously? She was doomed.

She swiped left and pressed the WhatsApp icon.

A smile crossed her face. All those messages she'd saved, she'd gone through them many times before. Simon was back in England but hadn't allowed a day to pass without a message, a Tweet, a picture. Most of them were pictures of scenery, beautiful locations, her favorite a cottage in the English countryside. She even decided to use those images to inspire her new book.

Yes, she was writing again. Funny how forgiving the drought becomes once the rainfall ensues. She had found her muse. Her main character was a man with a checkered past, hiding out in a small town in England. She hadn't told Simon yet—*you're the bad guy in my new book.*

They had a funny banter going.

"ET wants to call home." He would say before following up with a phone call. And yes, they had now graduated into phone calls. Video calls, most of the time. Skype or Facetime.

"Elliot here," she would respond.

It could be as quick as a, "Hi, what's going on? What? No. And why is that?" to "I'm thinking of you, what's new?" A word. A line. It didn't matter, as long as they kept in touch.

She justified it to Riley as the best of both worlds. He wasn't in her world, just passing through it, and it made her happy to know there was someone out there who didn't want anything in return. Even bloggers were only paying attention to her now because of her fame. She knew this was life, but it still turned her off whenever loyalties came at a price.

No one knew how lonely her world was. Except maybe him.

The chime of the hotel bell caused her to sit up unexpectedly, the water in the tub swishing back and forth until it overflowed on to the floor.

"Shit," she said. "They've got to stop with the A class service."

Quickly, she grabbed the robe hanging over the towel rack, wiped her feet on the floor mat and ran toward the door.

"Hey," Andrew said happily as he kissed her on the cheek.

"Andrew."

She wasn't surprised. She'd flown there with an army of people— she just hadn't sat with them. And yet, she couldn't hide her disdain about his appearance at her door. She made it obvious by peering outside of the room and glancing up and down the hallway to see if anyone else was there.

"Expecting someone else?" he asked.

"No, I—"

He stepped into the room and looked her over. Her bangs were clipped over her head, their ends dripping wet. "What?" she asked.

"How come you never modeled?"

His eyes looked rabid, hungry, tired, she didn't know what. *How was I ever attracted to that?* "Not my cup of tea."

Andrew walked to the couch and sat. "I figured since we have to look all lovey dovey at tomorrow's function, we should do a little practice."

She laughed out loud. "You lunatic. No."

She began to walk past him, intent on finding a towel to dry her hair.

He looked around the room and shook his head. "You need a maid, stat!"

Before she turned around, she saw him kneel to look through the pile of books on the floor. He picked up her Sudoku magazine and leafed through it.

"Shit, Tessa. You need to get a life. You're in your head way too much. If you're not reading, you're reading about reading. Or playing games by yourself."

When she returned, he grabbed the hem of her robe and pulled her toward him.

"Andrew! I said no."

"You used to like practicing!" he laughed. "What's changed?"

"Ha!"

With her luck, Simon would walk in right this minute. And then she was going to have lots of explaining to do. Even if they promised not to ask each other. If Simon was going to catch her with someone else, it would definitely not be with someone like Andrew.

"You're turning into a hermit."

"Not everything is about you." She scoffed. "Or sex."

"It used to be," he said, planting himself on the couch next to her. She never had to worry about him. He had the attention span of a fruit fly. "Okay, beauty. Mind if we just hang out?"

"Okay, but just for a few minutes. I have somewhere to be in an hour," she lied. She was afraid her excitement would give her away. She couldn't sit still. She was ready to see the man she had missed for weeks.

Andrew ignored her last statement and reached over for one of the magazines on the round glass table. "Look at this. This was the shoot I told you about. In Milan."

"Hmm." She took a seat next to him, her legs folded under her lap, a towel now wrapped around her head. She gladly changed the subject. "You look better without the facial hair. And those pants, they look painful. I—"

Another chiming bell. This time, Andrew was on his feet before she could react. She heard the voice of the man she had been waiting for.

"Sorry, mate, I must have—" Simon looked past Andrew and saw her sitting on the couch. "Tessa."

fourteen

Simon stood in the living room of Tessa's suite, staring out at the wide expanse of the sky with his hands in his pockets and a carry-on at his side.

Andrew had left. Still, Simon debated whether he should get his own room. He realized it was not something he wanted to do despite how he felt.

It had taken quite the maneuver to get here. He'd been asked to travel to Asia many times, and his supervisors were shocked when he'd finally agreed to schedule a trip to visit one of the research facilities in Kowloon. But since no one knew about Tessa, no one suspected his motives. To them, it was a blessing they'd be smart to take advantage of.

There he was, scheduled for a tour of the facility on Monday. But for now, he had three days to spend with Tessa. Their friendship had continued to develop after San Francisco. Somehow, it had become easier, freer, less constrained. They traded messages at any time of the day and night. They became experts at calculating the time difference. His WhatsApp profile would register his regular checks at 3 a.m. Chicago time and she would always reply to his messages at 3 p.m. his time.

And he continued his crazy life in London, putting in even more hours at work than he'd originally anticipated. He even made an effort to check in on Maxine. He found that there'd been no devastation on either side, just a bit of wounded pride on her part. Nothing that trips with her friends wouldn't cure with time.

No one in his family knew what was going on.

His parents had no opinion about what he was doing with his life. He'd always kept them close, filled them with pride for his accomplishments. They trusted that he knew what he was doing. You can't force love, they told him. Love isn't like the atoms you work with to manipulate surfaces and things, love just happens. And when it does, there's no guarantee that it's forever. And then his dad would follow it up by looking lovingly into his mother's eyes and mumble, "We're just lucky it's this way for your mum and I."

Not even Adrian was aware he was flying between continents to meet a friend. He didn't feel the need to explain these business trips. Even his logical mind had decided to bypass its propensity to explain everything. For the first time in his life, he was winging it.

But that day was not the day to wing it. He had caught Tessa by surprise by taking an earlier flight and arriving in Hong Kong sooner. And apparently, the man in her room as well. The same model she'd been with in Vegas. Simon's insecurities about their keeping silent about their life outside of each other began to surface. It wasn't her problem that he was too busy with work to screw anyone else. More power to her. If she had the time, that was great.

Fuck that.

Who was he kidding? He'd even stopped googling her after he'd seen her in San Francisco. He was afraid of what he would find, what he might discover. He didn't want to lose her to his jealousy, didn't want to pressure her so much it would scare her away. He was going to go with the flow for as long as he could.

He didn't even hear her when she finally leaned against his back and slipped her arms through his. There was something about her smell that drove him crazy. It was a personally crafted mix from a parfumerie in Paris.

She stood on her toes and leaned her forehead on his shoulder. Slowly, he turned around, enclosing her in his arms. He caught sight of little piles around the room. Clothes, books, a laptop, notebooks. He made a mental note to clean up when she wasn't looking.

"Are you mad?" Tessa asked, her brown eyes shielded by her dark, thick eyelashes.

"Seriously? Second cousin?" he asked in jest. He enjoyed watching her squirm over the introduction. She was so transparent; her face betrayed every single lie she'd ever tell. And every single truth. He wished he had taken a picture of her then. She had turned red with embarrassment. Definitely a Snapchat moment.

"I know!" she exclaimed. "Sorry!" She released her hold on him and covered her face with her hands.

"We don't look alike so I couldn't say we were first cousins, and then the word second just slipped out of my mouth!" she said, stepping backward and resting on the couch's arm.

"Crazy flackery mumbo jumbo."

"I'm supposed to know what you just said, right?" she laughed, twinkling eyes like the stars. He wondered whether they had something to do with his sudden shortness of breath.

"I've been subscribing to a dictionary since I met you."

"Stop." She placed her palms flat on his chest.

"Would it really be a big deal if he found out about me?" He stepped in.

"Yes! It would be! The press is playing off Andrew's and my supposed attraction to each other," she said.

"*Supposed* attraction?" he asked, gently pushing her down so only the bottom half of her body remained elevated.

"Oh my god. Really, Simon?" She frowned. "That's all work! You know how he gets on my nerves."

"And this? What is this?" Simon asked, kissing her again and again. She opened her mouth up and gave him access to what he'd been wanting since he walked in the door.

"Play." She giggled.

Simon stepped between her legs as she wrapped them around him. Gently, he tucked a strand of hair behind her ear. "You look different. Beautiful as always, but something's different."

"I'm growing my bangs out. Look." She parted her hair sideways with the tips of her fingers.

"And I can't see your pretty ears anymore," he whispered, leaning down to kiss her again. She pulled his head down and met his kiss. Every time he touched a part of her, it always felt like the first time. She

79

remained new, shiny, breakable. The moments they spent together after being apart were always intense.

"Simon?" she muttered against his lips.

"Hmm," he answered, still kissing her, tugging at her top lip with his teeth. He didn't like it when she pulled away.

"I was happy when you told me you broke up with Maxine," she said, caressing his hair as he nuzzled her neck.

"Good. So was I."

Tessa squealed as he lifted her roughly, intent on taking her to the bedroom. He went from door to door, opening a closet, and then the pantry, and then the guest bathroom. And not without tripping over a pair of high heels in the hallway.

"Jesus!" he growled. "If we don't find the bed soon I'm going to take you right here!"

She giggled, pressed herself against his hardness and pointed straight ahead of her. "There."

He kicked the door open and laid her flat on the bed while kneeling directly in front of her. He almost shredded his shirt in half, looming over her while unbuckling his belt. Their eyes never left each other. She took deep breaths as she lifted her tank top over her head.

There they are, my beautiful works of art.

His phone began to ring.

She motioned for him to answer it. "It's okay," she mouthed silently.

Irritated, he pulled it out of his pocket. "Two seconds," he whispered, leaning back on his feet to keep his balance on the bed.

"Yes!" he barked. "No, man, I'm not there yet. I'm still in London. I won't be landing until late Sunday evening."

He wondered whether cell phones announced your location to every caller. He still wasn't the savviest person when it came to technology. He cut the call abruptly; he couldn't take it anymore. He had to be inside her.

And as he looked up from his phone, he saw her. Turned on her side, her legs tucked under knees, her chest rising and falling in slow motion; Tessa was fast asleep.

fifteen

"Simon, please," Tessa gasped, almost out of air and struggling to hold herself up as she leaned on the marble counter top. "I want you."

When Simon announced he wanted to have breakfast, she'd had no idea his first meal of the day would be her. He had already taken her once that morning, vowing to make her pay for falling asleep on him the night before.

"Not yet, baby," he muttered, his lips against her skin. "I'm still hungry."

"But," she said, bending down to grab his head and pulling it up toward her. "I'm going, and I want you to be here with me. Please."

He shot upward, laid her on the counter and plunged hard and deep inside her. She held on to his shoulders, spurring him on, teasing him. "More." She breathed. "More."

"Tess," he groaned. "Take me, baby." He pumped faster, harder, lifting her legs and resting them on his shoulders. It wasn't long before he released, shuddering and shaking as he collapsed on top of her. Gently, he placed her legs down and held her up against him, supporting her with his arms. They kissed passionately, languidly, as if they were lovers who hadn't seen each other in a long while.

Tessa broke the kiss, caressing his face and wiping the sweat off his brow. "Now I'm going to make you a real breakfast."

"Okay, it says here," she said, tracing the map they'd picked up before boarding the Star Ferry, "that the shops are walking distance from where we get off."

"I thought you wanted to go to Ocean Park."

"I did, but with tonight's gala event, we don't have that much time," she answered. "I figured we could walk around Kowloon a bit, see Mong Kok or the Langham Mall before heading back."

She saw his blank expression.

"Sorry. Says here the Langham is a huge mall with lots of stores and places to eat. And Mong Kok is their outdoor bargain market. Sort of like New York's Times Square, only many more stalls."

His face still registered no reaction. She finally realized his expression had nothing to do with the shopping. She was obligated to take Andrew as her date to the gala event tonight, which meant spending a few hours without Simon.

This was clear, she told herself. I mentioned this to him even before he offered to meet me here.

Maybe she was reading too much into it. They were friends. Okay, maybe lovers. But with a common understanding. And obligations.

"No biggie," he responded as he took her hand and led her to one of the benches by the window. "I've got so much work to do; I should get started on my work plan while you're out."

"That's more than I can say I've done," she said. "I still have no clue about the arc of my new book. Zero. Zilch. Nada."

"Why is that?" he asked.

"I don't know. I'm just not forming anything coherent these days. It takes a while for the characters to find their voice."

"And how does that come about?"

She placed his hand on her lap, held it there and looked out at the harbor. "It just means I still haven't found the pivotal scene. It will come."

"Have you ever thought about writing an outline?"

"Me?" She laughed. "No way."

The ferry moved seamlessly across the water, bellowing its horn at passengers on a nearby yacht. Simon turned to get a better view of the skyline. He relaxed the full weight of his body against the wall and pulled her close. He looked mesmerized by the scenery, the buildings in all their majesty only to be upstaged by the mountains directly behind them. It was August, a summer month when the weather was hot and humid, and the forests were lush and verdant.

"Simon?" She squeezed his hand to get his attention.

"Hmm?" he answered, still staring off to the side.

"This is the third place we've visited together." She had no idea why she'd said that. She didn't want to sound mushy, but the calmness in the air left her feeling bold. Made her believe she could speak her mind with him. She was glad the third date rule had failed to rear its ugly head.

He pulled her to him and she settled her head on his shoulder. "I know," he answered with a smile she felt against her hair. "Is that your one truth?"

"Yeah," she declared, pulling his hand into her lap. "Yeah. It is. What's yours?"

"You smell really good."

After a two hour wait and with three shopping bags in tow, they commandeered a table for four at a dim sum restaurant in Mong Kok called Tim Ho Wan. It was a recommendation from a friend of Simon's who had spent a few years in Hong Kong when he first joined the company.

It shocked her that all she bought was a blouse for Riley and a wallet for Jacob. Simon had done most of the shopping, picking up a pair of shoes at Burberry and ordering a custom-made silk suit. Watching the ladies at the suit place fuss over him like he was someone famous amused her. She overheard one of the women telling the security guard by the door that he was a British actor.

She didn't blame them one bit. When he stepped out of the fitting room for the tailor to mark his alterations, she heard them giggle.

All the while, he kept his eyes on her, asking for her advice regarding the fit of the jacket and her choice of color.

She hardly looked like someone who should be stepping out with a famous actor, but she didn't care. Her hair was a bit grown out, and her jeans had way too many holes in them. This was her down time, her time with Simon, she reasoned to herself. Every time she was in the public eye, things always had to be in place. When she wasn't seeing people, she reveled in wearing what was now called street fashion. Loose, chic but comfortable.

"Pretty packed for a hole in the wall," Simon said, while digging his chopsticks into a basket of siu mai. He had taken care of the ordering, which pleased her to no end. She loved it when he took charge. Steamed baskets of assorted food filled the table—pork filled bao, chicken feet, shrimp dumplings, radish cake and pineapple buns. She tried everything except one.

"Those," she lightly touched his lips, "are definitely going nowhere near these," she pointed to her mouth, "after those," she looked at the chicken feet.

Simon leaned back in his chair and laughed. "I don't blame you."

She leaned back too, this time with her arms crossed. Just as she was about to ask whether anyone in Simon's family had ever been to Hong Kong, a thought suddenly entered her mind. "Who knows you're here?"

"You mean, specifically here? In Hong Kong?"

She nodded.

"No one. My family and friends think I'm traveling for work."

"Ah. So, if anything happened to you, how do they know where to look?" she asked, resting her chin on the palm of her hand.

"Well, when they find my phone and the one thousand pictures of you, they'll know," he said.

She laughed. Rather uncomfortably. This is what having an affair feels like. It's you and him and no one else.

"Adrian doesn't know I'm here." This time he leaned forward, closer to her. "Does Riley know you're here?"

"She has to. Even if I don't tell her directly, Jake knows. He's very protective that way. Needs to know where I go, who I'm with."

"You seem so attached, the two of you."

"He's the only constant in my life."

He stayed silent. She hadn't intended to offend him. But then she decided it was too soon to even think of his role in her life.

That was the real crux of the matter, and she wanted to keep it top of mind.

"What about you, your parents? Do you see them often while you're home?"

He laughed. "As a matter of fact, I have dinner with them every Sunday. They don't live far from my old apartment. I'm moving to Chelsea when I get back, which is a little further away, but I know my mum will find every excuse to come and visit. I'll be too close to the shopping area for her to resist. She likes to get out sometimes. Leave the farm."

"We're lucky we have family we can count on," she said.

"But none of them know we're together," he said, his tone lowered, quiet.

"Why does anyone need to know? Who cares?" she asked in defiance.

He picked up another dumpling and shoved the whole thing in his mouth.

"Okay, let me rephrase that," she said. "In time, they'll know."

He smiled. "Better."

He looked at his watch. She could tell he wanted to change the subject. And she didn't have to try. A round of applause filled the room. Tessa and Simon turned to see a man on one knee with his arms in the air, proposing to a very embarrassed woman.

"At a dim sum restaurant?" Simon smirked.

"Hey! You'll never know! Maybe this is a special place for them," Tessa said.

"Must be," he answered, pulling his wallet out. He motioned for the dim sum man to bring the check over.

The man counted the different colored plates, each with a code for the food they ordered, wrote with lightning speed on a pad of paper, tore it off unevenly and handed it to Simon.

As he examined the bill, Simon said, "I forgot your Twitter profile says, 'hopeless romantic.'"

"Love makes the world go 'round!" she said in response, pausing to follow up with an afterthought. "At least in romance books!"

sixteen

Simon abhorred spending this much time in front of the mirror. Normally. But tonight, he wanted everything to look perfect. He twisted his bowtie until it looked just right. It bothered him, not having a good set of cufflinks—who would've known he'd be attending a formal event while in Hong Kong? The event was being held to honor the Prime Minister of Canada during his visit to Hong Kong. Tessa had been invited as part of the Artist's delegation. Simon had not been invited, but a colleague named Nancy Ling had friends who knew the organizers.

He was an easygoing guy, never really one to care about what he wore, always believed comfort and fit came first before designers or brand names. But if anything came between him, his watches and his cufflinks, that would be another story. A man's image was reflected by his personal taste in those two items. That night, he had the watch, but not the cufflinks.

Renting a tux two-hours before an event was a production in itself. First, he had to leave the suite while Tessa was getting dressed to make a few phone calls. One call to the Asia Society for last minute seats to the event, and then another call to Nancy Ling, who had offered him tickets if he would go as her date. She even told him she'd meet him there, despite his offer to swing by her apartment on his way to the party.

Luckily, the hotel had an arcade filled with shops on the ground floor. Granted, they were luxury stores and he had been forced to fork over some serious cash for a formal shirt and shoes. Still, he felt pretty smug about pulling it off.

Tessa had been gone by the time he came back. Out of habit, he went about the room, picking up her discarded makeup, her hairbrush, her towels and her clothes. He put her things in a drawer by the bathtub and piled her clothes neatly on the sitting couch by the bed.

As he placed the finishing touches on his outfit, dabbing some cologne and straightening up his sleeves, he felt proud. There was no way he was going to sit in the hotel and allow his insecurities to get the better of him. It wasn't about her going with someone else, it was the fact that they'd be apart for a few hours. He only had one day left with her. And despite her seemingly hostile reaction to Andrew—she'd avoided his calls all throughout this trip—Simon's competitive streak just wouldn't let things be.

He arrived at the Asia Society Hong Kong Center one hour after the start of the dinner. He had read about the venue—a former British military site recently converted into a cultural hub. The rooftop garden, with concrete flower boxes and Chinese artifacts, had been transformed into an ancient Chinese palace, complete with a bridge over an infinity pool adorned with lotus leaves. Votive candles and paper lanterns lined the walkway from the entrance to the pond. Wooden tables and chairs were tastefully decorated with gold and red satin accents.

Nancy Ling waved at him from the bar. Her ebony hair flowed down the shoulders of her long emerald green dress. She was tall and lithe and graceful. He gave her a kiss on both cheeks as she leaned in to greet him.

"We're at table fifteen," she said.

He offered her his arm in response. They took their seats at a table with four other couples. To his left was the wife of the French ambassador and to Nancy's right was the husband of a local artist. Champagne was passed around and intricately plated Cantonese delicacies—shark fin, abalone, birds nest and squab—were served. Simon wasn't hungry, wasn't too involved in the tableside conversations. He busied himself looking for Tessa. Nancy made small talk, asking about the places he'd visited over the weekend and curious about his thoughts about her country. She would die if she knew that he enjoyed the eight corners of Tessa's suite more than anything else he'd seen.

Simon was gracious and attentive, making sure to react to whatever it was she talked about. But he kept looking. And glancing. And scanning the garden. He focused on women with short hair, ears perked up for that squeaky, quirky laugh. It was a full house with over one hundred fifty people in attendance.

The night wore on, the liquor flowed freely. Speech after speech was made. Some political, but mostly relevant to the arts and crafts of the Orient. And then it was time for the dancing. A hardwood dance floor rose out of the ground and the area quickly morphed into a club. By this time, Nancy was begging him to dance with her. He promised to do so after a quick trip to the loo.

Turned out that the loo was inside the building, through a maze of stairs and down a small escalator. It was on the way there that Simon saw Andrew. He looked every bit the model; dapper and exceedingly stylish, his blond, wavy hair greased back and tied in a ponytail. Andrew stood by the steps with a woman with shoulder length hair, her smooth silky back exposed in a long, flowing red dress.

He's dumped Tessa somewhere, Simon thought.

He overheard their conversation as he approached them.

"Come on, Tess. It's early."

"Andrew, I'm tired. I just want to go home."

"What the hell happened to you?" Andrew slurred. "You were fine a while ago."

"I'm just so jetlagged."

"I haven't spent any time with you during this trip." He stepped in toward her. She backed away. "Come on, Tessa. We used to have so much fun together."

"I'm sorry, I'm just not feeling too well. You stay. I'll Uber back to the hotel. Promise I'll call you tomorrow."

Simon knew that voice. And yet, when she turned around, he was struck by the most exquisite face he had ever seen—just like the first time he saw her. The almond shaped eyes, the thick full lips.

Tess gasped and tripped backward as their eyes met. Then slowly, she shook her head in a silent warning.

Simon kept walking, past the couple, down the escalator and toward the bathrooms. In less than a few minutes, he heard the clicking and clacking of high-heeled shoes. He felt a rush of excitement as he stopped in his tracks, swung around, grabbed her arms and pulled her roughly behind a large stone column in a darkened corner. He pushed her against the wall, pinned her arms up with his hands and kissed her, biting her top lip, muttering in her mouth.

"I couldn't find you," he said breathlessly.

"I know, I know. The wig," she whispered, planting kisses on his forehead and on his nose. "What are you doing here?"

"I got lonely," he said, slipping his hand into the front of her gown and squeezing her breast. His mouth remained latched onto her neck.

She closed her eyes but only for a second. "No!" She pushed him away. "I saw you with someone else."

She twisted herself to loosen his grip on her. Still he held on tightly. Mixed signals, that's what she was doing. He knew she was struggling to keep her wits. He wished she would just express herself, tell him what he wanted to hear her say.

"You're jealous," he taunted. "Just tell me you're jealous. Just like I am." He held her face and tried to kiss her.

She still didn't budge, ducking her head so his lips ended up in her hair.

"God, Tessa. She's nothing. She's a work associate. I used her to get in here, don't know anything about her. Don't want to know."

She stared at him blankly as he held her against the wall. He licked a trail down to her breast and bit her. "You're so beautiful, you're mine. Tell me you're mine."

"No." She was all contradiction, wrapping her legs around him as he lifted her up and pushed her panties to the side.

"Tell me," he ordered, this time opening her up with his fingers, as he looked into her eyes.

"No." She moaned. "You would've gone home with her. No. Let me down!"

"Tessa." He crushed her against him. "I'm blinded by you. I can't see anyone but you!"

She was ready. He wanted to cut through her defiance. "Tell." Deeper, he probed. "Me."

"Bastard," she said, pounding his shoulder with her fist. "Stop it."

Overcome with feelings he couldn't explain, he released her legs and gently set them on the floor. And then with both hands, he cupped her face tenderly and grazed his lips across her cheeks. "You're jealous."

"Yes."

The ultimate turn-on.

"You want something to write about?" he growled as he unzipped his pants and she took him in her hand. "Let me give you something to write about."

"Yes, give me…" She gasped as he entered her. "I'm yours, oh, I'm yours!"

This woman, he thought. She makes me do things, feel things, want things I never even knew I wanted.

Like a future.

Once every few weeks was no longer enough. He couldn't bear to be away from this constant pleasure. He was getting spoiled. As time progressed, as they saw each other more and more, she destroyed his senses. Made him crazy. All his thoughts were of her, and the ineffable madness she incited in him.

Simon shuddered with desire as he held her in his arms, sat her on top of him, lifted her up and pushed her down.

"Take me, Tessa," he sputtered. "Take me home."

seventeen

"**D**id you put away my hairbrush?" Tessa asked, agitated. She heard him draw a deep breath before he stood and walked toward the bathroom. "It should be in that drawer with everything else," he retorted, returning her tone with one of his own.

They rushed around the suite, packing up hurriedly, both sullen and exhausted. Tessa's car was coming in thirty minutes to take her to the conference. Simon's ride, along with Nancy Ling, was coming within the hour to take him to the Kowloon factory.

Tessa felt disoriented. Disconcerted. Something wasn't right. She was going to miss him. When she tried to assure herself the messages and calls would still come, it no longer served to comfort her. Maybe they were no longer enough. Maybe she wanted more.

Perhaps what fazed her was the lovely Sunday spent at Ocean Park, eating, riding and running around like little kids. She'd learned so much about him, tested his fear of heights once again, his reluctance to go on the cable car that crossed the mountain. And yet, he'd gone out on a limb for her, given in to everything she wanted to do, saw everything she wanted to see. He thought it was cute, her fascination for sea life. Dolphins and whales and her insistence on touching everything and trying everything, even the roller coaster that flipped over numerous times and made him sick.

By mid-afternoon, he had been ready to return to the hotel. But she hadn't. And so, they had taken the bus to Stanley Market and walked around for over an hour. Tessa had helped Simon choose a silk scarf for his mum and a leather tool belt for his dad. He'd carried bags full of magnets, tea cups and T-shirts for her fans. And then they'd found a special red and black Chinese pajama outfit for his little nephew.

They'd caught the sunset at Stanley Beach, laid Simon's new scarf on the grass and watched the windsurfers battle with waves. She'd sat between his legs as he held her, his chin on her shoulder. She'd finally told him about her ideas for her current book. They character casted, she outlined it all to him. He hadn't liked the fact that the main character had a checkered past. Couldn't he be a spy instead? A James Bond? He was British. She would already have that covered.

They'd kissed like teenagers under the moon and the stars and left only when the lifeguards announced the beach was closing for the day.

We drank too much, fucked too often and now it's time to leave.

"Next time it bothers you that my stuff is all over the place, just tell me and I'll put them away myself," Tessa barked.

Simon didn't bother to lift his head. He was too engrossed in reprogramming the electronic lock on his suitcase. She moved around the room to retrieve the red dress she had worn the night before. Wrapping it up in a plastic clothes bag, she then zipped it closed before laying it flat on the bed.

The more he ignored her, the more it maddened her. Reason told her he was just busy trying to get ready. Her foolish side told her he didn't care. Maybe she didn't either. Maybe she was just exhausted.

"I mean, you think I'm a slob, don't you? Did you ever think it's most probably because I had never shared a room with anyone before you?"

Simon finally got the lock to snap in place. He watched as she zigzagged back and forth, to the bedroom, to the living room, back to the bathroom. Picking up things and shoving them in her bag. Snatching her jewelry from the night table and placing it on her fingers, her neck and then her ears.

"I guess this is it," she muttered to herself, walking by Simon, who observed her from the floor. "All's well that ends well."

"Stop!" He grabbed her hand just as she walked past. "Tessa. Stop. Sit with me for a while. Sit down."

Tessa dropped to her knees in front of him. He placed his hands on her waist and pulled her close.

"What's wrong, Tess? Why are you so angry?"

"I'm not angry, Simon. I'm just stressed out because we're rushing."

"It's not ending, Tess. Nothing's ending. We had such a wonderful time, didn't we?"

He pulled her even closer. She held on to him tightly. She loved the way he smelled, his hard arms and shoulders, the grown-out stubble that rubbed against her face.

"I'll miss you, that's all," she said, her voice soft and calm.

"I'll miss you as well. In fact, you're the one who never wants to plan. I'm the one who has to wait until you Tweet your next destination, remember? I thought you liked this game."

"I don't know. It doesn't seem fun anymore," she said with a laugh.

"Where did all that spontaneity disappear to?"

"The last time I checked, it made you puke your guts out right by the panda forest."

He laughed out loud. She pulled away to look at his face. The sooner she admitted to herself she wished they had more time together, the better this would go. They only had a few minutes before the outside world would once again descend and take over.

"Why would I let you go?" He held her hands in his. "We could be beautiful. What we have, I mean."

She felt grounded, like she belonged in every moment they were together. But what he'd just said had rendered her speechless. Mostly because if she believed it, if she agreed to it, then it could take over her priorities. And she could easily see that happening now. Already, she was playing with ways in her head to ensure she saw him again.

"Okay, let's plan then. Let's try it my way. Where to next?" he asked.

She paused. Had a thought but hesitated to ask. It caused her to question her own resolve.

Were they planning where to meet, or next steps? Because she still couldn't do next steps.

Fuck it, she decided.

"How much time do you need to plan?" she asked sheepishly, fixing her eyes on the floor. Afraid to see his reaction.

He shrugged his shoulders. "Why?"

"A week from tomorrow I'll be in the Philippines at a secluded beach for a much-needed break. Do you think you can join me?"

eighteen

"Thank you." Nancy Ling flapped her long, dark eyelashes at him. "For agreeing to stay a few days to train us."

Simon tilted his head and squinted. "Not you, the scientists." His patience wore thin. Exhaustion, maybe. Withdrawals, definitely.

Nancy ignored his comment as they walked toward the observation deck.

Tessa's most recent text didn't help at all.

Boarded. Can't wait to pick another fight with you. Best make up sex ever.

Breakthrough! She was jealous!

Should he have told her he loved her before they separated at the hotel? The limousine ride had been a challenge, with Nancy riding in the back seat next to him, inching closer and closer as the ride wore on. Simon knew those messages were meant to distract him from spending the day with his coworker.

"Toxicology showed nothing concerning?" She traced her fingertips along his arm while they watched two long robotic arms inject substances into a giant test tube. One hour into their tour of the Kowloon laboratory and he just wasn't as attentive as he should have been. Even though he was witnessing his idea become a reality, he felt incomplete.

He stepped to the side, trying to put some distance between them.

"Not at all. In fact, the nanoparticles allowed access into the cell and various cellular compartments," he answered.

"Nucleus?"

"Particularly." He smiled.

She took it as another opportunity to make a pass at him, despite the presence of other lab technicians. "Brilliant, Mr. Fremont," she whispered into his ear while reaching her arm around his waist.

He grabbed her hand and untangled it from him.

"Nancy, no." He looked straight at her. "I have to make a phone call before checking out the rest of the testing area. Listen. I'll meet you in an hour by the front entrance."

He turned on his heel without waiting for a response.

As he walked along the long narrow corridor, he pondered his decision to meet Tessa at her destination. Coupled with the excitement of seeing her again merely one week after their time in Hong Kong was an apprehension he knew he needed to address. He had to tell someone in his family where he was.

Just in case.

He zigzagged through the halls, past glass enclosed offices looking more like fish bowls. Black couches, white desks. Very modern, tasteful, designed like an ad agency rather than a research facility. The government sure knew how to fund its investments.

Finally, he found what he was looking for. A Here and There Room, designed for teleconference calls. He sat at a long rectangular table facing a giant wide screen TV and plugged a long cord rising from the floor straight into his phone. Adrian's face popped up almost immediately.

"Hey, mate," Adrian said, his warm smile clear and radiating from the screen. Simon could see Ashleigh and the baby sitting quietly by the kitchen table. It looked like they were watching a movie on her iPad. "Hold on, I'm going to the living room."

Simon saw nothing for a few seconds.

"There. Can you see me?" Adrian propped the phone on something he couldn't see and leaned back on the couch.

"Hey. Yeah. I thought I'd call to check in."

"Where are you?"

"I'm staying in Hong Kong for a few more days. Thought you

should know," Simon said, running his hand through his hair.

"But I just saw you! What do you mean you're in Asia?"

Nancy Ling walked past the conference room. Adrian could see her through the screen.

"Fuck," Simon said, ducking his head instinctively, despite remaining unseen.

"Who was that? Holy shit, bro. I knew it! You've been bonking someone this whole time? No wonder, you've been quite chuffed lately. Is that her?"

"No! Adrian! Focus! I don't have much time here. I called because—"

Nancy Ling was back. And this time, she stuck her head in. She looked worried. "There you are."

Simon no longer cared about trying to accommodate her. This was too much. He was trying to get some time to speak to his brother. "Nancy," he said, his face grim, stern. His mouth in a straight line and every word enunciated. "I would really like some privacy to speak to my brother. Please leave."

She bobbed her head up and down and quietly closed the door.

"Okay, Adrian, listen. I need to tell you this. I was in Hong Kong with Tessa. The woman I mentioned months earlier. The author."

Adrian blinked. Once, twice. And shook his head. "Tessa? Talman?"

"Yes."

"Whoop whoop!" Adrian shrieked. "Since when?"

"March."

"March, as in six months ago?"

"Yes." He circled around from behind the table and leaned against it. He muted his voice, his head dipping low, his eyes cast downward. "I can't stop thinking about her. I have to see her again."

"And where is she now?" Adrian moved his face closer to the phone.

Simon had always trusted his brother. They'd been keeping each other's secrets since they were born.

"She asked me to join her on an island in the Philippines. I'm going to fly there in two days. I wanted to let you know where I was. But most importantly, I wanted to tell you about her."

He saw his nephew crawl over to his father. Adrian placed the baby on his lap.

"Hi Henry!" Simon continued. "Listen, she gets somewhat queasy about letting anything out about us, given her public persona and all. So please keep this to yourself for now."

"Of course," Adrian answered. "I won't tell a soul."

"I…" Simon paused to look into his brother's eyes. "I think I love her."

"Whoa!" Adrian whooped. Again. "How did this slip through us? How did we not know?"

"Stealth operation." Simon laughed. "A lot of travel!"

Adrian grinned from ear to ear.

He's in shock, Simon thought.

"Tell me about it," he said.

"I will, but for now I've got to go. I'll be home a week from today."

"Wait, no! Bro. You can't leave me hanging!"

"I'll be overseas for a few days, don't forget. Kiss mum for me and I'll see you soon."

"Fuck, man." Adrian bit his lip as soon as he said that. He covered Henry's ears. "Close your ears, son."

Simon laughed.

"Henry, say goodbye to Uncle Simon." Adrian took hold of Henry's hand and waved it in the air.

"Goodbye! I'll see you all soon."

the fifth goodbye

nineteen

#MeetMeBoracay

"How long, Tessa? How long do you plan on being there?" Revete's voice echoed in the air as Tessa sat at the edge of the wooden bridge, one leg folded and one leg dangling in the water. The speaker phone crackled each time the waves crashed against the break wall. There she was, on the island of Boracay. A beachfront cottage built on a rock and surrounded by the open sea. The bridge she sat on stretched to the edge of the resort—it was the only pathway leading back to her hut.

"I told you I was taking a few days off," she said calmly. "I'll be back in the States by Friday."

"Tessa, it was quite unprofessional of you to leave Andrew like that at the Arts event."

"I know I'm sorry about that. I should've called him the next day. It completely slipped my—"

"Granted, you were tired and all. I get it. But he was ranting about some guy he saw you leave with."

Facepalm. She should've been more discreet. "He's just a friend. We met while touring the park." More denials.

"All right. I'll call him to explain and let him know I've spoken to you about it."

"No. I'll call him myself." When I get back to the States, that is.

"Sweetie, you do know how important he is to this particular tour, right?"

"Of course, I know how important it is." Tessa played with her little toe, tried to see whether she could get it into the tiny slot between the bamboo floorboards. Now it was stuck. She placed the phone down and painfully yanked her toe out.

"He is. Him. Not it," Revete corrected.

"Yes, him." She winced. Her toe hurt, it throbbed and turned a greenish blue.

"Will I be sending the car over to get you at O'Hare next week?"

"Yes."

"Don't forget about the headshots Reggie wants to take of you the day you arrive."

"I won't forget." Tessa finally pressed END on her phone. A puff of air escaped from her lips as she leaned back on her hands. Nothing was going to ruin her vacation. Not the long sermon she had just received from her agent, nor the photos surfacing of her and a bearded stranger the night of the gala. Not even the fact Simon was somewhere far away, unable to meet her at her resort. They'd exchanged many messages since she'd seen him last week in Hong Kong. He was trying to find a way to see her.

What wishful thinking on her part. These crazy, silly feelings were made for her books. And yet, her disappointment at not having him there with her caused tears to pool in her eyes. When was the last time she'd even cried? What was there to cry about? She was resentful of the fact that she was always alone. Even in a deluge of a thousand people, she stood out on her own.

Simon had begun to fill a part of her she'd never even known was missing.

No crying, you weak, spineless hypocrite. You flaunt your independence and crave for his presence at the same time.

And so, she resolved to enjoy herself, take the time to write, finish her research so her story could take shape.

But at that moment, the sky reminded her of Simon. It was a cloudless day, the color of the sky only matched by the clear blue of the ocean. From where she sat, she could see all kinds of fish swimming around the wooden poles, vibrant colored corals illuminating the ocean floor. She wondered how in the world one could ever leave this paradise. She should tell Riley about it. Maybe they could plan a destination wedding and have it here. Jacob loved the beach, and this would be his bliss.

The warm wind blew her hair into her face; she closed her eyes and smiled. *There will never be a time in my life where I am this peaceful.*

Unfortunately, that solitude was short lived. Her phone began to ding.

DISCONNECTED: *What's the weather like over there? Are you having fun?*
GIRL IN 7C: *80 degrees and sunny. A little wind, but warm and wonderful.*
DISCONNECTED: *Funny, it's the same where I am.*
GIRL IN 7C: *Indian summer, huh. Won't last long.*
DISCONNECTED: *Well, I'm going to find other ways to keep the heat going.*
GIRL IN 7C: *In Lo-*

"Eeek!" She shrieked, her cares of the moment blown away by the wind. She slipped the phone into her shorts and swung her legs upward so forcefully that she immediately landed on her feet. And then she turned and ran as fast as she could. *Thump, thump, thump.* Her heavy footsteps and tiny stride had her running to the cottage, trying to maintain her balance on the concave bamboo surface with her slippery wet feet.

She was out of breath by the time she saw him standing by the door. With a sudden burst of energy, she sprinted up to him and jumped into his arms, wrapping both legs around his waist.

"You're here!" she burst out, hugging him with all her might. At another time and place, she would have controlled herself a little bit more. Not here. Not that day.

He carried her into the room and sat down at the edge of her bed, keeping her entwined around him and settling her on his lap.

His grin stretched from ear to ear.

"Of course, I'm here," he answered. "I'd follow you anywhere in the world."

She felt her heart spring to life. Coming from someone so focused, he was willing to take a detour, place his trip home on hold for her?

She looked up and traced his lips with her finger. "Oh, Simon." She sighed before pulling his head to her and parted her lips. He kissed her as if he hadn't seen her in years. And she kept the gates open for him, taking whatever it was he gave and placing her weight on him as he slipped his hands under her shirt.

The bareness he found with his hands elicited a salacious smile from him, lips upturned, mouth closed, eyes hungry.

Gently, she pushed him down on the bed until she was directly on top of him, her face only inches away from his, her elbows beside his ears. She held his gaze, his smile so infectious it made her cry. One teardrop landed on his nose, and then another on his lips.

"Ugh," she said, turning her back so she was lying right next to him. "I'm getting emotional in my old age!"

He rolled over, taking her face in his hands and interrupting her with another kiss. "What's the matter, old bird?"

"Nothing. Before you arrived, I wrote this emotional scene about Lionel meeting Carissa after ten years, and…" She sniffed twice and wiped her eyes. "I also hurt my toe." She held it up to show him. It throbbed, black and swollen.

He laughed. "Oh lord! What did you do to it?"

"I stuck it between the wooden floors. Don't ask me why. Revete made me do it," she giggled. She wiped her eyes.

He wrapped both hands around her foot and brought it to his lips. He kissed her little toe, lightly at first and then caressed it with his lips. "Better?"

"Mmm. Much," she said, pulling him back up so their faces were aligned. "How'd you pull it off?"

He loomed over, just smiling. "I never left Hong Kong. I told them I could stay and hold a training class for newbies last week. I had to deliver my report yesterday or I would've been here sooner."

"And then?" She twirled her fingers in his hair.

"I took this week off," he said proudly.

"But," she said with a glint of worry. "That's four days!"

"And?"

She could tell he knew where this was going. She felt him rising against her and so she lifted both legs up and wrapped them around his waist.

"Four days away from your work!" she teased. And then in a more serious tone, "This will be the longest we've been together."

"I highly doubt I'll have a problem with that." He burrowed under her shirt and settled his head on her bare skin. "Now, tell me what Lionel did to Carissa after ten shag-less years."

"I highly doubt he was shag-less," she argued, giggling.

"Pretend."

"He shagged her?"

"I'd prefer to think he made love to her," he whispered.

She sighed deeply and smiled before losing herself in the role of Carissa.

twenty

"So, I've known you for six months and you forgot to tell me this?" Simon yelled, his voice drowned out by the drone of the motor, the tooting horns and the whipping wind.

He held on tightly to Tessa, who sat next to him, her hand on his knee, as they bounced and bumped with every crack and pothole on the road. He learned the hard way that tricycles weren't built for people over five feet tall. These motorcycles with four-seater side cars were low to the ground. He felt like an American riding a burro.

Tessa turned to him, eyebrows raised.

"What? That my mother was half Filipino?" she yelled back. "I didn't forget. I just didn't think it mattered."

I see it now, he thought. Those beautiful exotic eyes. That perfect Asian complexion. He'd been fooled by the light eyes and the light skin.

"It doesn't," he answered, eyes fixed on her face. "And how do you know the language?"

"What?" she shouted. "Sorry. I can't hear you!"

"How do you know the language?"

"Oh." She leaned closer so her mouth touched his ear. He liked her being that close. "My nana—she was our live-in nanny, took care of Jacob and me even after my parents were gone. I only speak a few words."

The tricycle turned a sharp corner, slowed and sputtered to a stop in front of a muddy pathway leading to a few wooden houses.

"We're here," she said, paying the driver more than she should have. He knew this because the driver leapt for joy before taking off and leaving them alone.

Tessa took Simon's hand and led him down the dirt road. Three chickens strutted lazily in front of them, unfazed by two bony stray dogs trailing right behind.

"My nana and her family live here. She's expecting us," she said.

Simon watched her maneuver expertly down the sodden path, plodding through the dirt and the mud. She seemed oblivious to the squalor all around them, bouncing excitedly as she made her way down the road. She stopped to breathe in the air, smiling as she did it—like it was the most beautiful place in the world. They arrived at a wooden shanty with an aluminum roof covering only half of the structure.

"Nana?" Tessa peeked through a makeshift curtain door. "Nana, we're here!" she announced.

A weak but enthusiastic voice called, "Tessa!" A toothless old lady with snow white hair and a radiant, smiling face came out from under a ladder leaning against the rough cement wall. Her skin was dark and toasted, leathery from the sun. Her housedress hung loosely on her frame and she stood barefoot on the jagged tile floor.

"My baby!" she exclaimed, taking Tessa in her arms.

Tessa returned the embrace and shut her eyes tightly.

The old lady held on to her, consoling her with words Simon didn't understand. "*Anak ko*," she whispered. And then let Tessa go and looked up at Simon.

"Who is this?" she asked.

"Nana, this is my friend, Simon," Tessa said, wiping tears from Nana's eyes.

The old lady eyed him from head to toe. Up and down her head went, given that she was half Simon's size. "Boyfriend?"

Simon nodded. Tessa smiled at him.

Nana giggled, her seasoned eyes turning glossy. "Oh, Tessa." And then she offered Simon her hand. "Come and sit. My grandson is preparing our lunch."

They took a seat on a solid oak picnic table resembling a large, thick tree trunk that had fallen on its side. It jutted out of the living room and into the kitchen, leaving a minimal amount of space to move around.

Tessa pulled out her phone and dialed Jacob's number.

"Jake! Guess where I am?" she asked, then handed the phone to Nana.

Nana cried profusely as she spoke to Jacob, asking him questions, letting him know how proud she was of him, telling him how much she loved him over and over again. Simon didn't understand much of the conversation but the amount of emotion around him was real. She'd shared with him one aspect of her life that wasn't in the public eye. Her family. He was witness to a loving exchange, a warm reception. He felt welcomed.

After the call, the old lady shuffled back and forth, laying out a spread of rice and fish and fresh vegetables set on wooden plates lined by what looked like banana leaves. Simon had read about it in travel magazines, the use of these leaves for cooking, eating and wrapping food.

Simon waited for Tessa's lead. He wondered whether they had forgotten to bring out some silverware. Tessa lifted one knee while she sat. Simon thought maybe he should do the same.

"What's with the knee?" he whispered.

She laughed. "Nothing! Nana used to sit this way when she ate. My mom was so big on table manners, that whenever we would eat with her, she allowed us to get away with everything."

She reached for the plate and began to pick the food up with a pinch of her fingers. "We use our hands here, babe," she stated, as a matter of fact. Like he was supposed to know that.

"For real?"

"For real. Go for it."

At first, he found it quite squeamish, the feel of mashed rice between his fingertips. He observed quietly as Tessa brought the food from her fingers to her mouth. He didn't do it quite as daintily—he shoveled it in with everyone else. He couldn't get enough of the delicious food. Good thing they kept on coming. They must have made a hundred batches, the way they just kept reappearing on the emptied-out plates.

As time progressed, the room began to fill up with people. Nana introduced them to Simon as her children and grandchildren. Tessa broke into animated conversation, a mixture of English and Tagalog, the language spoken by the people of the main island of Luzon. He could tell that her pronunciation was very different from theirs—she couldn't escape her American accent. Nevertheless, there was laughter and giggling and much joking around.

"Leny just asked what country you were from," she turned to Simon. "And Nana wanted to know what you did for a living."

"Scientist," he heard her family say. "Mautak." Tessa leaned in and whispered. "Intelligent."

Before he knew it, an hour had passed. He devoured freshly fried fish they called pompano and inhaled the delicious vegetables, cooked in coconut milk and soy sauce. He got the hang of eating with his fingers. Once in a while, Tessa would dab the ends of his mouth with a napkin.

He had never seen this side of her. For a while, he could swear the sadness in her eyes had completely disappeared. She stayed relaxed and animated, just like when she was with him, but a little more demonstrative. She touched, she caressed, she embraced everyone she came in contact with. She impressed him with her candor, her ability to adjust to her situation. Here was a woman of the world, purely ensconced with people from another culture. He watched her in her element, loved how at ease she was with this family. She transitioned so easily in different conditions, and he was amazed by the authenticity of her actions no matter who her audience was. She wasn't like a chameleon that changed with the environment—she adapted to people in such a genuine manner, with depth and sincerity. He witnessed the many facets of who she was and was suddenly humbled by the presence of the strangers who made him feel like family.

He was told that Nana had stayed in the US with Tessa and Jacob for a few years after their parents had passed away. When her husband got sick with cancer, she had to leave them with an aunt, so she could come home and care for him. Despite the opportunity to migrate to the US, she'd chosen the happiness and togetherness of a family rather than the material fruits of a first world country.

"Tessa! We still have the Karaoke you sent us! Do you still sing?"

She sang?

"Tessa, remember the time you broke your front tooth doing a wheelie on your skateboard?"

"Jem, it wasn't a wheelie."

He learned more about her at this one lunch than he had over the entire time he'd known her.

"What about your Miss Cheerful award in high school?"

"Okay, enough, guys!" Tessa laughed. "You're going to make Simon regret this!"

"On the contrary," Simon said, reaching out to rub her back. "I'm totally absorbed."

The sound of a crying baby silenced the group. Tessa looked toward the stairs. "The baby's here?"

Nana nodded. "She was taking a nap."

Tessa stood up quickly and made her way up the stairs. "Be right back, Simon!"

The family quickly dispersed, some following Tessa, others retreating to the kitchen. Nana stood up to retrieve a large glass bowl filled with oddly shaped condiments, crushed ice and topped with purple ice cream. "Halo-halo," she said. "You will like it. And this time you can use a spoon."

Simon obliged and began to dig into the glass bowl. Some of the mushy delicacies were sweet, all decadent. Crushed ice and milk were mixed with coco and crunchy bits of caramel, beans, pineapple and sweet plantains.

"She's a very special girl," Nana began. "Not so good with relationships. Afraid of loss."

"I've never met anyone like her," Simon replied.

"She looks happy for the first time in her adult life," Nana said. "It must be you?"

"Tessa is extraordinary. Her life is coming together, and she deserves it," he said.

"She looks at you different. You make her happy."

Simon was speechless. He wanted to say so many things, ask a multitude of questions. But he wanted to ask them of Tessa. He wanted to go back to their little hut, to their little world. He wanted her to weave him some stories, and it was her voice he wanted to hear.

"Don't stay if you're just going to leave," Nana said. It was an order, not a request.

He remained silent, finishing off the last of the purple ice cream.

Tessa descended from the stairs with a baby girl no more than three months old in her arms. Tiny with a head full of hair, dressed in nothing but a onesie. Tessa took a seat back down on the bench with her back to Simon, leaning the baby's head on her shoulder.

"I just fed her," she said, addressing Nana. "She looks just like Leny!"

The baby's wide eyes stared right at Simon, a little trickle of milk slowly slipping down her chin. Simon lifted the edge of the blanket and wiped the baby's mouth. Tessa cooed and swayed until Leny came over to take the baby back upstairs.

Tessa stood, circled the table and placed her arms around the old lady. "I think we have to get going," she said.

Nana tilted her body toward Tessa, who lovingly caressed the top of her head. "Take care of yourself. I'll come visit again soon, okay? Don't cry. I'm okay."

"Are you, Tessa?" Nana asked. "I just want you to be happy. You and your brother. I love you both so much."

Tessa turned to Simon and smiled.

"Are you using the computer I sent you? I'll email you again and you can ask Leny to teach you how to Skype, okay?"

"Okay," Nana said, sniffling.

"And here," Tessa said, reaching into her purse. "Use it to get Papa's medicines. And I think you need an air conditioner upstairs for baby Shirley."

Nana shook her head. "No, Tessa, this is too much, please, I don't want anything from you."

"This is hardly anything," she said, pushing the large wad of bills into Nana's hand. "And this." Another large envelope. "This is for the school I told you about. Jem said he already had the architect submit some plans. Two classrooms. Math and reading, okay, Nana?"

"Okay, Tessa. God bless you, my baby. I will miss you."

Simon watched as the women spent a moment of silence. He wished he knew what Tessa was thinking. She became composed, almost too impassive. He felt like she had rehearsed this scene before she'd gotten there. It wasn't the same person he saw just a few minutes ago. This was more the woman he met in New York months ago, guarded.

"I'll miss you too, Nana. I'll be back soon."

Tessa offered Simon her hand, and together they bid goodbye

before hailing another tricycle to take them back to the resort.

The rented villa was too quiet. Simon began to miss her again, when he returned from the gym to find it empty. He walked out to the balcony and saw her on the beach. Wearing a white cover up and a black bathing suit underneath, her eyes were closed, toes pointing towards the water. Lying on her back with her arms stretched to the side, she looked like she was doing snow angels, only on sand. Quickly, he made his way to where she was, running down the spiral staircase from the balcony to the beach.

There was no one in sight for what seemed like miles.

"Hey," he greeted. "Have you been here all this time?"

She looked at him and smiled. "Why do you have your shoes on?"

"Because I always do."

"Lay on the sand with me," she instructed, arm outstretched, fingers reaching out to him. "The stars are out in full force tonight." She tapped his knee and laughed as he crouched. "Lose the shoes, dude. And the clothes."

She sat up and peeled her cover up off and lay back down in her bikini.

"Tessa," he uttered, amused. He'd never lain on a beach before, never felt the sand between his toes, never allowed himself to be so out of control. Except with her.

"Live a little, Simon. Look, there's no one here but us. And the moon and the stars."

He looked around again and realized their only light was the one from the sky. He stripped down to his underwear and laid down next to her. She reached out her hand, and he took it. And then he followed her lead and stared at the sky.

Little lights twinkled all over, shimmering like droplets of gold spreading like fireworks exploding in unison. The sand felt good on his back, the rolling of the waves mesmerized him. The rush of the tide against his skin made him feel invincible. Like it would wash his sickness away, so he could spend an eternity holding her hand.

There they lay for seconds, minutes, almost an hour. In silence. He was dying to break it. To tell her that if that night were his last, he didn't leave this world without touching the sand.

"Is that the Big Dipper?" she asked, still gazing into the sky.

"No, just a group of stars."

"The moon looks huge tonight."

"Well, that's not the moon. That's Jupiter." He turned his head and smiled at her. She flashed a grin before squeezing his hand. They stayed as they were, supine on their backs, chins pointed toward the heavens.

They lost themselves in the music all around them. He could see the sounds clearly, despite being ensconced in the darkness. He wondered if she was pondering the events of the day. He had so much to ask her, but that was not the right time.

"Simon?" she said, lifting her head up to untie the straps of her top.

"Yeah." Her voice catapulted him to the moon. He turned on his side to face her.

"Take me to the stars with you."

twenty-one

Tessa moved around quietly, careful not to wake Simon, who slept soundly with his feet sticking out of the covers. She'd learned he didn't like to be bundled up at night, the comforter constantly bunched up and piled on her side of the bed. She'd also learned that he always gravitated to the middle no matter the size of the bed. And that he kept jetlag pills on the corner of the bathroom counter, but she never saw him take them. She liked to think it was because he never needed help falling asleep.

She wrapped his present in the bathroom, intent on surprising him first thing that morning. Like clockwork, his alarm would go off at 7 a.m. and he'd get dressed and go for his daily run. She had ten minutes before then.

They had one whole day left together. His disposition was concerning. He hadn't spoken much the afternoon they returned from visiting her family the day before. He seemed pensive, deep in thought. Tessa was sure he was just worrying about work. She knew he'd never taken that many days off before. Even the extra night in Vegas had him taking the first flight out the next day.

Many times, on the beach that night, she'd caught his stare. And when she smiled back at him, he returned it with a grin so wide, so warm and bright.

"What?" she'd asked when he'd reached to touch her face.

"Nothing. You're ace."

"I'm what?"

"Awesome."

Touchy. That was the best description she could find for the way he'd acted that night. He couldn't get enough of her, he wanted her close to him, even while he worked on his computer, made phone calls, confirmed his returning flight.

They'd made love three times, his movements gentle but urgent. She'd seen him like this before, but that night, she felt like he'd wanted to tell her something. And she was sure it would be something sad. A goodbye, perhaps. Maybe he'd decided to marry Maxine in the end. He was pushing thirty. She knew that eventually men like him would choose to settle down. Was it time to ask where this was going?

Tessa wasn't sure she wanted to yet. She'd committed to too much that year. It was only September and she still had four more tours to complete before Christmas. Lionel and Carissa were beginning to take shape and their voices filled her head more often than not. She really needed the time to finish their story.

Beep, beep, beep.

Tessa placed the finishing touches on his final gift. She removed her robe and wrapped an enormous velvet ribbon around herself. Then she grabbed his present off the floor, silently stepped into the room, and settled herself on his side of the bed. She turned the alarm off and kissed the back of his head.

"Morning," she said. "Happy birthday."

He turned to face her. "Hi."

She leaned down to kiss his lips. They were warm and soft.

"My birthday was last week," he mumbled. "And you greeted me over the phone, remember?" He smiled at her while vigorously rubbing his eyes. "Complete with virtual hugs and kisses." He deliberately changed his tone, low and gruff. "And pictures."

"Yes, and you better not have stored those on the cloud!" she laughed. "But here you are in the flesh! And I got you something."

He sat up and turned on the lamp next to him. "Wow." He saw what she wore, the red ribbon placed exactly over her chest. He tugged at the ends until she became exposed. "Get under the covers with me," he instructed, sliding over so she could scoot next to him.

"What about your run?" she asked.

"My what?"

"I have a real present."

"Why? What's wrong with this one?" he asked, chin on her shoulder, his front pressing against her bare back.

She laughed, turning to face him, arms in front, hands together, her knees folded between his.

"Tess?" He looked at her, searching for something.

She stared back, silently urging him to see through her. She had nothing to hide.

"What's wrong, Simon? You seem so troubled." She traced along his cheek. "I've put you over the edge, haven't I? All this traveling is just too much for you."

"What?" He growled. "No!"

"What, then?"

"Yesterday, I learned more about you than ever before."

"Is that good or bad?" she asked.

"It's great!" he answered. "But I want to know more. Yesterday was the first time you introduced me to the people who love you, and it showed me so much about who you are. I want more. I wonder... would you tell me about your mom and dad? What really happened?"

"It's supposed to be a happy time." She snaked her hand between his legs. "I want to give you your birthday nookie."

"Tessa, please." His face was so serious, eyebrows in a straight line, eyes slightly crossed.

"Ugh, okay. Where should I start? As you know, my dad was a urologist, a surgeon. My mom was a pediatrician. We lived a normal life. My mom gave up her career early on when I was born and stayed home to take care of me and my brother. I had everything I could ever ask for—a nanny, ballet, hula, piano lessons. My parents held hands when they walked through the grocery store. They kissed and cuddled openly in front of us. We had a home filled with love, Jake and I."

"When did they pass away?" He took both hands in his.

"Fourteen years ago. And do you know, I still haven't remembered everything? The principal pulled me out of class and then asked me to walk with her to get Jacob. And then as she led us to the office, I saw my aunts and uncles waiting by the door. That's when they told us my dad had crashed his plane. He'd just bought a little six-seater; a

Beechcraft, I think. He named it Aurora after my mother, and he was ecstatic about completing his flying lessons. He took her to Wisconsin for the weekend."

Simon's face filled with dread. He wasn't sure whether this was just too much for Tessa. But she pressed on.

"I remember asking them to get my nana, and then chaos ensued because my relatives started fighting about who would be taking us home."

"Where did you live after that?" he asked, his voice in an almost whisper. He continued to caress her fingers.

"This is the first time anyone has asked me about this."

"What do you mean?" he asked.

"No one has cared enough," she whispered sadly, "to ask me about my life."

"I," he leaned over to kiss her forehead, "find that hard to believe. Everywhere I look, you have people telling you how much they love you. You're surrounded by followers, fans, people who idolize you. You have a solid family here and they all adore you."

"Oh, Simon!" she laughed. "Yes, I have a family here but they're so far away from me and Jake. As for the fans, they're not real friends. If I was in a bind today, tomorrow, none of them would come to my aid. It's not their fault, but they've got their hands full with their own lives. I'm an abstraction to them, that's all I am. People are fickle, life is fickle."

He nodded his head and waited for her to continue.

"Let's see. I was twelve and Jake was two years older. I was just getting out of middle school and he was in eighth grade. So, we finished the school year with my aunt who lived in Chicago, and then moved in with relatives—four places in four years. By the time I went to college, Jake moved in with an older cousin and I stayed at a dorm. And the rest," she concluded, her voice strong and even, "is history."

"Did they take good care of you? Your aunts and uncles?"

"They had a fund from my dad's estate and a salary to take care of us. In other words, they got paid to love us." She smiled weakly. "Nana had to leave to take care of her sick husband. As soon as Jake finished school, he bought an apartment downtown and moved me in with him. He graduated with honors from Northwestern and went straight into medicine."

And that was when things between them had shifted.

Tessa closed her eyes, vowing to remember this moment. Because Simon sat up, placed two pillows against the headboard and leaned against it, pulling Tessa close to him so that her head rested on his shoulder. He locked her in an embrace so tight she felt her skin mold into his and whispered. "You'll never be alone again."

Tessa raised her head up and leaned the palm of her hand on his chest. "No promises. Just one day at a time."

twenty-two

They talked about everything. She filled him with stories about her childhood, about her mom and dad. Simon loved listening to her voice, loved watching her express herself. With her hands waving, her fingers spreading out and then closing in, her voice inflecting at certain points she animatedly recounted parts of her life when she'd been happy. She was so open, so honest. Her laughter was infectious.

Simon had so many questions for her before they said their goodbyes again.

"When we left, why didn't you tell Nana that you loved her?" he asked.

"What do you mean?" She looked stumped. She lilted slightly to the side.

"It's just that you're so genuine with your actions, but you're short on words."

"Are you kidding me, Simon? Why do I have to verbalize it? She knows I love her."

"But it helps to hear it," he argued.

By then she was sitting up, still facing him, her legs crossed under her and her back straight and rigid. Before he could say another word, she straightened her legs, sprang off the bed and stomped out the open

119

door onto the veranda. The concierge had dropped off a continental breakfast—a pot of coffee and a tray of assorted breads waited on the glass table next to the rattan couches. By the time he followed her outside, she was pouring herself a cup of coffee.

"Did you cry when you heard about your parents?" he kept on.

"What's with the third degree, here? You meet my family and now you have the right to cross examine me?"

He was indignant. He leaned his back against the balcony. "Pretty much."

"I don't remember," she answered.

"Come on, I think you'd remember if you did."

"Then I didn't! Jesus, what is this?" The porcelain cup clattered as she laid it on the plate and stood.

For the past two days, he hadn't been able to bear having her out of sight. He was sure she'd noticed. He'd had to have her close, no matter what it was they were doing. And he realized he wanted—needed—to hear her say how she felt about him.

But he also realized he was out of line. Slowly, he walked toward her and reached out to hold her.

"I'm sorry, baby. It's just that you're a woman of many words. You write about love, and yet, when it comes to yourself, you don't articulate much."

"Am I disappointing you?" she asked, her voice shaking.

He pulled her in an embrace. She willingly stepped in. "No! Of course not." He tried hard to keep an even tone. He really didn't want to fight. He wanted to hear her say things were changing. And yet, he knew she wouldn't. He had to tell her the truth. He'd been thinking about it even before this trip, right after he'd seen her in Hong Kong. He pulled away, enough to look at her face, his arms remaining wrapped around her.

"It's not enough for me anymore, Tess."

There. He'd said it. He couldn't bear to wait around until the next trip, the next adventure. Sure, they communicated often through the phone, or text or the infamous WhatsApp. But living from one trip to the next was not what he wanted from her.

Then again, he had to be very careful about this—too much too soon could also turn her away. He had many goals to accomplish. What did he know about her, anyway? Always noncommittal, sometimes self-absorbed.

Beautiful, enticing, smart, free-spirited.

What the fuck. He was confused.

All he knew was that he was falling, falling, falling. Fast.

"What, Simon? What's not enough? Me? I'm no longer enough for you?" she asked, her eyes filled with pain.

"No! This. I need to know what this is. Fucking fifteen hours a day, saying goodbye and then meeting weeks later, only to do it all over again."

Now she stepped back. They stood facing each other, an arms-length apart.

"I've been too afraid to ask at the risk of hearing your answer. But I need to know. Tess, where is this going?" He looked in her eyes as he said it. She avoided his gaze and cast her gaze at her hands. She stayed silent for a few seconds, her shoulders hunched, eyelids fluttering nervously. She braided her fingers first in one direction and then in the other.

"Simon, you're asking me for next steps, I don't know what to tell you."

He grabbed her hand again. He seemed to be doing that a lot lately, on to her tendency to take her stress out on her hands. Wringing, swinging, twisting.

"I didn't say I had the solution." He smiled. "I just know I have a problem."

"Is it really a problem? And why do we have to talk about all this now? I don't want to spend our last day talking about this."

"It's a part of who you are and it's definitely not stupid. It's a process, Tess. When two people try to get to know each other, the past matters."

Her head jerked back, and her eyes widened.

He continued, "In fact, Riley, Jacob, Revete, even Andrew. Someday, I'd like to meet them all too. Like we did Nana yesterday. In fact, maybe I should Facebook friend her."

That made her giggle. "Add her to your eleven friends?"

"Something like that."

They both laughed. Detours, detours, detours. She was an expert at deflecting. Now to get her back on track.

"Seriously though, Tess. I'd like our lives to intersect." A slight pause. "Eventually."

"We're not there yet."

This is it, he thought. *This is where she cuts ties.* Simon released her hands, turned around and walked back to the nightstand where her gift lay waiting for him. Maybe he was over thinking this. She was right about the fact that they both had so much going on.

"Let's see my birthday present," he said, reaching for the tiny box on the night table and before sitting on the bed.

She followed him back into the room and sat beside him. "Simon, I'm sorry. I—"

"Is it okay if I tear the paper?" he asked, ignoring her latest attempt to apologize.

"Of course," she said with a half-smile; the sound of crinkling paper permeated the room, providing them with respite from words. Gently, he opened the box and held up a pair of cufflinks. They were white gold shaped globes, intricately etched with the different continents of the world. He lifted his legs and scooted back on the bed to lean on the headboard. She slid in closer to him, legs still hanging off the floor.

"They're great," he said, gently caressing the back of her head and pulling her in for a kiss. Whenever his lips touched hers, everything that happened right before had been erased from his mind. "Thank you."

"Now you'll remember me whenever you wear them," she said, holding his eyes in hers.

"Why? Where are you going?"

For the first time in so long, he felt lost. He wanted answers, but she wasn't offering any.

"Nowhere, silly. I just wanted to tell you how much I enjoyed seeing the world with you."

"Me too."

Whatever it was she had to give at that moment, he was taking. He would follow her lead—shoot now, ask questions later. It seemed to work for her. Maybe it wouldn't be half as bad if he quit planning.

She lifted herself and straddled him. "You do, huh?" she whispered, planting a kiss on his forehead, his nose, his lips. "What." Kiss. "Else." Kiss. "Do you." Kiss.

"This," he interrupted, sliding down against the sheets and burying his face between her breasts. "I love this."

twenty-three

As hopeful as she was, Tessa knew that the morning's conversation was far from over. She tried to make it up to him, she really did. It bothered her too—the fact that they were going to part ways in less than twenty-four hours. She was at a loss for words... had run out of verbal assurances. So, she showed him how much she trusted him—that her body, soul, and heart were all his.

Do this to me. Here, yes. Use this. Yes. Please, do what you want. I'm yours. Yes, Simon. You have me. Of course, you have me. Do it.

They stayed in bed for a few more hours, watching two Madrid teams play against each other. He told her who the teams were; she couldn't really remember.

"The guys in the orange costumes are hot," she commented.

"You mean uniforms, not costumes."

"Whatever."

What she remembered was that he told her he'd love to take her to Barcelona one day to watch his favorite team. They ordered lunch in while she forced him to watch *The Holiday*.

"I couldn't really get into a Christmas movie in early September," he said when it was over.

"It's only Christmas towards the end," she argued. "Besides, don't you like where it's set?"

"My country house is nicer than that," he said. "Smaller, cozier." He wrapped his arms around her tightly to get his point across.

She asked why he liked making her feel like such a glutton when he always ordered vegetables and she always ordered bread.

She also asked about his family, and he told her all about his brother Adrian, his wife Ashleigh and their baby, Henry. He'd sent her pictures of his family before, but she never tired of hearing him speak so excitedly about them. There was *uncle* this and *cousin* that, and a pub in the middle of here and a baby coming out of there. There seemed to be a whole nation filled with Fremonts.

He was never alone, he said. He always had family around him.

She told him again that morning how lucky he was. He kissed her on the nose and said nothing.

"I have an idea," she declared, as Simon tried to catch his breath after another make out session. "Let's go parasailing. Jem's friend from high school owns the company that runs the best tour."

"No." He stretched both arms over his head.

She lay on his chest, keeping him inside her. "Please?"

"Tess, I'm still getting over that cable car in Hong Kong."

She laughed before burying her nose in his neck. He smelled musky. Sexy. "Okay. Didn't think it would hurt to ask."

"I think you should do it. I'll take your picture for your Instagram. If you're nice to me, maybe I'll make a video too."

She shrieked as Simon flipped her on her back and held her arms down. She felt him growing inside her. Parasailing will just have to wait. She was about to see the clouds and the sky without leaving the ground.

It was mid-afternoon by the time they found themselves on a tiny speedboat in the middle of the ocean. First, it was an island-hopping tour in a fishing vehicle called a Bangka—a motorized boat shaped like a canoe with a makeshift roof and outriggers made of bamboo. It bounced in the air with the waves and took in sprays of water against the current. Not far from their hotel in White Beach, they visited a tiny island known for its shells, aptly called Puka Beach. The waters were rough, and the sand was coarse and dense. Simon laid out on the shore while Tessa carried on a conversation with the locals. She watched him revel in his element, bonding with the sand as if it were his new best friend.

It was always the same routine. Small talk was scarce during the last few hours of their time together. They touched, kissed, held each other in the silence, the sounds of the environment allowing them to immerse themselves in their thoughts.

A yellow speedboat took them to the deepest part of the ocean. Tessa was nervous and uptight. There were so many things she wanted to say to him, but the time for that had passed. When he'd asked her all those questions, when he'd told her he wanted more, she hadn't reacted the way she should have.

Why did he always want to talk about feelings? It's not like she had none. She certainly spoke, wrote and thought about emotions every single time; honestly, they were overused. Didn't everyone on Facebook profess their love for their fellow strangers with every single post?

How unfair. Pushing and provoking when she wasn't prepared.

The guide slowed the boat and allowed it to idle in the water. They sat side by side, his arm around her shoulder, her hand on his thigh. All around them, different hues of blue touched the sky and the sea. Cloud swirls in different shapes scattered throughout reminded her of drawings on a chalkboard.

"Miss," said Arturo, the guide who looked no older than sixteen years old. He handed her an orange harness weighted down by a heavy black belt. "I can help you get into your gear, if you'd like."

Tessa nodded absentmindedly, standing before releasing Simon's hand. He reached behind the seat to pull out his backpack. "I'll take your pictures."

She nodded again and held her arms out to Arturo. He slipped the harness straps over her shoulders and pulled the cord tightly around her waist. She remained focused on Simon. He smiled at her before turning his attention to his phone and scrolling for the camera.

"Ready anytime you are, miss. You can get in the water using the ladder in the back or you can dive right in," Arturo instructed.

She gestured at him by blinking her eyes and he tipped his head toward her in agreement.

"Pull this cord once you're airborne."

Tessa nodded. "Gotcha."

Simon pulled her into an embrace. "Have fun, babe. Wave at me from above. I'll be waiting for you right here."

Slowly, she turned around and walked toward the edge of the boat. She heard Arturo shuffling toward the engine, getting ready to shift it back in gear.

"Wait, wait!" she yelled, turning on her heel and running back in the opposite direction.

Simon jumped up. He ran toward her until she pressed against him, her hands on his chest, his arms locked around her waist.

"Tessa, what—"

"Simon, wait! It's not fair, you're never fair! You ask me these really tough questions when I'm not ready to answer. Now I have to go on this thing and what if the cord breaks and I get eaten by sharks, and then I never get the chance to tell you what I feel?" she blurted. She was out of breath before she even started. Arturo was going to lose serious money if she didn't hurry up and get in the water.

Simon took a deep breath and held her tighter. She worried for a moment when he didn't say anything. But what the heck. Poor Arturo. She had to hurry up.

"Here's the deal. One truth!" she said loud enough for him to hear. The motor kept humming. The sloshing waves threatened their balance. "Whenever something wonderful happens to me, you're the first one I want to call. And even when something not so good happens to me, you're the only one I want to complain to. So, I'm changing too."

She stopped to take a whiff of his shoulder. He smelled so good, she began to lose her composure.

"But I'm scared, Simon. I'm not good at this. I've moved around so much in my life, that's the only way I know how to live. I don't want to disappoint you. I'm afraid if I commit to something, I won't be able to see it through. Because the reality is, I love to move around."

She looked up at him and trailed her finger across his cheek. He was smiling at her. And she smiled back.

"One more thing. I wanted to cut that bitch Nancy Ling the night you took her to the gala. I was so jealous! I couldn't see straight. I had every intention to punish you that night, but I couldn't resist you."

He kissed her. Oh god. It made her change her mind about going in the water. Maybe if they just paid Arturo to go swimming while they made out? She was about to suggest that when he took a step back and pulled away.

"Oh, Tess. It's okay. You don't have to worry about anything at all. I know if I push too hard, I'll lose you. I'm going to give you time to figure it out. But don't take too long because I'm there."

"You are?" she asked, her tone soft. She felt comforted now, knowing he still wanted her no matter how crazy she'd been acting.

"I am."

"Promise?" she asked.

"Promise."

She stood on her toes and kissed him one more time. "Okay, the sooner I get my ass in the water, the sooner we can be back on dry land."

She turned and walked toward the end of the boat. "Tell me your one truth later!"

Tessa gave Arturo a thumbs up and plunged feet first into the ocean. She heard the engine rev up and slowly, the slack of the rope holding her down began to pull her across the surface, until her feet no longer touched the water and the sound of the wind lapped against her ears. She pulled the cord, felt a slight whiplash backward. And then there she was, soaring above the boat, Simon standing by its edge, smiling, taking pictures. She drifted up into the sky, waving in an effort to touch the clouds.

The loss of gravity, like the loss of control, was liberating. There was nothing she could do to change direction—she was at the mercy of the heavens.

The sound of the boat began to fade, and an overwhelming sense of peace washed over her. She imagined her mom and dad reaching down to touch her. She wished she could stay there forever, soaring alongside her parents, soaring above the man who was changing her life.

And then she remembered.

Her one last surprise. How could she almost forget?

She pulled at a tiny red string that opened a secret pocket within the harness. In it was a sandwich bag—Arturo's secret little touch, which she opened and emptied out. Confetti began to litter the sky like rain, falling slowly around her. They disappeared into thin air, pulled down by gravity—touching the tips of the waves, little glitters of light. And then she unfastened another piece of tape—a large banner unfolded by the wind hung from her waist and moved together with the balloon across the sky.

She wanted him to know how special he was to her.

HAPPYBIRTHDAYSIMON!!!!

She looked down to see him laughing, clapping and shaking his head. Arturo jumped up and down, clearly excited his plan had worked. She moved her head from side to side, losing herself in the moment, taking in the omnipresent view of the universe.

This is what it looks like from their vantage point, she thought. *They are watching.*

And then a voice in her head. Look down. Simon is trying to tell you something.

She focused her gaze back on the boat. He stood looking at her, waiting for her to look back at him.

And then he did it. She didn't believe it at first. Had it happened? Had he really done it?

Yes, he had.

"Happy birthday!" She waved her arms frantically, her body tipped forward slightly, her legs still swinging in the air. She stared at him, her anchor, her foothold, the only one who could make her want to come back from the sky. He lifted his index finger in the air, paused as if in thought, and then gently tapped his slightly parted lips.

One. One lip? One teeth? One tooth? Oh my god. One truth! Yes, yes, I understand! She nodded in a frenzy.

And then slowly, he lifted his right hand and placed it over his heart. His words were unmistakable. He had formed each syllable with his tongue and his lips, making sure she saw his words because he knew she couldn't hear them.

"I." He pointed to himself.

"LOVE." Hand back on his heart with his eyes closed.

"YOU." Palm up towards the sky, extended toward her.

the sixth
goodbye

twenty-four

#MeetMeAthens

There's no way she could be in the middle of this bloody mess, Simon thought while elbowing his way through the sweaty drove of partygoers. Shame on him for not knowing who this Tiesto guy was. Some world-renowned DJ playing live at a nightclub in Athens called Venue. Adrian apparently had friends in pretty high places, considering he'd gotten Simon's name on the doorman's list at the very last minute.

Simon was livid. He'd found out through Instagram that Tessa was all the way in Greece, something she had conveniently forgotten to mention to him the last time they spoke. Which was last night. He was done following her around the world. So, he followed her to this part of the world to tell her. He thought they'd made progress in Boracay. Apparently, he'd been mistaken.

Tiesto stood atop his DJ table, arms outstretched, holding up two smoke guns and ready to go. The audience followed suit, lifting their arms and waving in hysteria. There were circular pedestals scattered around the area, women in skimpy outfits dancing on top of them, some shedding more and more clothing while everyone cheered them on.

And then the smoke was released, first shooting up in the air and

131

then covering the entire stadium until nothing was visible. How convenient. He couldn't help but laugh at the clever staging of it all.

This was quite the shindig. And the music was pretty good. If he weren't in such a nark, he might have enjoyed it.

She must be here somewhere. Obviously, in a VIP lounge of some sort. The latest picture posted by her publicist looked like they were outdoors, with trees and shrubs in the background. Tessa was sitting on a black velvet couch. Above her were mini Christmas lights and tiny paper lanterns against the backdrop of the dark night sky.

It took him well over forty-five minutes to plow through the raging horde until he saw an exit sign leading to the outside of the club. It was cordoned off, blocked by a large heavy red rope that extended itself from end to end. There was a low drone of endless conversation—the music was no longer blaring. It played subtly in the background, low techno beats still resounding through the walls, but people were able to hear each other speak.

There was no way he could get through the rope, and so he stood a few feet away from it and surveyed the patrons. A waft of air crossed his nostrils. Weed. Cigarettes. Smoking was supposedly banned here, like in most places in Europe. But no one ever paid much attention to the rules. The place was dark, he struggled to make out faces in the light. He pulled out his phone to look at her picture once again. Maybe he could situate her table now that he was looking at the actual location. Slowly, he thumbed through the screen, adjusting his sight to the dimness and making out her surroundings.

"Simon?"

He looked up to find her standing on the opposite side of the rope. It had only been a few weeks since he'd seen her, but her hair had grown out, her bangs now to the length of her chin. She looked stunning; he had an instant erection just seeing what she wore. Her shiny top was tied at the waist. It had no buttons, no enclosures. The front was open, revealing a lace black bra underneath. She wore ankle length wide leg pants that showed off her five-inch stiletto heels. She held a cigarette between her fingers.

"Simon! What are you doing here? I'm so happy to see you!"

"You smoke?" He had to focus on being pissed off.

"Oh, no." She threw the cigarette to the ground. "Only socially. First time in a long time."

She reached for him, he took a step back.

He looked away without saying a word. It was all he could do to cast aside the pull he felt toward her. It was a normal reaction, to touch her, to hold her. He couldn't do that there. He had business to take care of.

A waiter saw what she was doing and rushed toward them. She held her hand up and motioned for him to stand back.

She lifted the rope up. He made a note to tease her about it when he wasn't so mad anymore. Even with her those heels, she only got it up to his shoulders. He had to duck to get under it.

She grabbed his hand and laced her fingers in his. "Come with me, I want you to meet everyone."

He pulled his hand away and followed her. His resistance surprised her, she paused to read his expression but continued to lead the way.

They sat at a booth surrounded by bottles of Cristal and Vodka. There they were—a sultry blonde-haired woman, extremely well-toned, perfectly made. That must be her agent. And the knobhead was there too, looking all coiffed and blown out. He glared at Simon as he saw him approach and took a swig of whatever it was he was drinking.

Three more people occupied the table, two men and one woman. One man's eyes matched Tessa's. He looked reserved, wearing a white button-down shirt and gray dress pants. The woman had long, straight black hair framed around her face like an Egyptian goddess. She was also dressed like one.

"Sayy-mon!" the woman squealed. "Is this him?"

Tessa smiled and snaked her arm around his. He stepped aside but allowed her to hold him. "Yes! This is my friend, Simon, everyone! That's Revete, and you know Andrew," she said, avoiding his eyes. "And this is Liam."

That didn't slip past me, he thought. She called me her friend. And she's been here for three nights. Has he been keeping her company?

"It's the second cousin!" Andrew cheered and clapped.

Liam offered his hand out and Simon shook it. "Nice to meet you, mate."

The Egyptian princess and the man with Tessa's eyes stood. "I'm Jacob, Tessa's brother," he said. "And this is my fiancée, Riley."

Riley slid out of the booth and gave Simon a hug. "I'm so happy to meet you," she said quietly, as if not wanting the others to hear their secret.

"They just got engaged! Tonight!" Tessa squeaked with excitement. "We're celebrating!"

"Oh wow! Congratulations!" Simon said. He felt like an ass. Could it be she wanted this trip alone with her brother because she'd known of his plan to propose? No, wait. Still. If they were that close, especially after their last trip together, she could've told him.

The flurry of activity continued around him—strangers stopping by on their way to their own tables to congratulate Jacob and Riley, servers rotating around with appetizers, no one staying put for very long. When their party squeezed back into the booth, Tessa, under the watchful eye of her agent, moved away from him but stayed close. Tessa poured him a glass of champagne and they toasted to Jacob. He watched as she chatted happily with everyone. Patrons who recognized her handed her their napkins to sign and she scribbled a few words on them in addition to her signature.

Simon had so much going through his head.

He was happy to see her.

He wanted her.

He couldn't go on like this. She kept her distance.

He was an idiot for showing up on impulse. Another one for the books. *The Year That Simon Lost Himself.*

Andrew was a twit; he found every opportunity to touch her skin.

Riley was fit. She glowed from the inside. Liam kept stealing glances at her.

Revete tolerated him. She was like a mother bear protecting her cub. "Tessa, this is the owner of Venue. Pose for a picture with him. Tessa, there's so and so. Let's say hi."

Try to smile. Be cool. So, what if you've been working twenty-hour days and you're completely knackered. Just keep up until you can get her alone.

"So," the twit began, taking a big gulp of wine before pounding his glass on the table. "Simon. Tell us what brings you to Athens." Another tip of his glass.

Way to get sloshed, Andrew. Keep it up because you're going to be sleeping alone tonight.

Everyone was interested in Simon's response. They leaned forward, anxious to hear him speak. "Well," he replied. "It's kind of a silly story, actually. I found out Tessa was in my neck of the woods by seeing a post on Instagram."

Tessa sat up straight. Her hand began to play with the rim of her wine glass.

"So, you decided to fly over three hours from London just to see what she was up to," Andrew said.

Simon was mistaken about this guy. He wasn't all beauty. He had balls. Although to Simon it was a misuse of his bollocks—fighting for someone who wasn't the least bit his.

"Pretty much. You know, Instagram is such a good source of communication between friends."

Revete poured more champagne. Liam wiped his mouth with a napkin. Andrew stared at Simon.

"Move!" Tessa stabbed her elbow at Riley. "Move. I need to get out."

She was obviously furious, her eyes rolled into the back of her head, her tone turned cold. Her movements were jerky; she remained facing forward, refusing to look at anyone. Riley nudged Jacob, who nudged Simon, and they all slid out of their seats. Tessa snatched her purse and looked directly at Revete. "I'm calling it a night. I'll have the car come back for you all."

She leaned over to wrap her arms around Jacob. "Night, baby. Congratulations. I love you." And then she lightly brushed Riley's arm. "See you tomorrow, Rye."

"Okay," Riley answered.

Tessa waved her hand at a big, burly man who led her through the back exit.

It's now all or nothing, Simon decided.

Riley wrote on a slip of paper and then slid it over to him. "King George Hotel. Syntagma Square."

Simon leaned over to kiss the top of her head. And then he, too, was gone.

twenty-five

Tessa hadn't realized how late it was until she'd checked her phone in the car. It was 2 a.m., and there she was, back in her hotel suite at the King George, too wired to even think about going to bed. The view of the Parthenon and the Acropolis did nothing to make her feel better.

She kicked off her shoes and sat cross-legged on the high back chair facing the grand window. The front desk had just called to let her know that Simon was waiting in the lobby. He hadn't wasted any time coming after her. She was relieved in one way, but still so very pissed off in the other. How dare he show up out of the blue and embarrass her in front of her brother!

And what he'd done was laughable. He just made himself out to be a dick in front of the one who needed to approve of him most of all.

Jacob had planned this trip right after she'd returned from the Philippines, and she'd been all for it. When he'd asked her whether she would be inviting Simon to join them, she'd decided against it for many reasons.

I have to explain it to him. No sense in delaying the inevitable.

She called the front desk and asked the receptionist to send him to Room 624.

In one minute, there was a knock on the door.

136

"Hi," he greeted.

She stepped aside. He didn't venture very far inside. He stood frozen in place, arms behind his back as she shut the door.

"Nice suite," he said.

Tessa settled herself on the same chair facing the window. He sat right across from her, on a couch by the fireplace. He faced her, she looked away from him. She couldn't contain her anger any longer.

"Why don't you look around and check my bedroom—that's what you want to do anyway, right? Maybe you'll find some of Andrew's things in there. Then you'll have the excuse you've been trying to find."

"Tessa! Don't be ridiculous!"

"Oh, come on, Simon. You're telling me you're not here because you were worried about him!"

She rose from her chair. She wanted to see his face, gauge his reaction. And when he didn't say anything, she kept going. "How dare you accost me like that, say those things in front of Jacob! It was a happy occasion. We were celebrating!"

"I know. I'm sorry," he said, his tone somber. "But you didn't tell me you were going to be here. When I spoke to you last night, you acted like you were home!"

"I didn't act like anything! Jesus, Simon! I didn't lie. I just didn't tell you because it was a trip with Jacob. And—" She stopped, erecting the usual walls around her.

"And what?" he asked.

"Nothing."

"There you go again."

The way he leaned back with his arms crossed while exhaling loudly told her he was agitated. She knew that part about him, always taking deep breaths as if trying to fill his lungs. He kept on.

"Can you blame me? Can you blame me for always feeling left out? I'm the one who keeps on having to find you!"

She really didn't understand what she had done wrong. She traveled around the world for a living. He should know that. And be okay with it.

"You knew this was my life. You knew this is who I am. I like to disappear. I like to be free to come and go. It has nothing to do with the way I feel about you!"

"Dammit, Tessa! I can't do this anymore!"

"Do what?" she shouted back. "You were the one who told me you were okay with this!"

"Sod it! I realized I'm not. I'm sick and tired of you asking me how I am, what I do when you're not around! I only exist when we're together, Tessa. Which means I don't exist often. And it's not a life I want. It's not a life you should have either. I came here to let you know I got the job I applied for. I'll be staying in London permanently, in R&D. No travel, which is what I have always wanted."

"Well, I'm happy for you!" she exclaimed. "Case closed. Have a good life." This was ridiculous. Here she was, egging him on when all she really wanted to do was jump across the ornate brass coffee table and demand that he hold her.

Her voice cracked. And she was having none of it. Be strong, she told herself. You knew it would come to this. They always leave. They always say they can't have this life. And you're never willing to compromise.

Are you?

Tears began to pool in her eyes. She turned away from him. She heard his footsteps certain he'd be walking in the opposite direction. She held her breath, waiting for the sound of the door. But the only sounds she heard were those right next to her. Even more she wanted to cry. He always fought for her. Why couldn't she do the same for him?

"What does that mean, have a good life?" he asked. "So, that's it? You're giving up on us? Just like that." He knelt on the floor. "Face me, Tessa. Look at me. I think I deserve at least that. Have the decency to tell me it's over to my face."

She didn't feel the need to defend anything to him. And so, she remained silent.

"That's all this was to you? Just the sex? Answer me. Is this all we had? Good sex?"

"Fuck you," she said, raising her middle finger in the air. "Leave."

Two large, heavy tears rolled down her cheeks. She swiped them with the back of her hand and slowly turned around to look at him.

"You're crying?" he asked, surprised. There was a lilt in his voice which made her think he was happy about her tears.

"Why wouldn't I cry, you fucking bastard? What do you think I am, a robot? We spent seven intense months together. Do you think it was nothing to me? Fuck you! Go away!"

She tried to push him away. Pride. Silly pride.

He smiled at her, actually pleased about her suffering. Bastard.

"And by the way, for your information, I haven't slept with Andrew since Las Vegas. Or anyone else, for that matter. You must have been sleeping around and thinking I was doing the same thing as you! And the reason I didn't tell you about Greece is because every memory I have is with you! I thought I should start making some on my own, just in case."

He stepped in. She swatted him again.

"And I was miserable. I planned to call you tomorrow to tell you I could go to London to visit, if you had some time. But you beat me to it! You saw a post and thought I was cheating on you! You suspicious jerk!"

She couldn't stop with the name calling. She was on a roll. Next up was *asshole*. She wanted to use it in a sentence.

"I'm a cock-up. A bastard and a jerk," he said. He pulled her hands and kissed them. "I'm sorry, Tess. I should have trusted you more."

"It breaks my heart that you don't think I value what we have. Sure, I admit, I'm slow at defining things, but I can't even keep up with your oversexed ass, why would I give myself more problems?"

Seemingly he found her hilarious, because he broke out in laughter.

"Stop laughing, dork." It should have been *asshole*.

"I haven't slept with anyone since Vegas either," he said.

"Good," she responded, still holding his hands. He kept his eyes on her and she smiled at him.

"Tess, we still have to decide where we go from here. I'm no longer okay with this. We have to commit to something more."

Say something, you screw up. You'll never know if you don't try. You're nothing like your parents. They believed in taking chances. Why don't you?

"Okay."

"What does okay mean?" he asked, puzzled.

"Just that. We're in this together," she answered. "I'm going to try, Simon."

"That's all we both can do. We can try to be a normal couple."

"Define normal," she said. "Let's get this clear once and for all. Six months later and we're still confused about what we want from each other."

"No traveling to any part of the world without telling me," he said, still kneeling on the ground but this time with his arms around her. Their foreheads touched. "I want to be with you and you want to be with me. There is no one else. And we are in a relationship."

Being in a relationship came first before next steps. She was okay with that. She nodded in agreement. It was amazing, how her mood had shifted from anger to doubt to lust. She could feel her insides begging to be touched by him.

"Where did you leave your bag?"

"That's it." He pointed to his backpack by the door. "I was only going to stay for one night."

"It's your call. I either go to London with you tomorrow or we can stay here for a few more days."

"My call?" He smiled, leaning sideways to slowly push her down the couch until she held the full weight of his body.

"Then we stay," he whispered, pulling on her top lip with his teeth. "Here."

twenty-six

Simon half-opened his eyes, drowsy and relaxed at the same time, while people moved about the lounge. He turned to his side to find Tessa still asleep. She stirred slightly, eyes still closed, arms crossed. They had passed out as soon as the Blue Star Ferry had left the dock at Piraeus. The 6 a.m. ride on bus X96 near the Athens airport was easy but way too early.

Tessa had everything planned out on her itinerary, except she was supposed to be visiting Santorini with Riley and Jacob. When they'd found out Simon had decided to stay in town, they respectfully offered to book their own tours and to meet her in Athens for the flight back to the US. Simon made a mental note to ask her why she hadn't invited her brother to join them on their tour.

Tessa lightly placed a hand on his arm. "Hi."

"Hey," he greeted. "How'd you sleep?"

"So-so." She sat up straight and turned toward him.

"I heard someone say we're going to be passing another island soon. I think we missed Syros," he said. "Want to step outside?"

He read from the guidebook that they'd be passing three islands on the way to Santorini—Paros and Naxos were coming up.

They gathered their things and climbed up a flight of stairs leading to the outdoor deck. It was filled with tourists. Many stood by the white metal railing while others enjoyed their meals on the deck chairs and tables. Simon found two chairs and pulled them as close as possible to the edge of the boat. Tessa removed a plastic bag from Simon's backpack—food they had purchased at the bus station. She handed him a pork gyro. They'd ordered the same thing, except she had it plain while he had it loaded with tomatoes and tzatziki.

"You sure you want to eat that much, considering?" she teased, just as he took a large bite of his food. It had been his idea to take the eight-hour ferry ride instead of using Tessa's pre-purchased flight tickets.

"You mean the ride? Yeah. It's not too bad. I'm just glad we didn't take the high-speed ferry. This one's already pretty bumpy and it's the size of a cruise ship!"

She nodded her head and zipped up her sweatshirt. They held onto their food as the strong wind threatened to blow them away. "Good thing we changed from cabin to outside deck," she chomped. "I think we have the best of both. We can hang out here for a while and then go back into the lounge later."

They continued to eat silently, observing the constant stream of passengers moving around the deck. The waters were rough, and he was glad he'd given in to her appeal to take some Dramamine as soon as they'd boarded. It was making him very sleepy but kept his food down without feeling sick.

He stared out into the sea—shades of blue, markedly different in some areas, open water with islands and cliffs way off into the distance. He had no familiarity with the ocean, but he'd striven to learn about it growing up. He began to speculate on various reasons why the Mediterranean waters had an imposing deep blue color unlike the Atlantic Ocean, which looked green under the sun.

Before getting carried away with more technical pondering, he turned to see Tessa playing with her phone.

"Who's texting?" he asked. He took the empty bag from her hand and headed to the nearest trash bin.

When he returned, she looked up to respond. "I let Revete know I'm taking a different flight back to the States."

"Way to piss her off again," he teased, leaning over and placing his hand on her knee. He was ready for another kip. And she knew it.

"You're worth it," she answered, placing her phone back into her purse and taking his hand. "Let's go back to the lounge. I'd like to do some writing for the next few hours."

When Simon awoke, she was sitting next to him, banging frantically on her keyboard. She sat up straight, legs stretched out on an ottoman, her computer in her lap. He slouched down on the couch, head on the backrest, legs straight out on the floor. He didn't call her attention, content on watching her work, seeing what she was like when deeply immersed in her zone.

She muttered to herself, swiped her touchscreen a few times, clicked the search button and then wrote notes on a shredded piece of bar napkin. *This is her world,* he thought. *How privileged am I to share in her creative moments?*

That wasn't the way he worked, let alone the way he conducted his studies. He made outlines, maps and diagrams, and handwrote his essays before typing them. And here she was, so free flowing, so organized in such a disorganized manner. Type, mutter, swipe, type, scribble. Intermittently, her lips would curve up in a half smile as if she was pleased with what she had written.

He sat up.

"Oh, hey." She smiled before leaning over to kiss his forehead. "Still okay?"

"Never better," he answered, rubbing his eyes and looking over her shoulder at the screen. He had never asked to look at her work, and she had never really asked to see his. He didn't want to overstep boundaries, cognizant of the way she segmented her life from the part they shared together. But now more than ever, he wanted to see if she was willing to lift open that gate.

It may be the Dramamine talking, he thought, but things are shifting between us.

She'd become much more open, more transparent. He'd never seen that side of her.

She'd bought him medicine at the drugstore.

She'd prepared his lunch.

She was proud to introduce him to her circle of friends. If you can call them that.

She'd given up her time with Jacob and Riley to be with him.

She was willing to go to London to see him.

What would his parents say about her? He needed to break it to them soon.

I'm in love with someone, Mum and Pop.

"One hour to go. You didn't miss much," she said. "Now that you're awake, do you remember if that lady ever told us who made the yellow glass blown chandelier we saw at the coffee shop yesterday? Or where it was from? I started writing about it. Our day. It was an eye opening one."

They had hopped a bus from Syntagma the day before, hoping to end up at the Attica Mall, a recommendation by one of the locals at the club the other night. They'd gotten off at Omonoia instead and walked around an empty square, looking for someone who could give them directions. Finally, they'd found a neat looking coffee shop named Meet Me. Tessa, excited about the name of the store as well as the pastry display, insisted they take a break and hang out there for a while.

"Oh gosh! This is fate!" she'd squealed. "A restaurant named after our story! Meet Me!"

She'd proceeded to take pictures of everything—the sign, the walls, the menu, the sugar packets. Anything that had its name. They'd sat outside on wooden folding chairs with maroon covers after touring the shop, admiring the various art deco on the wall and the outlandishly styled chandelier. Omonoia Square, a historical area built in 1846, had been the site of many sporting events and art exhibits in previous years. More recently, the economic hardships in Greece had given the area a bad reputation as a symbol of despair and social collapse.

"Venice. It was from Venice," he'd recalled. "The chandelier."

"Hmm." She'd jotted something down on the napkin. "Venice, huh?"

Progress. She might want to visit Venice in the very near future.

He'd let out a chuckle. "Glad you found getting lost in a shady part of town fateful."

"I'll admit, I was a little scared," she'd said. "But they said it was a transportation hub, and we did find our stop eventually."

"And the pastries were delicious!" he'd added.

She had ordered a cappuccino and took three bites of her spinach pie. He'd ordered an orange pie topped with caramel ice cream and licked the plate clean.

Tessa had taken notes on her phone, intent on writing about the images of their day. That afternoon, they clearly saw how homelessness, drug addiction and prostitution had penetrated the once-thriving area.

Last night, when they'd been nestled safely in their hotel, she'd told him how bothered she was about those immigrants sleeping on the steps and scattered around the streets. "They can still be the future of Greece, if only they were given a chance. Adversity makes a country stronger," she had said.

He'd wondered if she was referring to her own childhood and the loneliness she had survived.

twenty-seven

The Santorini caldera was a submerged volcanic crater surrounded by high cliffs on three sides. Their hotel, the Andronis, sat squarely at the edge of a cliff, its rooms directly above the sea.

"Absolutely breathtaking!" Tessa exclaimed as she stood on the terrace of their luxury suite. Directly in front of her was an infinity pool extending itself into the horizon. Everything around them was white, contrasted only by the varying hues of blue—aqua for sky, blue green for land and indigo for sea. Heavy stone furniture and fixtures gave their room the much needed respite from the bright sun and the warm temperature. Cycladic architecture at its best—simple and airy, with minimal aesthetics. Whitewashed cube houses had been built on top of each other, some carved inside the hills with volcanic rock to keep them protected from the seasons.

"Sure is." Simon sat on the stone bench directly behind her. She heard the smirk in his voice and turned around to catch his gaze. It was fixed on her and not on the view. She noticed how handsome he looked, rested and relaxed unlike any other time she'd been with him.

With every trip they'd taken together, she found herself experiencing a myriad of emotions. That evening, she refused to think about anything else but what was happening there and now. Her mind kept drifting back to the day he said he loved her. Or the day he'd signaled that he loved her. She'd seen him clearly as she flew over the clouds. Granted, he'd probably just been overwhelmed by her birthday surprise, but it didn't matter. She had heard those words spoken to her many times but hearing it from him had filled her with joy. Simon had given them new meaning. For once, she wasn't writing about it. She was living it.

She extended her hand and called to him. "No, come look!"

She held his hand and stood at his side, overtaken by silence and awe. The drone of the motorboats below them and the sound of merriment coming from the neighboring balconies was hypnotizing. And the wind. It constantly reminded her of its presence. In a way, that was how she saw their relationship before their confrontation the other night. Coming together and then parting ways. No more wind to pull them apart. No more doubt. They were going to try for normal.

"Penny for your thoughts," she said, squeezing his hand.

"I beg your pardon?" He squeezed back.

She laughed. "What are you thinking?"

"Well, not about work for the first time ever. You first," he said.

"I guess that's a good thing, huh?" Still he stared out into the horizon. Addressing her, without turning toward her. He looked serious, eyes deep set and brows furrowed. Tessa grew nervous. Her normal paranoia set in. Will this be the time? She wondered. Will this be the time he says goodbye for good?

"I was just thinking about the wind. Everywhere we've gone, the wind has been there with us," she said.

"That's because you love high places. Of course, wind would be a factor."

Ferris wheels. Cable cars. The baths above the beach.

"Good point," she answered with a smile. "Okay, now your turn."

"What would you say if I asked to read about Lionel and Carissa once you're done with the draft?"

She tilted her head toward him before scrunching up her nose. "You don't have to do that! I know you don't read romance."

"But I'd really like to," he answered. "I'd really love to read it, if you're okay with it."

No one had ever read her manuscripts before submission. She guarded them with her life. It was more an insecurity, really. She didn't think she was of the same caliber as the other authors, and often attributed her rise in the book world to hard work. And luck. Allowing him to see her vulnerability would mean just that.

"Of course." Two words on the matter. For now.

"I enjoyed *The Last Dance*," he said. "Your words are very lyrical but also sad."

"Get out!" she squealed. "You read it? When?"

"After San Francisco." As he said this, he began to walk toward the room, still holding her hand. He guided her toward a stone bench lined with gray throw pillows, directly facing the window. Simon took a seat before pulling her down on his lap.

Tessa thought the room resembled a cave. Or an igloo. An arched doorway with a flowing white organza curtain gave the bedroom its privacy.

He held her in his arms and she stretched her legs out on the bench. "I have this insatiable need to know everything about you. Maybe it's the scientist in me. I want to be able to figure you out," he said, brushing his lips against her ear.

"But you do!" she argued. "At least compared to anyone else," she followed up. "I haven't hidden anything from you, Simon."

"On social media, though," he began. "You're pretty open with the world."

"That's not me. It's a persona I must maintain. You know that."

Her tone softened as she caressed his face. "You have to know the person I am with you is the real me."

Before she could utter another word, he drew his lips to hers and opened her mouth with his tongue. She allowed him to play with her, taste her, claim her lips before consciously pulling back. "Let's do something special together. Here."

"I thought that's what we were doing," he joked.

"No, no. I mean here in Fira. What have you always wanted to do but never got to do it because you're trying to save your reputation as a logical scientist/nerd?"

He laughed. "Run with the bulls, but that's in a different country."

"What else?"

"Do the Ironman. Try archery. Trek the Inca trail. Check out astral projection. Win a chess championship. See the northern lights."

"Jesus. Uber nerd things. What else?"

"You next," he answered.

"Ride an alligator. Swim with tiger whales. Hot air balloon. Climb

Kilimanjaro." Slowly, she pushed him sideways and gently placed her weight on him until his back was flat on the pillows and she was directly on top of him.

"Here we go with the heights again."

"There's one more," she whispered into his mouth. "But that can wait."

He held her head in place while she played with his lips, kept her eyes closed and pressed against him.

"Mmm, Tess, hold on," he said. She sat back, surprised. But before she could say anything, he swooped her up and carried her to the bed. Gently he laid her head on the pillow.

"Do you know." He placed a finger on her forehead and gently trailed along her nose, down to her lips, along her neck. "I've tried to memorize every part of you while you sleep?"

Tessa took a deep breath and closed her eyes. Savoring, feeling, wanting his hands on her.

"Every time we're together, I discover something new about you. Look." He leaned down to kiss her shoulder. "These freckles." He lifted her arm and kissed the side of her breast. "This mole." His lips brushed against her skin until he landed right below her bellybutton. "Here, your little tiny scar."

Tessa flinched in response, stiffening to leave a space between his lips and her skin. She'd never told anyone about the medical scare. How they'd found a germ cell tumor on one ovary and how Jake was adamant it be removed. Because it was contained to one side, she was left with one good ovary.

I always thought I'd have lots of babies, she'd sobbed.

You will. Jake had assured her. Between us, we'll have so many kids, we won't know what to do with them.

Her hands flew to her stomach. She covered the area defensively.

"Simon, please. No," she begged. It was a part of her life she willed herself to forget. In her younger years, she'd always told her mother all she wanted to be was a housewife. That mark was a souvenir of more broken dreams.

"I know what it was for, Tessa. But I still wished you'd told me about it."

She shot up like a bullet, back straight, hands to the side.

"Why do we always have to visit my past?"

"Oh, baby." He pulled her gently to him and enclosed her in his arms. Her sobs were muffled tightly against his chest. "That's not what I'm trying to do. I want you to be able to open up to me. Your past is what makes you who you are. It's not something you run away from."

Someone had told her once the scars one carries are the most beautiful part of one's heart. If he felt that way about them, then why should she worry?

"What about you, Simon? Did you have a perfect past?"

He stroked her hair, let a few moments pass. She didn't push for an answer. Her breathing began to relax, she closed her eyes and hid in his arms. What was it about him that made her feel so safe? He tipped her chin upward with his hands and met her eyes. Slowly, she laid back down on the bed and pulled him toward her.

"Tess, we don't have to do anything now," he said. "We can just stay like this." He held her close to him.

"I want to feel you," she whispered. "I want you to take me over like you always do."

"Here's my one truth." He brushed his lips against her neck. "I'm addicted to you, Tessa Talman. I meant it when you were waving at me from the clouds. I mean it more today, when you're down here with me. I love you."

Tessa nodded her head and took his hand. "Look. Look at how much I want you," she said, pushing his fingers inside her and then releasing him as he brought them to his lips. She tasted herself on him pushed him down, urged him to devour her, to help himself to her. Which he did. He bit, he licked, he consumed every single part of her. When she couldn't wait any longer, she flipped herself over and sat up on her knees, opening herself up so he could take her. He growled and pushed hard, she whimpered and gasped and moaned with pleasure.

"Hold on, baby." He grabbed her sides and slammed continually into her. "Oh god, Tess," he said gruffly. "You're my heaven. This. This is heaven."

He loved her. She believed him. His words of love equally as strong as his movements. She wanted to soar in his love, take flight because of it. It wasn't the physical pleasure that overtook her. It was the fullness of her heart, the excitement she felt at the sound of his voice, at the meaning of his words.

"Fly with me," she moaned. "Let's never fall back to the ground."

twenty-eight

Simon would be lying if he didn't admit that it bothered him. Slightly. No, actually, quite a bit. He must have told her a hundred times the night before he loved her. He had fucked her, made love to her, played with her and enjoyed her. And she had given so much of herself, allowed him to take her over and over again. Smiled lovingly as he said those words, held him gently, kissed him with all her might.

But nothing.

No words.

She hadn't said she loved him back.

And now there they were, on a seven-mile hike from Fira to Oia. They had started out at 8 a.m., intent on taking their time as they trekked through the cobblestone streets, hiked up some trails and climbed a few hills.

Jacob and Riley walked in front of them, chattering happily about their ferry ride to the port of Athinios. That Tessa had invited her brother to join them was a monumental achievement. Case in point.

He should stop insisting she become someone she wasn't. He loved her, her words were hers. She could keep them to herself if she so wanted to.

Their first stop was a gyros place along the road lined with shops and restaurants and villas. Both couples sat on the ground along the narrow sidewalk and feasted on souvlaki.

"What kind of sauce is this?" Riley asked, wiping off the pink gravy dripping from her mouth.

"Something like thousand island—ketchup and mayo," Jacob answered.

Everyone was casually dressed. The women wore their bathing suits under floor length caftans. Simon noticed how many heads they turned—European men could spot American girls a mile away. They exuded an openness often missing from European women.

"Are we going the right way?" Tessa took Simon's hand as they followed her brother and his girlfriend. "We're heading towards... uhm, that village that starts with an I, right?"

Simon nodded his head, desperate to show apt attention. He'd become a little short of breath. It happened sometimes, when he couldn't get enough air in his lungs. Besides that, he wanted to snap out of his reverie. She was quiet too and he was happy to hear her break out of hers.

"We're supposed to follow along the caldera to Prophet Ilias."

"Jake!" Tessa called out to him. "Can we please have the map?"

The couple slowed down to allow them to catch up. They walked in tandem, the four of them, catching the ire of the tourists going the opposite way along the narrow road.

"Yup, we're going the right way," Simon assured them as they continued their walk.

Slowly the clusters thinned out. The farther along they went, the less and less tourists there were.

"This must be it." Simon paused to view the map. "Yes, this is Imerovigli."

To their left was the most picturesque view of the Aegean Sea.

Two hours slipped by quickly. Tessa and Riley paired up for most of that time. They spoke animatedly about everything under the sun. Simon noticed how close Tessa was with Jacob and Riley. He noticed Jacob consciously taking a step back to allow Simon to take charge - whether it be reading the map, ordering their food, carrying Tessa's stuff. What Jacob would normally do, he deferred to Simon. And often, Tessa would include Simon by looking back at him, taking his hand, reaching out to touch him, making contact.

He felt her affection.

I just wish I could hear those words.

As they continued their trek along the caldera, they stopped to take pictures against the backdrop of the iridescent view.

"Hey, babe!" Riley called to Jacob, who walked alongside Simon. "Didn't someone say we have to climb the Skaros peak to see the view? There it is right there!" She pointed. Jake scurried over to her side.

"Are you guys heading over?" Tessa asked, wrapping her arms around Simon's waist. He kissed the top of her head in response. "We want to get in the water as soon as possible, so we'll keep going. We'll meet you at the dive point."

"Sounds good," Jake responded, leading Riley toward an uphill trail. "We'll see you there."

"See you lovebirds later!" Riley teased, before challenging Jacob to a race up the hill.

Tessa and Simon soldiered on. Hand in hand, they strode in silence, except for the crunching sound of their shoes on the uneven rocks and pebbles. The majestic view had simply taken their words away.

"Have they come up with a wedding date yet?" Simon asked, wanting to hear her voice. He expected this—their mood somber once again, one day before having to say goodbye. It was getting difficult for him to keep up with their traveling. His new position was going to keep him local; there were no longer any travel plans in the near future. Lately, the effects of the time in the air and the harried schedules had been taking a toll on him physically too. He was due to see his doctor in Essex, but the waiting time for an appointment was a few weeks away.

"Yeah, I think next October. One year from today," she answered, lost in her own thoughts. He had hoped she would follow up with a statement alluding to him being at the wedding. But nothing.

"Did she say where she wanted to have it?"

"They want a destination wedding. Just a few friends and family. Riley wants to go to Paris next month to check out some places over there."

Stomp. Crunch. Stomp. Crunch. More small talk. About work and her upcoming schedule. About his new position. How he was getting a new office and how he would be able to work from home a few days a week. She teased him about working from his weekend cottage in

South Woodham. He agreed he should probably make those arrangements.

"I wish I could visit your home someday soon." There, she'd said it. It made his heart skip a beat.

"What's stopping you?" he asked. They reached a downhill trail with a torn up wooden sign saying Amoudi Beach. They arrived in Oia after only three hours. There was a single path to Amoudi Bay, a narrow, stony trail along the water. They walked all the way to the edge of the island, past an outdoor restaurant called Sunset, until their passage became nothing but a bed of crusted lava. Simon spotted the diving cliff to the right, aware that they would have to swim to it.

"Let's sit here first and wait for Riley and Jacob," Tessa suggested.

Simon placed his backpack on the ground and helped her climb a boulder.

"Tess, let's not change the subject. Fly back to London with me instead of going back to the States."

"I can't tomorrow, but I can see you in a few weeks after I wrap up some things at home."

"How about acting on impulse? Does it only apply when I'm the one following you around the world?"

"That's not fair. Here you go again. I can't just drop everything and move with you!" she said "Don't you think I hate saying goodbye as much as you do?"

"Then why do we keep having to do it?" he asked, searching her eyes for answers. She looked sad, about to cry. Only he knew her well enough. She was going to suck those tears back into her eyeballs if it was the last thing she did.

"It isn't any easier for me. I've never done this before, Simon. Never had to reorganize my life for somebody else. Please, please give me time to ease into this. I'm getting there!"

Off in the distance, he saw Riley and Jacob approaching. Simon had two minutes at the most to settle this. He pulled her close to him and stroked her hair. "I'm sorry. You must know, more and more, I die with every goodbye. It used to be okay. It used to be easy to separate you, keep you in a different section from the rest of my life. Now, all I want is for you to be in it."

Tessa clutched his collar and pulled him in for a kiss. "I want that too."

"The view was amazing!" Riley ran toward them with Jacob at her heels. "We took a lot of pictures. If I didn't like Paris so much, this place would be it!"

Jacob took her hand and kissed it. Simon watched Tessa cast a forced smile and fake enthusiasm.

"Let's go!" Tessa said, swinging her arms.

"Sis! Isn't this the place where Mom and Dad met?"

"You mean in Santorini. At a resort," she corrected him.

"Well, wherever it was, their story is still the most beautiful love story I've ever heard," Riley piped in.

"Yeah, Simon, do you know that my mom was e—"

Tessa waved her hand. "I want to be the one to tell Simon about them," she said, caressing his arm and smiling lovingly at him.

He was touched by her gesture. She had really come a long way. Slowly, she was beginning to share the most important people in her life with him.

"Mom was engaged to be married to some guy she was dating in med school. My grandparents had taken her to Greece for the summer. My dad had some commitments related to his fellowship at Mayo and so he rented an apartment and stayed for three months. She met my dad at our same resort in Santorini one weekend, only it was named something else. They spent time together and fell in love. They eloped and got married three days before she was supposed to go back home to Chicago. And the rest, as everyone says, is history." She spoke with familiar longing in her voice. He heard it every time she mentioned them.

"That was the Cliff Notes version," Jacob said with a chuckle. "There was more drama in between that, all the way to the day Tessa was born."

"I have all the time in the world to tell him about the drama," Tessa answered. And for some reason he felt comforted by those words.

What he was about to do was even more shocking. He was going to show her he was open to the challenge. That he was willing to live on the edge, be more like her.

She removed her cover up and carefully skidded down the walkway. "I'm so excited to get in the water! Let's go!"

twenty-nine

"You're actually going to do it?" Tessa asked in disbelief. There they were, sprawled out on deck chairs under a tiki umbrella on Kamari Beach. She'd found old pictures of her parents on this black sand beach but never imagined how emotional it would be for her to finally be there. Everything was just as they'd described it. It was a place for falling in love—and she realized there and then she was in love with him. Somehow, she knew then there would be a connection between her parents' past and her future.

She watched as Jacob and Riley frolicked by the shore a few feet away.

"At sunset, remember? We talked about it." Simon turned on his side to face her and rested his head on his elbow. She did the same.

"Yeah, but you never told me why."

"Just so if anything happened to me—if I died while doing it—I would have already spent the day with you," he teased, his smile turning into an impish grin. "I don't lose my whole day."

"Stop it!" she said, giggling.

So far, so good. The angst of their earlier conversation had been washed away by the rush of the waves. When Tessa told Simon about the fifth item on her bucket list the other day, all he had done was shake his head. She wondered what changed his mind. There had been many moments of silence between them that afternoon, but there was never a minute spent apart. Whether it was standing in the middle of the sea or sitting by the shore, there was a need to hold on desperately to each other. A kiss, a touch, a loving embrace. It didn't matter that Jacob was there. It didn't matter that their interaction confused her brother, made him constantly furrow his brows at her. She loved that he had the biggest smile on his face as he watched them, his eyes warm with love and consent.

"Tess," he'd hissed at one point when Simon left to order them a drink at the bar. "Since when have you been serious with this guy?"

Riley intentionally excused herself to the ladies' room.

"It's still new," she answered.

"It's serious. Stop patronizing. The only time you've mentioned him was during your trip to the Philippines. And it wasn't even you who told me. I found out through Nana."

Tessa shrugged and rolled her eyes at her brother.

"Look," Jake said, sticking his hands into his back pocket and taking out his wallet.

"Jake, you're going in the water, what are you doing with your wallet in your shorts?"

"Don't change the subject," he said, pulling out a photograph. It was of her as a teenager, with a group of friends including Riley. "Look at them. They're all wearing your clothes."

"We traded all the time. What's your point?"

"You were so generous. You gave everything off your back to everyone you met. I think it was because you just wanted to be loved. Remember how you'd give all your things away at school and Riley and I would take them back when you weren't looking?"

"You did?" she asked, her hands flying to her cheeks. "I just wanted to fit in. I had so much stuff. I didn't need them. I wanted people to know I didn't need them."

"You are no longer that girl in the picture. You're an accomplished woman. You've weathered through so much, but you don't have to be afraid. He loves you for you. He's here for the long haul."

"Sorry," she said with a sheepish grin. "I swear, Jake, this wasn't planned. I thought I could keep him separate, leave him outside the fray, but he keeps wanting in."

"Do you want him in? It's you. It's what you want that matters,

Tess. But let me tell you—from a dude's POV, there are so many sharks in the ocean these days, a guy like that will get snatched up in no time. Believe me, this looks serious."

She shook her head. "I just need time to digest it all. I'm afraid."

"Time?" His eyes were dark, despite being in the sunshine. "As a doctor, that's something life can never have enough of. You think you have it one day, and the next, you're on an operating table fighting for time." He took her hand. "Is he in your heart, sis? If he is, the first step towards acceptance is admission. Admit it to yourself. And if he isn't, admit that to yourself too."

Simon's voice strayed into her thoughts. "Babe?" He gently stroked her arm.

"Sorry?" she asked, a bit lightheaded from the heat.

"Your brother asked me what was going on with us," he said.

"When?"

"When you and Riley went to get towels," he said. "He pulled me aside and asked me what my intentions were."

"Oh my god!" Tessa gasped. "He had no right to do that, I'm so sorry. Let me—"

"Tess," he interjected, lightly grazing her arm. "It's okay. He's your brother, and he cares about you. I told him what I told you this week."

Tessa didn't dare ask for clarification. She just nodded as a warning for him not to dabble in this any further. Over and over again, he had told her he loved her. And she tried her best to show him how she felt, not in words but by action.

It wasn't enough. His eyes begged her, pleaded with her to return his words. But she couldn't.

She lived in a world where those words made a difference. She wrote those words on every page, made up stories for all the women out there who might never get a chance to hear those words.

Her heart was protected. Guarded.

Once she said them, she knew it meant she had allowed it to take over her life. And allowing it to take over her life would mean what exactly? The loss of her freedom? The loss of her mobility?

"You should see yourself," he began. "The way you stiffened up and pulled away."

"Come on, Simon. My back was kinking, I had to sit up straight."

"Uh-huh," he said, not sounding the least bit convinced. He paused before she detected a shift in his tone. "Tessa, I'm not going to come in between anything you've worked so hard for. I myself, have my goals, my dreams. I have my focus. But it doesn't mean I can't open my heart up to you. You know how I feel. Tomorrow, we get to say goodbye again. Until when? Next month? Your next book event? In between your public appearances with Andrew? When?"

"Amsterdam? Next week?"

This time it was his turn to sit up. Suddenly, she felt a wall between them. "You don't get it," he said with clenched teeth. He dropped his legs on both sides of the chair and tapped his foot on the sand.

She stood, circled the hut and squeezed herself next to him. "I was kidding." She leaned her head on his shoulder, her right knee folded over his hips, her arms wrapped tightly around him. "Simon, tell me what you want. Please just tell me." Then, more than ever, she didn't want to leave the next day without giving him what he wanted.

"No more goodbyes," he whispered, voice weak, weary.

She lifted her head, touched his lips. "Give me this time away from you, please. Give me a few weeks to wrap up my life. The next time I see you, there won't be any more goodbyes."

His eyes grew wide. She scooted herself up to kiss him. He kissed her back with a vengeance, grabbing her head and tugging at her lips with his teeth. "Promise me," he said. "Make that your one truth."

"One truth." She placed her lips on the side of his ear. "I promise."

He was actually going to do it! Tessa almost couldn't believe it. She beamed as she sat at the edge of the cliff, hanging her legs in the air. Riley and Jacob were long gone, leaving them in their hesitation and cruising across the water on their backs. It was a short swim from the shores of the main beach to the jumping point, a cliff formed from volcanic crusts on the right side of the island. Its colored strata, a sight in itself—various shades of brown, red, yellow, orange and white filled the layers of the ashes that burned and cooled and compacted to form this massive rock. To climb to the top, the four friends had discovered a steep and bending path that eventually led to the landing.

"Oh, wow," Simon said, his excitement showing in the glimmer of his eyes and the stretch of his smile. They arrived at the top to catch the emergence of dusk. The view of the sunset was magnificent. They watched in awe as purple streaks began to fill the sky, followed by a transition from yellow, to orange to red. As it skated across the water, its reflection burst into tiny images that illuminated the sea and all the little islands around it.

It warmed Tessa's heart to see him so happy, so content. I am like the sunset, she thought. I skim and fleet and glide away only to wish I'd stayed instead.

The dusk began to settle in.

She stood to join him many feet away from the ledge.

"Simon, we should do it now, before it gets too dark."

He took a deep breath and grabbed her hand. She grimaced from the pain of his fingers crushing hers.

"We don't have to do this if you don't want to," she said gently, her hand numb from the strength of his grip.

"No, let's go," he said, inching his feet up toward the end of the platform.

She nodded her head and moved forward with him.

"Wait! Tessa!" he wailed. "What if I die now? What if—"

"Do you have to be so morbid?" she shouted. The wind was getting stronger and stronger. All she could hear was its howling.

"Oh my god, I think I'm going to be sick!" Simon looked as if in prayer.

Tessa wasted no time in distracting him. "Let's just do it! Let's go!" With all her might, she raced toward the edge of the cliff, huffing and puffing, pulling him along with her. He was right. What if this was their only chance?

She loved him.

She loved him with all her heart.

"Let's do it! Jump, Simon! Jump! Close your eyes, and jump. I love you! I love you, Simon!"

And together they leaped into the air and soared with the wind.

thirty

The timer went off just as Simon was placing the finishing touches on the strip of crown molding above the entryway. The smell of fresh paint infused the foyer, while the aroma of roasted meat filled the rest of his apartment. Simon neatly laid the brush on a thick pad of newspaper, washed his hands and slid the heat pads over his fingers. Time to get the food out of the oven. His family was due in any minute.

"We're here," Ashleigh's voice rang merrily through the intercom. Simon pressed the button to let them in. He heard the pitter patter of tiny footsteps, as slower, heavier ones followed right behind.

"What's that smell?" his mum asked as he opened the door and swooped Henry into his arms.

"I just repainted the door," he answered, leaning over to kiss her on each cheek. "Do you like it?"

"Changed the color, huh? Yes, I like it," she said, kissing him back. "I need to get Adrian and your father to do that for our kitchen."

Adrian walked past them and began setting up Henry's pack and play in the living room. "You've really fixed up this place. I was just here a..." He paused when he realized Simon was up to something. "Three weeks ago." His voice trailed off. "Why the rush for all these changes? You're not planning on selling, are you mate?"

Simon cocked his head to the side and grinned.

"There was no parking!" his dad announced his presence as he hurriedly shuffled in through the front door.

"Hi, Dad," Simon greeted him with an embrace. "So glad you and Mum are here."

Ten minutes later, dinner was on the table. Simon looked around, pleased with the happy exchange going on around him. Instead of traveling down to Braintree for the usual Sunday lunch, he had invited them over to see his new place. It was a far cry from his apartment in Chelmsford. Not only was he now living in Chelsea, he had also upgraded his lifestyle. The new patent had given him enough money to retire.

But that wasn't the point. It was important he break the news to them about Tessa. She had finally come around, and he was counting on her promise at that last goodbye. The words she'd finally said to him had kept him buoyant, afloat, high, during the three weeks they'd been apart. He was back to his old self, the dude who lived every aspect of his life with a plan.

But this time, she was with him. She loved him. She'd said it herself when they'd taken the plunge from the cliff, when he'd kept his eyes open and they'd held hands until they'd landed in the water. He might have shed his fear of heights right there and then.

"You've been doing a lot of work to your place lately," Ashleigh said, leaning over to clean Henry up, after he emptied his cup into a bowl of carrots. "What's the rush?"

It was then or never. Simon wanted to give her the respect she deserved. Finally let the world in on their secret. "I've met someone," he began. He paused to assess a reaction. There was none. His father continued to slice into his chicken and his mother continued to butter her roll. Henry banged his spoon on the table and Ashleigh was busy trying to grab it from his little hand.

His mum finally looked up from her food. "Oh?" Her tone flat. It told him she wasn't about to indulge him.

"That's good, son. Did you meet her at work?" his father added.

Simon shot his brother a look of concern, his eyes narrowed, and his lips pursed. It wasn't going to be easy to convince them she'd become part of his life. In all fairness, they'd never even known she'd existed.

Adrian nodded and encouraged him to continue. When this all started, Simon had made him promise not to tell a soul.

"Well, not exactly. But the reason I wanted to let you guys know is that she will be here soon to meet you," he said with pride, rubbing his hands together before looking around the table for a reaction.

"Hence, the sprucing up around the house," said Adrian.

"When did you have time to meet someone with all that traveling?" Ashleigh asked.

Adrian coughed.

"Well, I kind of met her during one of my trips," Simon admitted while looking pointedly at his brother.

Silence again.

"It's not what you think, guys," he stressed. "I've been seeing her for eight months."

"Eight months," his mom echoed.

"Eight months," his dad confirmed.

"Eight months?" Ashleigh asked.

"It's pretty serious," Adrian chimed in.

"Define serious," Ashleigh said, glaring at Adrian and clearly upset he had kept this secret so well.

"He loves her," Adrian answered.

Why was it when Adrian said it, everyone listened? Ashleigh lifted Henry off his seat and placed him on her lap. His mother took a sip of water and laid her utensils on the place mat. His father crossed his arms on the table and leaned forward.

"Okay," his mother began, her voice now calm and soothing. "Tell us about her, Simon. What is her name and where is she from?"

"Her name is Tessa Talman and she lives in Chicago. I met her at a convention in New York. We've been seeing each other exclusively ever since."

"Not really exclusive, dear," his mom inserted. "Maxine was still in the picture."

"Thanks for the commentary, Mum."

"Oh, Mother," Adrian snapped. "Let him finish."

Simon brushed over their comments. He knew he'd been wrong to continue with Maxine. He himself still wondered how he'd fallen for Tessa so quickly. "I want you all to meet her, I know you'll love her as much as I do." He smiled at his parents and turned to his sister-in-law. "Ash, she's a writer—she writes romance books."

"Oh," Ashleigh responded. "Holy. Shit."

"She's famous," Adrian said.

"That she's famous isn't important," Simon explained. "But she does have obligations and commitments because of her career, so we never really had the time to introduce each other to our families." He paused. "Well, she doesn't really have a family. Her parents are deceased, but she has an older brother."

"So, you left the other woman you were dating for this one?" his mother asked.

"Her name is Tessa, mum," Simon snapped.

"Tessa," his mom repeated.

"And yes," Simon answered truthfully, avoiding her eyes. "I felt awful about it. The day I met Tessa, I found myself wanting to get to know more and more about her. I broke it off with Maxine as soon as I returned home."

"What else do you know about her? Eight months is eight months," his mother said

"I know enough," he said defensively. He knew where his family was going. He expected this from them. In a way, they'd only seen each other six times. Six reunions. Six goodbyes. And each time, he'd gotten to know a few snippets about her. About her life.

But he knew he was taking a chance. That she could bail at any moment. But he had to believe she loved him. "I know her enough."

"Simon." His mother shook her head.

"I love her, mother. And I want you all to meet her."

"Of course," his father reassured him. "When does she get here?"

Henry held his arms out to Simon, who didn't hesitate to reciprocate. Soon enough, Simon was bouncing around the room with a sleeping baby on his shoulders.

"We were at the park all morning," Ashleigh said.

Simon smiled and turned his attention back to his parents. "I don't know yet. She's tying up loose ends right now and will cross the Atlantic, hopefully soon."

"And then what?" his father asked. His mother nodded and they both looked up at him.

"I think." He took a deep breath and exhaled loudly, running his fingers through his hair. Everyone waited with bated anticipation. Henry began to stir but his parents ignored that development and focused their gaze on Simon too. "I'm going to ask her to stay for a while."

thirty-one

Back home in Chicago, Tessa hurried into the topnotch sushi place in the River North neighborhood and stopped by the bar to collect herself. Jacob and Revete sat at a booth, the hustle and hurriedness of a work day all around them, loud and cacophonous, waiting for her to arrive. Jacob shifted uncomfortably in his seat and a moment later Revete did the same thing. A large bottle of cold Sake surrounded by plates of sushi and sauce platters cluttered the table.

Tessa hadn't given them a clue as to why she had called them to a lunch meeting.

Tessa waved as she approached. Jacob stood up and embraced her, while she leaned down to give Revete a kiss.

"Hi!" she said cheerfully. "Sorry, I stopped by the washroom first." She slid down to the end of the booth by the window. Jacob sat next to her. "Thank you for coming, guys."

"I ordered you some uni," Jake said.

"Thanks." Tessa took his hand and squeezed it.

Revete smiled warmly. Her perfect white teeth and sun kissed hair flashing in the natural light. She was all Miami, all the time. Impeccably dressed and continuously plugged in. This was the type of person you always want on your side. But Revete didn't love just anybody. And to her, Tessa was family.

"You look rested, honey," Revete said. "Glowing."

"It's been great just being in town for once," Tessa said. "I actually got a few Chapters in. I may have a title change I want to discuss with you."

"Is this why we're here?" Revete asked. "Did your PA tell you there's an event we should be attending the week of Thanksgiving?"

She adjusted her gold cuff to slip over the sleeves of her Emilio Pucci dress.

"No." Tessa said. "And that's not why we're here."

Her anxiety returned. Thanksgiving was in three weeks and she didn't plan on being in town. She was going to be in London. With the man she loved. She loved him. Granted, she'd told him at the weirdest time, in the strangest moment, but it had unleashed a firestorm from inside her heart. Feelings she'd never known she could have, words she'd barely uttered to another human being.

When they'd separated the next day, she couldn't breathe. It was never going to be the same again.

Jake noticed when she began to twist her fingers around each other.

"It's okay, sis. Just tell us. What's wrong?" He placed his hand on hers. Revete's eyes searched hers for answers.

Tessa exhaled sharply. "I'm so happy, I can't even begin to tell you!" she shrieked, bringing her hands in a praying position toward her face. "I'm going on an extended vacation. Take a break for a few weeks."

"That's great. But weren't you just in Greece?" Revete asked. "Maybe we can squeeze in a tour if there's a place you'd like to visit."

"I'm going to London for a couple of weeks. Maybe longer. Depends," Tessa said.

"On what?" Jake asked.

Jake and Riley had headed back to Athens the night of their trek to Amoudi Beach, leaving Tessa and Simon to themselves. Tessa knew Jake and Simon had exchanged a few words and her brother could see exactly what was going on that night.

"On where Simon and I decide to take this."

"Take what?" Revete leaned forward, hands on the table.

Tessa turned to glance at Jacob. She knew her brother detested the way her agent handled her. She was kind and generous to a fault, but she also did not let anything get in the way of Tessa's career.

"Tessa, I need to remind you that this is your year," Revete said.

"Your time to shine. Opportunities like this won't wait for you. You need to be focused enough to set things aside temporarily. Andrew is a big part of the success of your book. The women who read your book read it because he was on the cover. You have book two due to the editor in just forty-five days. If it's writing time you need, I—"

Tessa could see Jacob squirming. He lifted his hand up, palm facing away from him and pushed it toward her agent. "Revete!" he barked.

"Jacob, talk some sense into your sister. Now is not the time to go on a fuckfest with her lover."

Jacob slammed his fist on the table. "Revete! Stop!" he shouted. "Apologize to my sister right this minute!"

"It's okay, Jake. She means well. This is kind of out there, I get it," Tessa protested.

"It's never a good time, sis. If this is the time you need to get things figured out with Simon, then this is the right time," Jacob said to Tessa before turning his attention back to her agent.

"Listen Revete, may I just remind you that all this"—he traced an imaginary giant circle in the air—"has nothing to do with the book. Tessa can survive well into her old age with the money from my parents. She writes because it's her passion. Nothing more, nothing less. As her friend, aren't you happy for her? Are you not seeing a remarkable change in her and does it not make you proud?"

Revete reached out to take Tessa's hand, her eyes misting, her tone soft and quiet. "Yes, of course. I have always been proud of you. I just thought this was what you wanted."

"It was," Tessa answered. "Maybe it still is. But I can't lose him. I've pushed him away enough and he's not going to wait forever for me to get my act together. I promise to keep you posted on what our plans will be as soon as I can. We don't have to cancel any of my appearances next year. I just need these next two months."

"Two months," Revete repeated to herself, as if verbalizing it would actually make it better. And then her face lit up. Tessa could tell she had turned the corner. "Tell me about him," she said.

"Well," Tessa lovingly turned to her brother, "Jake's been able to spend more time with us. But I met him in March in New York, as you know. And—"

"He's been there at every signing you've done after that," Revete finished her thought.

"Yes."

"What was the big secret? I get that we had to play up the Andrew angle, but you never told me anything about him either." The challenging began before too long. "And the three-date limit?"

Tessa laughed. "That's the million-dollar question. I guess the fourth date should have been a sign it was going to be more than that for me. And as far as the secret goes, at first it was for the fans, but afterwards, I was afraid more than anything to change my lifestyle. He's very stable—even his profession isn't like mine at all. And I didn't know how it would work. But as time went by, he really put himself out there for me. And then it was my heart. I didn't know how to give it away. It just got harder and harder to say goodbye."

"I'm sorry, sweetie. For what I said earlier," Revete said.

Tessa tipped her head forward.

"So, what's next, sis?" Jacob asked.

Tessa heaved a sigh of relief. It felt good to stand up for herself, to speak of plans and goals and to be able to share her feelings with the people close to her. "I love him!" she exclaimed. "I love him, and I need to spend some time making it up to him. He's loved me all this time and I want to love him back." She leaned her head on Jacob's shoulder and he pulled her close.

"Tell your best friend to plan her Paris trip in the next few days so we can join you while we're there."

"Deal!" Tessa answered, her smile reflecting the happiness and peace she felt in her heart.

the seventh
goodbye

thirty-two

Simon stood by the arrival gate at Heathrow, questioning his decision not to bring a bouquet of flowers. He figured he would do that later. His focus was on keeping his arms free to hold her, touch her, squeeze the bejesus out of her. And when he caught a glimpse of her exiting the gate, a light among the ordinary people, the excitement, the anticipation—all felt as thrilling as it had when he'd first met her. The difference this time was that he knew those earlier reunions would lead to excruciating goodbyes.

Today would be different.

"Hi!" Tessa ran up and folded herself in his arms. He held her tight, swearing to never let her go again. She stood on her toes and kissed him. "I missed you," she whispered before taking his hand and leading him away from the gate. "We need to go to Baggage Claim 10."

It surprised him. "You have checked baggage? In addition to this carry on?"

Please, God. Make it mean she's staying.

She rolled her eyes at him. And then she smiled. "I'm going to be here for a while."

"Wow! This place!" Tessa squeaked, wandering into his apartment while he held the door open for her. He saw her reaction as she reached the hallway. Ashleigh had done a great job. Where she found one hundred long stemmed yellow roses, he had yet to ask. "Oh my god, Simon!" she cried, as he came up from behind to wrap his arms around her.

"I was being selfish at the airport. Wanted both arms free to hold you, so I'm making up for it here."

She laughed. "They're beautiful! Your home is beautiful!" She surveyed his place, walking back and forth, from the living room, to the kitchen. He leaned against the counter and enjoyed the sight of her. Her short hair grown out just below the ears this time, her neck lean and long, her limbs endless. He couldn't believe she was in his home.

"What did you call this place again?"

"A maisonette. Kind of like a two flat in Chicago terms."

"I love the white exterior. And the inside is huge! How big is this and where are we exactly?" She stood with him in the kitchen as he began to uncork a bottle of champagne.

"It used to be a restaurant," he said with a chuckle. "It was a good investment with my share of the latest patent. Two bedrooms, two living rooms and three baths. I made an office downstairs and I wanted enough room for my family to visit."

Simon placed a glass in front of Tessa and began to pour her a drink. "We're on the Fulham and Chelsea border on Waterford Road."

"When am I getting my tour?" she teased.

God, she was beautiful. He still couldn't believe she'd come to see him.

"How'd it go?" he asked. "Did you have to take some time off?"

"It went well, actually," she said. "I think I gave them less credit than they deserved."

She leaned on the marble counter and played with the discarded cork laying by the wine glass. "I've taken the weeks at least through the Thanksgiving holiday."

"That's great, Tess," he answered, a wide grin pasted on his face.

"Is it okay with you? That I stay here?" she asked. "Riley and my brother will be in Paris next week. I've got to meet them there for a few days—just some wedding stuff. I'd love for you to come with me. We can make it on a weekend when you don't have to work."

"There's nothing more important to me than the fact that you're here. And that you're staying. Let me work my schedule out so I can go to Paris with you."

He didn't really want her to know he could now afford to quit working for good. He wasn't going to do that anyway. She inspired him to work harder, earn more money to start a family.

"Thank you." She smiled, raising her glass in the air.

He followed suit, clinking his glass with hers. "Welcome home, baby. Cheers."

"Cheers," she answered, then took a big gulp. She pulled him away from the kitchen and towards the spacious living room.

Okay. Enough time had passed. He'd given her ample space, sufficient time to digest her presence. In his home. He hadn't wanted to freak her out or anything, and so he'd reluctantly backed off, allowed her to enjoy the sights on the way from the airport, to walk in without fear of being immediately carried off to the bedroom. He couldn't wait any longer—couldn't imagine the early months when seeing each other after weeks apart had been acceptable.

"Oh, there's Henry," she said, pointing to a round picture frame in the middle of the custom-built shelf spanning the entire wall. Its red oak finish contrasted the white oak floors. "And are those your parents?" she asked, turning her head excitedly. "You look like your dad." She lightly trailed her fingertips along the edges of the frame as she walked past it. "Oh, is that us?" she asked, inching closer to the fireplace mantel to lift up a silver light box. "It is us! At Stanley Beach."

Simon stepped and leaned his chin on her shoulder. He pressed himself against her, felt the warmth of her body through the silk dress she wore. "That's us," he whispered back. He brushed his lips against her ear and took her earlobe between his teeth. She leaned back to give him access to her neck.

"Hmm." She moaned. "Simon."

"I love you," he muttered, reaching down and trailing his hand from her stomach to the hem of her dress.

"I love you." She turned to face him, looping her arms around his neck. He pressed his brow against hers. He held her face in his hands and kissed her. Nothing had changed. Not the tingling feeling of her skin, nor the sweet taste of her lips. Every goodbye served only to increase the intensity of his feelings for her. Seriously, he asked himself again, how had he survived without her in his world?

"So, how 'bout that tour?" he asked, lifting her up, fingers searching underneath her dress.

"After this tour," she whispered against his lips and wrapped her legs around his waist.

thirty-three

Tessa sat on the couch facing the windows, affording her a view of the small backyard, while Simon lay sprawled out on the bed, asleep. On the floor were discarded bottles of wine and an empty tray filled with bread and cheeses from the night before.

The tour of the apartment never happened—the kiss in the living room led to a night locked up in his bedroom. And so, at the break of dawn, she slipped out silently and wandered around his home on her own. The layout was functional, a wonderful use of space. Natural light seeped in through the skylight above the living room and through the white metal paneled windows. An open floor plan with customized white wood floors and French windows led to an outdoor terrace.

The appliances were first class—modern and sleek—and everything—music, lighting, cooking and washing was integrated within a centrally controlled panel. Simon had gone all out for this house and it showed. She was immensely proud of him and his accomplishments, felt almost inadequate when she compared his stature in the intellectual world with hers. Here she was, all art and words. And there he was, making a difference in the scientific sense, accomplished and celebrated at only thirty years old.

She turned her attention to the pile of clothes on the floor and smiled to herself as she spotted the silk necktie hanging on the side of the bed by his foot.

She felt victorious. Huh. He didn't clean up this time. He must be spent.

A flashback of the night before made her want him again. Right at that moment. Slowly, she made her way back to the bed and placed her body on top of his, head on his shoulder, skin to skin. His arms shot up, hands grabbed her behind.

"Morning," Simon greeted, his voice still gruff from sleep.

"Hi." She lifted her head to look into his eyes.

"What did I do in my life to deserve waking up to this?" he asked, pressing her against him. She felt his desire against her, reveled in his reaction to her. They read each other so well now. Most of the time, words were no longer needed.

"I'm so proud of you, do you know that?" she asked, grinding into him.

He arched his back upward, thrusting inside her. "Where's this coming from?"

"I don't know," she answered, eyes closed, the palms of her hands on his chest. "I was looking around your home this morning and you truly are self-made. You're so intelligent. I find it so sexy."

"Oh really?"

"Really." She mumbled, moving herself back and forth. "Yeah, super." She leaned back and placed all her weight on him.

"God, Tess, you feel so good." He held her by the hips and slammed her down on him. "Do you feel that? Do you feel me?"

"Yes!" she moaned. "Yes, Simon."

He thrust upward even more, extended his arms and grabbed both breasts. "Shit, Tessa, you fill me. Every single part of you, fills me." He lifted his head and sucked on one and then the other.

She bounced on top of him. "Simon?"

"Yeah, baby," he gasped.

"I think I'm there."

"Let go, baby. Let go."

"No. No! Next steps. I think I'm there," she said again.

That was her one truth. He was too far gone, too involved in their ecstasy to understand what she meant. It didn't matter. It was more for her, anyway. She wanted to say it out loud.

I think I'm there. I'm ready to stay in one place. With you. Only you.

"Ride me, baby. Hard," he ordered. His mouth on her, one hand exploring, the other pinching, hurting, pulling.

"Si—"

In one fell swoop and without separating from her, he flipped her on her back and pounded in so hard, she screamed in pleasure. And in pain. She screamed his name, over and over again, until he covered her mouth with his.

It took them a few minutes to catch their breaths, and she was happy to keep him inside her for as long as he wanted. "Do English people always like to spoon?" she asked, breaking their gratified silence.

"Do all Americans love to yak non-stop? Are they always this full of beans? Hyperactive?"

She squealed as he pressed himself harder against her back when she pushed him away in pretense.

Simon pulled away only when his phone rang. After hanging up, he told her his mother had confirmed dinner at their place that night.

"I didn't know how long you'd be staying so I planned this dinner with my parents sooner rather than later. I hope you don't mind. Don't let it scare you. It's just in keeping with what we agreed on—to open up our worlds to each other," he explained. She had her head on his stomach as they both lay crisscrossed in the middle of the bed.

She kept her gaze up toward the ceiling as he stroked her hair. "I'm not scared. I'm fine. But do you think it's a bit too soon?" she asked, knowing she risked a change in his mood. In ordinary circumstances, this was going way too fast for her. She'd never really met a man's family before. Well, Andrew's maybe, but that was because they were doing a book tour in Los Angeles once and they had all come to see him.

But this was Simon. He'd pursued her from the day he laid eyes on her and she tried her best to wrap her head around it. Dating on steroids. She couldn't quite figure out why he had such an accelerated timeline.

It was just as she expected. He rolled on to his side, still cradling her head but keeping his hands to himself. "Do you think it's too soon?" He took her question and volleyed it back into her court.

"I know how important your family is to you," she answered.

"They are."

"Then I'd love to meet them."

She could tell he wasn't completely convinced. He shook his head and squinted at her. "How did it change so quickly? I mean how did it go from you being so freaked out, to this?" He made a sweeping motion with this hand.

"I think it had been decided months ago. You scared me, Simon. You were always so determined, so sure of what you wanted. But in the end, when I began to dread the end of our visits, I knew."

"That you loved me?"

"That I love you," she agreed.

"Well." He began touching her skin, trailing his fingertips along her sides. "I'm quite easy to love, you know."

Gently, she slapped his arm. "Persistent is what you are."

"Believe me, this is not like me at all. Before you, I was methodical and focused. I couldn't survive with no plans, no goals, no schedule. I booked flights months in advance; I wrote everything down, planned every hour of my day. And then you came along. And all that went out the door."

"I know. It drove you nuts I never knew where we were going to see each other next," she said with a chuckle. "Me and you, we're quite the opposites, huh? Those days you worked in the hotel room, your maps, your charts. I used to get overwhelmed by so much organization!"

"And I used to get overwhelmed by the extreme lack of it! You're my girl with her head in the clouds," he said, gently touching her face. "If we have a daughter, I will name her after the heavens. Because that's where you're from, and that's where you take me, each and every time."

Daughter? Kids? That wasn't the shocker. What surprised her was she liked the sound of it. She liked it so much, she wanted to ask, *why a girl, not a boy? When did you want to have them? Where will we live?* She wanted to hear him say those words again.

"Simon," Tessa whispered tenderly. "I love you."

"I love you too," he answered, bending down to kiss her. "But now I have something else to tell you. My apologies in advance."

"Oh no," she muttered. "Now I'm worried. What happened?"

"Adrian. He asked if Ashleigh's mom could stop by while you're at my parents."

She laughed, relieved. And flattered. She never stopped appreciating the fact that people actually enjoyed reading her book. "That's it? Of course! I have a few extra books in my luggage. I can certainly bring one for his mom!"

thirty-four

"Are you going in there, sometime?" Adrian whispered to his brother as they stood hovering around a pile of dirty dishes in the kitchen. "Hand me the gloves."

"No, I'll do them," Simon offered, stepping toward the sink and slipping on a pair of floral pink, blue and yellow gloves. He held them up for Adrian, whose mouth turned up in a smirk. The kitchen was the most updated place in their parents' home, gutted and retrofitted with the most modern stainless-steel appliances. Of course, his mother still had her whimsical flower babies by the window and misshapen picture frames taking up any available space. Magnets on a whiteboard held up sheets of poster paper covered in Henry's colorful doodles.

Adrian walked over and sat on the countertop directly adjacent to the sink while Simon started on the dishes. At first, he tried to whisper, but it was difficult to hear themselves over the rush of the running water.

"Poor Dad. He didn't make it past nine. He's gone to bed, the old guy," Adrian said.

Simon turned the water off and began to load the dishwasher. He grouped the plates by their size, neatly lined up the forks and knives, and separated the wine glasses from the cups.

"What do you think they're talking about in there?" He pointed to the dining room where Tessa and his mother were huddled together, whispering. Laughing. He watched his mother place her hand on Tessa's as she spoke.

Adrian read his thoughts. "She's lovely."

"Yeah, she is," Simon answered. "I really want you guys to like her."

"She's the one, isn't she?" Adrian said quietly. It was more a statement than a question. Simon could see his brother was pensive. All throughout the dinner, Adrian observed rather than participated in the conversations.

Simon knew where Adrian was going with this. "I'm going to tell her."

"When?"

"When the time is right. I'm feeling fine, there are no symptoms. I've given up everything. Not her, mate. Not her."

He had worked so hard. He followed the orders, ate well, given up life's indulgences, made sure he stayed on track. He deserved the one thing he wanted to keep in his life. He wasn't going to risk losing her because of something out of his control.

Not Tessa. No. He had given up so much. Couldn't he keep just one thing? His heart had been besieged with rules. Just this once. Let him keep the one thing.

When he finally entered the dining room, both women were talking animatedly about Henry. He never left Tessa's side, and it was an ordeal to get him to leave her for bed. Tessa laughed as his mother recounted when Henry was addicted to eating ladybugs. She leaned into him as he sat next to her and encircled her in his arms. A few minutes passed. There was much happy banter about his nephew, their home, some of Tessa's crazy fans. His mother was fascinated by the tall buildings in Chicago. She wanted to hear all about Tessa's childhood and the places she'd visited with her parents. Maybe it was her maternal instinct that drew her close to Tessa, motherless since she was fourteen. His mother had her own career, and so she was a strong proponent for independence and individual accomplishment.

"Do you want children?" Kind, soft, buttery brown eyes, assessing her, searching for the right answers. "You seem to be very good with them."

Visibly shaken, Tessa straightened and pulled back slightly. Relaxing only as Simon rubbed her back.

"Mum—" Simon protested.

"It's okay, Simon." Tessa turned to face his mother. "Yes, Mrs. Fremont. I would love to have children."

"That's wonderful to hear," his mom said. "I was beginning to lose hope with your guy."

"Mum!"

"Well, isn't it true?" his mother said defiantly. Chin up, a haughty, playful tone. "You've never brought a girl home before this one. And I truly like her. You're a lucky man, Simon Fremont."

"I think I'm the lucky one," Tessa said, smiling. She took his hand and held it in her lap.

"Well, he's grown up to become such a wonderful young man." His mother pointed at an elongated oak cabinet across from where they sat. Vibrant blue porcelain jars lined up next to family photos and trophies and plaques. Simon shook his head at Tessa, raising his eyebrows to ridicule his mom. "Look how little he was when he was born! Barely four pounds. In grade school, he was bullied for being so tiny, so meek and frail. But he worked hard on keeping healthy and now—"

"Look at who he's become," Tessa interrupted. "He must make you so proud."

Simon watched as she focused her gaze on one of the pictures.

"We should get going, Mum," he said. "We have an hour drive back to the city." He stood and walked to his mother, who held her arms open for him.

"It was so nice to meet you, Tessa," she said. "I hope you come see us again before you go back to the States. Come during the day. We can walk around the lake, see the flowers and get to know each other a wee bit more."

thirty-five

"Ooh! Is that Henry?" Riley asked, her fingers locked with Tessa's as they held up Tessa's phone. It was a picture of a little boy in a sailor top and navy-blue shorts. "He looks so British!"

"God, he's adorable," Tessa said, leaning closer to whisper something in Riley's ear. "He's the only one I understood from that whole clan."

Riley burst out laughing.

Simon rolled his eyes as Tessa lovingly placed her hand on his thigh. "Yeah, Tessa had a little bit of trouble with the accents."

"That's because I didn't realize that you'd break into full Cockney on me."

"The formal word is Estuary," Simon corrected her.

"Last time I checked, it was still English," Jacob piped in.

"Uh-huh." Tessa rolled her eyes.

Together, they looked at more pictures, huddled around a round table on the terrace of a restaurant on Rue Destin, located in one of the busiest districts in Paris. Earlier, they had walked around the *Place de la Bastille*, checked out the 11th arrondissement for the two women's favorite designer store and art gallery and ended up at a place called *La Belle Vie*. The place was small, hardly quaint, with solid wood fixtures, built in brick walls, a regular jaunt frequented mostly by locals. They had chosen an outdoor table overlooking the street, their backs to the blue green wooden framed windows and underneath brass pendant lamps. The street was dark, cars and motorcycles separated from them by removable metal railings. Bicycles were parked along the trees that lined the road.

Simon rubbed Tessa's shoulders while she pulled her sweater tight against her. "You cold?" he asked.

"A little bit. I know it's heated, but there's a draft somewhere," Tessa answered.

"I feel so French," Riley joked.

"I know, right? Just like the internship days. Dinner right before bed," Jacob answered.

"Oh, shush," Tessa quipped. "Hanois was fully booked, and this was the only available time. Besides, it's not that late. We've eaten later before."

"What was wrong with Sushi Maki next door?" Riley asked. "I kinda felt like sushi."

"Full," Tessa responded. "This had outdoor seating and was first come first serve."

"Nine o'clock is definitely not late," Simon said, defending his girl.

"For you!" All three friends piped in, breaking out in laughter.

"Seriously though," Riley teased. "Tessa feels right at home with the beautiful people. They all look like artists."

Their server, a pretty French girl wearing a tight black dress and thick black tights, set wine glasses on their table. Music from the neighboring establishments syncopated through the air. Men in berets, women in trench coats, cigarettes, ashtrays, bottles of wine, lovers, couples, boots, scarves. Beautiful people, all of them. Tessa played a game in her head, tried to find as many objects depicting Parisian culture, tested herself to see how well she'd acclimated to her favorite place.

"Still better here than Bastille," Tessa said. "Nice to get away from all that energy for once." She looked pointedly at Riley. They had checked out the rows of clubs, pubs and bars the night before at Riley's insistence.

"Seriously, thank you for coming salsa dancing last night," Riley said. "It was fun, wasn't it?"

And when no one replied, Jacob took her hand. "Yes, it was, babe," he said before leaning over to give her a kiss.

Tessa looked at her brother, and then his girlfriend and then glanced sideways at the man sitting next to her. This, right there, was her home. The three people who mattered. At a time and place she wanted to remember forever.

"Okay, where were we?" Riley slid Tessa's phone toward her. "More pictures."

Tessa complied happily, opening her camera and swiping left. The two men leaned sideways as well.

"Henry wanted to sit with me the whole time!" Tessa bragged. A picture of the little boy in her lap.

"Is that Simon's mom?" Riley asked.

The screen showed a beautiful woman with blond hair, her arms around Tessa, the corners of her eyes crinkled into a loving smile.

"Yes! Isn't she gorgeous? And this is his dad," Tessa swiped left again. An elderly gentleman with Simon's sandy brown hair.

"Your brother is hot!" Riley squeaked.

Jacob reached over and swiped left again. "Move on," he said, smiling. They all laughed.

"Did your mom and dad like meeting Tessa, Simon?" Riley asked just as the server was bringing out a plate of escargot.

"Oh, my, it went bloody well, I would say. My parents thought she was the bees' knees."

"Bees' what?" Riley narrowed her eyes, looking confused.

Tessa caressed Simon's arm. "He means they liked me."

"Ah. They don't say that in Spain," Riley muttered, defensive.

"They have a really warm and cozy home," Tessa continued. "You would have liked it, Rye. His mom is a middle school teacher and his dad just retired from the farm. They've sold it to a developer and are moving closer to Adrian."

Simon nodded his head. "In Chelmsford." He wrapped his arm around her shoulder and pulled her close. She watched his reactions as he continued to talk about his family. She never imagined she would love someone like that. Never thought she would be one of the women in her books, so hopelessly in love. She had to admit, the visit with his family had gone exceedingly well. They were welcoming of her. Not only had she been able to keep up with their queries, but she'd really enjoyed meeting his mother. His parents were hardworking, warm and shared their love openly. They were such doting grandparents to Ashleigh's son. He was most definitely the light of their lives.

Her parents would have been the same way. Had they lived.

And as the minutes flew by, both couples were engaged in conversation about everything under the sun. There was laughing and teasing and a whole lot of affection. She noticed Simon watching her too. Every so often, he would turn to look at her, as if wanting to say something. And when his eyes bore into hers, she swore she saw her parents, his parents, her future. She saw love.

And he saw it too.

"Are we there, baby?" he asked, ever so softly. He had heard her that night after all.

"Yes. I think so."

"Marry me," he murmured in her ear, out of the blue, as Riley and Jacob talked. Tessa jerked her head and turned to him, her eyes squinted, her mouth agape.

"Marry me," he said again, this time out in the open. "I'll go anywhere with you. I'll put in for a job in the States, move there with you. Anything!"

The sights, the sounds, the air around her. They no longer were. It was just her and him. Standing at the edge of the cliff, her lungs filling with air and her heart about to explode. She didn't see Riley bring her hand to her mouth in surprise or Jacob smiling from ear to ear. She saw him. She saw him on the day she'd met him, him on the night he looked lost and alone in the lobby of the Vegas hotel. She saw him as he sat on the plane with his reading glasses on. Him somersaulting in the Aegean Sea, the sweet sound of his laughter echoing through the mountains after completing the jump of his life. He who had touched the sand for the very first time.

Only him.

She nodded. First slowly, up and down, up and down, and then rapidly, eyes fixed on him.

"Yes?" he asked, a hitch in his breath attributed to nerves.

"Now you know how the dim sum dude felt," she teased. She placed her hand on the back of his head and drew his face to her. He found her lips, grazed her teeth with his tongue. But then he pulled away, looking from side to side in earnest.

"Wait," he said. "I need to make this official." He slid his chair back and stood up. "There's a pharmacy two doors down. I'll be right back!"

"Oh my god! I'm so happy for you!" Riley wrapped her arms tightly around her friend's shoulders for a few seconds and lunged away from the table. "Wait, Simon! I'll come with you!"

Simon ran back toward Tessa and kissed her loudly on the lips. "Be right back. Don't move."

Jacob slid over to Riley's empty seat. He took Tessa's hand in his and kissed it. "I'm so happy for you, sis!" he exclaimed.

"Oh, Jake. I hope I'm doing the right thing. I don't know anything right now except that I love him. And you said it, right? There's nothing wrong with taking a chance. He's worth it."

"You're doing the right thing."

"I love you, Jake. We've been such a good team. I don't know what I would've done if I didn't have you with me through all these years without Mom and Dad. Whatever the future brings, we have each other, right?" she asked, almost trying to convince him to stay with her through this new phase in her life. "I might have to move to London. How will I do that without you?"

Jake locked her in an embrace and kissed her forehead. "With or without me, you were bound for happiness. You deserve it. And your future will be great. It will be filled with love because that's all you've ever given and that's what you've earned. It's one thing to write about it, true love. Now you can live it. He's the one for you, Tessa. I know he is. He's the one."

POP. POP. POP.

Tessa and Jacob separated only when they heard a woman's scream. And then another. And another.

Chaos ensued. The wooden tables and chairs were thrown around, people were crying, running, hiding under the tables.

"*Sous les tables!*" A man yelled at the top of his lungs. *Under the tables.*

POP. POP. POP.

The sounds were deafening, close enough for her to feel a gust of wind every time it happened.

Everything moved in slow motion, sounds and images floated across in a dreamlike state. Things flew in the air and landed away from her, people ran in the opposite direction.

By the time she realized what was happening, it was too late.

Masked men with guns, maybe four or five of them, stood merely a few feet away.

Tessa could hear the clicking of their heels as they moved about, using their bearing to loom over all those cowered on the ground. She saw black masks on all of them but one. It was him, the one in a bright orange mask who locked eyes with Jacob. She saw his steely, beady eyes flicker back and forth before he moved forward.

Her heart pounded in unison with the man's steps, every beat brought him closer to them. For a split second, he turned away from them to address one of the other men in his group. She thought he would forget about them. Maybe her brother believed it too.

"Run, Tess," he whispered. "Run now."

She gripped Jacob's arm tightly with both hands, frozen with fear and disbelief. Somehow all she could do was hold on to him, out of instinct, loyalty, love. She wasn't going to leave him.

But the man—he didn't forget them. He looked at Jacob and then at her, before adjusting his orange mask for a better view.

She saw the dismay in her brother's eyes.

But two seconds later, she saw his look transform into defiance.

She saw the man mock Jacob's stance by pointing his gun at them.

And then she saw nothing more.

Oh, my Jacob. My handsome, beautiful Jacob. You stand out wherever you go. Because you're brave. And valiant. And strong. And you always know what to do.

Jacob yanked her under the table and pushed her head down roughly toward his abdomen, his forearms feeling like heavy ropes against her head. He covered her with his coat. She was rolled into a ball, her eyes in complete darkness.

"Jake, no!" she cried. "Let me out! No! Jake!"

The more she cried, the more she pummeled him with her fists, the harder he crushed her against his chest.

He had formed himself into a human shield, rocking back and forth, his arms tight around her.

"I love you," he said. "I love you, be happy. Tell Riley I love her so much. She always—" He paused and took a deep breath. She could feel the rise and fall of his chest, before he rambled so rapidly as if trying to say everything he could. "She always says I'm her home, but the truth is, she is mine."

thirty-six

"**S**ayyyy-monn!" Riley squealed as she hooked her arm in his. She literally skipped along the cobbled street that led away from the restaurant and toward the pharmacy. "I can't believe this is happening! I'm soooo sooo sooo happy!"

He laughed out loud as she repeatedly pulled on his arm.

"Simon! Yay!" she squealed.

"I hope we can find something," he said as they entered the store. "Anything I can place on her ring finger until I can get this sorted tomorrow. You can help me find something you think she'll fancy."

"Cartier, of course," Riley announced.

He was dizzy with hysteria. He couldn't believe his fortune. He'd been wanting to ask her since she'd arrived in London the week before, but if there was anything he knew about her, it was that she was slow to adjust. He knew he had to tread lightly, but at the same time, he couldn't imagine letting her go ever again.

She would have to leave for the States soon. Life was like that. They both had to figure out how to make their careers work. He had to make it more permanent. And after he'd seen how enamored his parents were with her, he knew she was made for him.

"I'm just so fortunate to have met someone like her. I can't imagine waking up without her next to me. I don't even know what I did before

189

I met her."

"Aww," Riley said. "Tessa loves you, Simon. No matter how much she tried to push you away in the past few months, you stuck around. You were the only one who's ever been able to turn her around."

"Why do you think that is?" he asked.

"It's because you didn't give up on her. You waited patiently for her to be ready while tearing those walls down. She was different after the day you met in New York. There was something about her that changed after that trip. When I think about it now, I can point to that time in March."

They stood in the middle of the pharmacy, trying to read the signs in French.

"I'll go this way. You go there."

He nodded at her before turning in the other direction. Simon turned into the candy section, hoping to find Kinder Eggs. He'd grown up on those chocolate eggs with a surprise hidden in them. But even if they had them, how would he know which one contained a toy ring? Quickly, he scanned the shelves. Bonbons, Sucrets, bubble gum cigarettes. Bubble gum cigarettes? Seriously? He chuckled at the thought. *I've unearthed a time capsule.*

"Sayyyy-monn!" That irritatingly endearing screech rang through the aisles. "I found it!"

Simon zigzagged in and out until he found Riley standing in the middle of the toy section. "Here!" she shoved a plastic jewelry kit in front of him. "There's a ring in there, look!"

He held the plastic box up to find many little things—a princess crown, a silver necklace, many different colored bangles, and there it was—a ring. "It's small enough for her tiny fingers too," he cracked.

"Yeah," Riley laughed. "Let's go."

Simon tore the package open as they walked out of the store. He handed the rest of the toys to a little girl and her mother and slipped the ring into his pocket.

The piercing sound of sirens and horns met them as they hit the street. The flashing of lights, red, blue and white, blinded them. "Oh my God!" Riley screamed. "What is happening?"

French police, dressed in all black, with shields and guns were everywhere. People, men and women were wailing, screaming in pain. They were crying, bellowing out in agony.

Simon grabbed Riley and held on to her tightly. Shards of glass, discarded tables were strewn all over the street. Thin yellow plastic strips cordoned off the two restaurants next to the pharmacy. Ambulances, police cars, trucks everywhere. There were people on stretchers. But there were also many white sheets scattered on the ground.

"Tessa!" Simon yelled at the top of his lungs, tightly clutching Riley.

"Jacob!" Riley cried. "Jacob! Where are you?" She was a cyclone, spinning in place, her hair thrashing against her face.

A mass of people had spilled into the streets, held back by a line of yellow ribbon. Simon lifted Riley up, carrying her, running past the police and paramedics.

"*Non, Monsieur*, you cannot go there."

A policeman in armor stopped him.

When Simon continued to push past him, the policeman screamed, "*Non, monsieur! Ne pas entrer! Il y a des morts!*" *There are dead bodies.*

"My girlfriend and her brother are there. Let us through!" Simon yelled, pushing, shoving, hitting everything in his way.

And when the obstacles cleared, they stood in the street, directly facing the restaurant.

"Jacob!" Riley screamed before her knees gave way and she fell. She crawled toward the table, now turned upside down, its round edges rolling like a wheel back and forth on the cement floor. "Jacob! My Jacob!"

Simon rushed toward Riley, trying to hold her up, lift her off the ground. And then he realized what Riley was running to.

She was running toward her ruin.

Tessa was covered in blood, her hair, her face, her hands, sitting upright and oscillating back and forth, side to side, her eyes drained of all signs of life. She stared straight ahead into nothing.

Next to her, on the ground, was the man she loved most in her life, his dignity preserved only by the thin white sheet that covered him.

Tessa fiercely struck at anyone who tried to come close, like a mother bear fiercely protecting her cub. She kicked and screamed and cursed at the paramedics. "I need to be with my brother! You don't understand. I have no one. I have no one!"

Those were the last words Simon heard her say. The broken girl who feared love because of loss had been destroyed. This time for good.

PART II:

When She Forgets
(The Present)

thirty-seven

The sound of the door shutting as Will and Ciela leave is music to her ears. Time to sit in silence and savor that one cup of coffee, to revel in the comfort of a hot shower before starting her day.

She looks forward to this on most mornings, when dreams don't consume her and sleep eventually gets its way. Today, she feels fresh and hopeful. Like every other time she's decided to start over, begin with a clean slate. As she sits on the fourth step of the grand staircase, she gives herself the luxury of time. In the past years, since returning from Paris and deciding to settle down, she has sat on this step to look over the expanse of her home. Everywhere a sign of her accomplishment and proof she has made the right choice.

In the living room is a massive stone shelf filled with books, trophies and awards. The walls are plastered with movie posters and paintings. Her heart on display, a story all too familiar to her. She smiles as she turns her head toward the family room. What she observes pleases her, makes her heart ache with love. Dolls in pink dresses, a shopping cart filled with plastic groceries and actual packages of food from her pantry.

Work, career, motherhood.

A man's black leather jacket is slung across the armchair in the family room.

Because love. She has that too. It's beginning to take the form of a tall, dark and handsome man. One she'd met the year before. He hadn't stolen her heart. Someone else had and run the hell away with it. And although she'll never get that heart back, she thinks this new guy might give her a new one.

Who would have thought she would settle down? Find a home, stay grounded? In a forgotten time and in a place far away, she left that life and started over.

Through the tall bay windows, she sees the sun. It's trying with all its might to break through the clouds. There's snow everywhere, ten feet of it, and all signs of summer—the grill, the deck chairs, the potted plants—are buried underneath massive lumps of ice.

The shrill ringing of the phone startles her. No one ever calls her landline. She hops down from the staircase and runs into the living room. What is it about phones? You can never find them if your life depends on it.

Ah, here it is. She fishes the cordless phone from under the fluffy couch cushions in the family room, but she's too late. The call goes to voicemail. It's a 617 area code.

Boston.

She has no business thinking about Boston. Or who used to be there. Or what that meant to her at a time in her life when all she wants is to move forward.

The subsequent ringing annoys her.

"Hello?" she answers, glancing at the clock on the mantel. She has thirty minutes before she has to be out the door.

"Tessa?"

It's a man's voice. The accent is unmistakable. But it's the way he says her name that sinks her. It was the way he called her name when she saw him last. Full of sadness, of longing. She doesn't remember much, but she remembers the way he called out to her before she looked away.

Impossible. He left me. Walked away and left me.

"Who is this?" she says.

"Tessa. It's me."

She's reluctant to say his name. It took two years to cast that name out, eradicate the feelings brought about by those two calamitous syllables.

"Simon?" Her voice echoes, resounding against the high vaulted ceilings before settling in her heart.

"Yes. It's so nice to hear your voice. Can you talk?"

"I... Where are you calling from?" She begins to move helplessly around the room. Back and forth, in a circle, to and fro.

"Doesn't matter now, does it? How have you been?"

"Fine. I've been fine. Is everything okay?"

Stop it. Sit down and stop.

"Yes. I'm sorry for worrying you. I just wanted to hear your voice. There's something I need to tell you."

She collapses onto the couch. "This is... this is unexpected. What is it?"

"Three years. I've been visiting our places, trying to remember your face. Been trying to remember everything about us. I guess I just called to say thank you."

"For what? *What's wrong?*" she asks, her heart sinking. She cradles the phone, afraid to let it go. And then she closes her eyes tightly, praying for a vision, a memory, anything that will help her remember why they both had to leave.

"What we had... It was the stuff of romance novels. I wanted to thank you for that. No one else, Tessa. There was no one else that I would have wanted to experience true love like that with but you."

She's stunned. And filled to the brim with so much regret, she doesn't know where to start.

"It was love at first sight, wasn't it?" he's saying. "We were just too selfish to admit it."

I have to tell him. But something else comes out of her lips. "Yes. Yes. It was."

"Will you write about us? Write our story?"

His request stuns her. "Simon, I—"

"That's all. I hope everything is going well with you. I wish you the best."

A dial tone bursts through the dam, and the rushing flood drowns her in the past.

thirty-eight

"Mama?"

Her daughter's voice rings through the hallway, six hours after the phone call from Simon. Tessa remains shaken, understandably so. Hearing his voice, remembering who he had been to her, those memories had been locked away for a while now. They were relegated to the same place where she had stored her life's most precious moments. She just couldn't think of him without thinking of Jacob. To her, they were one and the same.

"Coming!" she yells back, running down the stairs.

Will and Ciela stand by the front door, unbuttoning their coats and kicking off their boots. Tessa wonders if it's just her or if they're beginning to look more and more like each other. Will's got a crew cut, his hair shaved close to his head. But the tiny spikes of blond hair are difficult to miss. His eyes are the greenest of fields. *Refreshing.*

Next to him, Ciela looks like a little peanut, barely up to Will's knees. Her curly hair the color of wheat and her eyes as transparent as the sky. Their similarity. Could it be because she no longer remembers what Ciela's father looks like?

Will lines up their boots neatly on the splash pad. He reaches out for Tessa and skims his nose along her neck. "Mmm. Hi. How was your day?"

She pulls away. "Good." She touches his face with one hand and leans down to kiss her daughter.

She knows he doesn't notice her apprehension. He leaves her with Ciela and ambles into the living room, picking up the remote control by the coffee table.

"Wook!" Tessa unrolls a piece of paper that announces Ciela as Super Kid the following week. Tessa can't help but smile at the thought. Super Kid chosen to be Super Kid. Ciela had started the Advanced Preschool program as a result of her high aptitude test results. The test placed her at a first-grade level! Who would have known she would take after her father?

"You are? That's great! We have to start making your poster, okay?"

Tessa sits on the floor and folds Ciela into her lap. "We'll take some of your baby pictures and add some of the puzzles you put together. How about that?"

Slowly, her world stitches itself up together again. She has mastered the art of living in the moment. It's been her survival instinct for the past three years. Focus on right now, her therapist teaches her. When you find your mind wandering, rein your thoughts in. Look down at your hands, your gloves, the dishes. Feel the soap through your fingers as you're performing life's daily chores. See, hear, touch, smell. Here and now. Not the past. Not the future.

But it's really Ciela who brings her back to the present, no matter how far into the past she might regress.

"You have a few minutes to play with your babies before I come up to start your bath."

Ciela gallops upstairs to her bedroom as Tessa sets her backpack on the floor and makes her way into the kitchen.

Will is pouring himself a glass of red wine. "What's for dinner?" he asks. He pulls the oven door open, expecting to find something cooking.

"Sorry, my meeting ran late," she replies. "I figure we could just order in tonight."

"Sounds good." Will smiles. "I'll call Rosatti's."

Tessa nods absentmindedly. "Sorry."

"By the way, the plumber called me. He said he stopped by to drop off the bathroom tiles, but no one answered the door."

"Hmm. I wonder if that was when I ran out to the cleaners?"

The truth is, she'd sat in the same place on the floor for hours after that phone call. She heard the mailman. And the delivery guy. And even the plumber who rang the doorbell as if there was no tomorrow. But she'd been paralyzed, immobilized by so much emotion, she couldn't lift herself from her misery to save her life.

He had called her after almost three years apart—why not sooner? Up to then, the details are murky. How she let him go, how he let her go. How she even got this far after losing her brother.

"I'm going upstairs to—"

"How about I give her a bath tonight?" he offers, touching her shoulder.

She nods and gives him a grateful smile before he turns away. Will knows her so well, well enough to sense when something is wrong. It's not like he'd have to have ESP. She tried to freshen up before they arrived, splashing water on her face, but her eyes are swollen and red and she's still in her pajamas.

Of course, Will has seen her like this before. It happens every year, right around the time of Jacob's death anniversary.

That's months away.

Ciela is finally in bed, and Will sits on the couch flipping between the Travel Channel and ESPN. Tessa clears up the dinner table, stacks up some papers in her office, cleans out the pantry before returning to her desk to review the screenplay for her latest book.

She can't get past the first sentence.

In place of the words, she hears Simon's voice. "When we get back from Paris, I'm going to ask to be assigned to the States. Girl in 7C, we're going to stay put in one place and have the most gloriously boring life together," he had said.

When had he said that? Was it before or after Ciela had been conceived? Did he even know about her? Will he hate Tessa for keeping this secret from him? Where had he been all these years?

She's been working on herself, trying to remember. For now, she knows nothing about what happened after Jacob... After Jacob.

Why now? Why now, damn him!

Will clears his throat, and she jumps. He wraps his arms around her shoulders. "Something happened today."

She swivels her chair around to face him. "Will." Her eyes begin to sting. "I love you."

"I know," he answers.

An uncanny calm fills the room. She knows he's been waiting for the right moment. He's been trying to get her to this, to talk about what happened, how she felt, but in the past two years, he hasn't really been able to skim the surface. Like everyone else left to speculate on her life, he knows the details as they were published in the news articles. She'd never really talked about it with him.

She stands up and makes as if to tie her robe together. "I must be getting sick. I think I'm just going to go to bed. See you tomorrow?"

He opens his mouth to say something but doesn't. For a few seconds, he just stands there, dislocated, an intruder in the wrong house. She can see it's not what he wants to hear, especially when she's so clearly upset—she fell in love with him partly because of how well he takes care of her. But she also loves him because he's so good about respecting her boundaries.

"Sure." He kisses the top of her head and she responds by encircling her arms around his waist. "Do you need help with Ciela tomorrow?"

"No. Thank you. I've got her for the rest of the week. It was just today, with that meeting."

The meeting she had missed. The biggest meeting of her career. Isn't this reminiscent of the way she was years ago, the impulsiveness, the lack of a plan? There's no time to analyze at that moment. All she wants to do is to once again get lost in her memories. In the peace and quiet of the fortress she had built for her and her daughter.

She listens intently for Will's footsteps, replaced by the ding of the keys as he picks them up from the antique tray sitting by the foyer. She even hears him zipping his coat before his footsteps start up again. A sigh of relief passes her lips as she hears the closing of the door. And then she covers her face with her hands and releases her very soul through her tears.

thirty-nine

"What's so important that you had to drive all the way to the suburbs to see me?" Riley asks, unfolding a napkin and placing it on her lap. The lunch regulars at the high-end mall have just begun to fill up the empty tables around them.

"You look like shit," she adds. "Are you up all night writing?"

Tessa smiles weakly. A day has passed since the call. Nothing makes sense anymore. She just has to speak to someone, anyone. The years have given her more than she can ever imagine, and yet nothing has ever felt right. All she wants is a reprieve. Had she been fooling herself? Until yesterday, she truly thought she was finally starting to move on with her life.

"Ciela's at a playdate. I figured it would be easier to drive out here than to have you meet me downtown."

She glances around the room and smiles to herself. Three years ago, she wouldn't have been able to sit alone in a public place for very long. These days, people don't even know who she is. Some washed up author with one movie to her credit. Paris had taken away everything from her. Her inspiration, her career, her sense of self.

You're only as good as your latest book, her agent always reminds her. It had taken her quite a long time to finish Lionel and Carissa's story. And now they were just about to make it into a movie.

Due to her publishing delay, she'd lost her notoriety. In the past few years, her fans have moved on to the greatest and latest book, to the latest author whose words have touched them. She was rebuilding her fan base, trying to organize some local book tours that wouldn't take her away from Ciel.

Don't worry, your time will come again. Once you get your words back, they will be there waiting.

"Did you want to go shopping? We can walk over to Neiman after lunch. I have some time." Riley reaches out to touch her shoulder. Tessa notices the pain in her friend's eyes every single day. If you didn't know Riley until that very moment, you'd see a beautiful woman with a quiet reserve. Little would you know this woman was once vivacious, gregarious and full of life. The years have changed her friend. Her tone is somber, monotonous. She has no spark for life.

Tessa gets lost in her thoughts once again, carelessly turning her water glass repeatedly. Exhaustion begins to take over, her mind is empty. She can't string together a thought for very long.

Although Riley has told her what happened, she draws a blank each time she tries to remember what happened after she was rolled into a ball in Jacob's arms.

Look at us, she thinks. We are two friends who commiserate in agony. That's what holds them together.

And now, Tessa is worried she may upset Riley. Maybe she shouldn't have been so impulsive to run to Riley for comfort. Riley has no comfort to give her. At least Simon is alive. Jacob is gone forever.

"How 'bout this snowstorm?" Tessa says. "We thought we were over it and then, boom! Ciela has cabin fever. We all need spring to come soon." She forces a laugh while nervously brushing her hair back.

Riley shakes her head. "You didn't come all the way here to discuss the weather with me."

Tessa runs her fingers down the edge of the tablecloth. "No. It's about yesterday," she starts out. She looks at her friend. "Yesterday." She chokes back tears. A fork slides off the table, and when she reaches down to grab it, her wine glass crashes to the ground. A server runs over, dustpan and broom in hand.

"Tessa!" Riley exclaims. "What's wrong? What's happened?" Quickly, she runs to Tessa's side, gently taking her elbow and lifting her off the seat. "Let's go outside."

They stand right outside the revolving doors, not far from the valet station. "Yesterday, what?" Riley asks.

"Simon called the house. I heard his voice and…" She takes a deep breath. "And I missed him so much, I thought I would die all over again. He sounded off, I think something's wrong. Oh, Rye, he might be in trouble or something."

Riley leans forward, interested in hearing more.

"I haven't stopped thinking about him, I can't. I won't. I won't stop thinking about him. I have to find him. I want to know what I said, what I did to make him leave. You told me all about it, but I still can't remember!"

"Oh, Tessa!" Riley cries. "You didn't do anything! The doctors felt it was best!"

Tessa begins to sob. "I'm sorry, Rye. I know this brings back so much for you."

It isn't fair that Jake had to give up his life to save her. Jake was their hero, and yet Tessa would've rather had a coward who was alive than a brave man who'd lost his life. She'd lost her brother, and Riley had lost a future with the only man she loved.

Tessa has something of Simon, a daughter, a reason to live. But Riley? A year after Jake's death, she'd married his friend, Liam. Liam who was there for her through the tears and the breakdowns, the anger and the acceptance. The same Liam who was in love with her from the very first day they'd met.

Riley has a husband, a career and a home, but Tessa knows it's surrounded by a thick, heavy fog that hasn't lifted since the terrible evening in Paris.

"How do we find him?" Riley asks. They sit on the sidewalk, outside the restaurant in the arctic air, everything dead around them. Gray clouds have swallowed what's left of the afternoon sun. Nature gives no sign of life. The trees are barren, their branches brittle from the suffocating weight of the ice. Spring is way beyond their reach.

"It was a Boston number," Tessa answers.

"Do you think he's working there?"

"I don't know!" Tessa lifts both hands up in frustration. She has no answers.

"Okay, what about Will? What did you tell him?"

Tessa clenches her teeth, the cold beginning to seep into her bones.

"Nothing. He probably assumes it was just a bad day for me yesterday. He's been really careful about pushing too much."

Tessa digs her numb hands into her pockets.

"What do you want, Tess? What do you want to do with that phone call?"

"I don't know. I feel like I slept through the past three years. I lived in the present, sank myself into raising Ciela. And now that phone call's woken me up and nothing feels right. I want to find him. I want to know he's okay. It's time to remember what happened."

"There's Will. There's your career. There is your daughter. How will you manage all that—this life—and reconnect with the past at the same time? Listen. I know it's been a living hell, not being able to remember what happened. But it was a mutual agreement between the two of you."

"And he never tried to come back," Tessa answered, the pain of Riley's words going straight to her heart.

Clouds of cold air emanate from Riley's lips. They look at each other and acknowledge the need to get indoors. They stand, hold hands and walk out toward the parking lot.

"I have to be home before Ciela gets there," Tessa says. "I have no answers today. Give me some time to digest it all. And then I'll know what to do next."

Riley nods. There's nothing they could do today. Tessa would have to tie up loose ends before pursuing the threads that would lead back to her past.

forty

The weekend drags on. Tessa is forced to shroud her anxiety, mask her apprehension, forget her pain. It feels worse than when she first lost Jake. The panic attacks have returned; she can hardly breathe, makes every effort to function.

A week after the phone call, Ciela has a birthday party at Chuckie Cheese. Tessa can't decide whether spending time with the other mothers in the midst of carnival music and screaming children would kill her or help her. But then she reminds herself: she's been dead for a while, so what does it matter? Ciela is the only one who reminds her to pull herself back up. And Will's love for her makes her feel like she still deserves to live. Two people who have no clue they've saved her.

Tessa sits motionless on a bench facing a musical helicopter ride rising and falling a few feet from the ground, its propeller churning slowly as her daughter bobs up and down in its seat. A small sized cheese pizza and two paper cups of root beer are placed neatly in front of her.

"Sit still, Ciel," she orders, "or you might hurt yourself."

Ciela nods and lifts her arms up in the air. "Go, go, go!"

Tessa has grown accustomed to seeing him in her daughter's eyes. Today, she longs for him so much, the physical pain is debilitating. It's too difficult for her to stand, to sit, to interact.

The ride's motion mesmerizes, hypnotizes her. She clears her mind of everything—lord knows she's learned to master the art of shutting off. Of storing away the memories of the day that changed everything. Not like she hasn't tried to remember. But there hasn't really been any time to dwell on it. She molds herself into the mother she's always wanted to be and makes sure the past no longer has a hold on her life. She's given up every semblance of the person she was before. And now, all she wants is to free herself from all this pretense. Before she completely loses herself. Does she even know who she is anymore?

The party progresses, the lunch alarm goes off and all the kids are corralled in an area with tables in front of a large stage. Chuckie and his friends are about to do their dance. Ciela bounces excitedly in her seat. More pizza is served, and then a birthday cake. Chocolate and fudge and everything sweet, devoured by parents and children alike.

Tessa and Ciela dance with the mascots, take pictures and go on more rides. Three hours pass and the world around her swirls in music and camaraderie. No one bears a mark of sadness in this place. Everyone's secrets are hidden for the sake of their children.

"Wiw!" Ciela jumps up from her dance and races in the opposite direction. Will sweeps her in his arms and gives her a kiss. Tessa follows her daughter until the three of them are side by side, a perfect picture of family and togetherness.

Will leans over to kiss Tessa, and she takes his hand.

"Hi."

To the parents in Ciela's school, they are a couple. In fact, everyone has assumed Will is Ciela's father. They think it's cute that she addresses him by his first name. Tessa and Will play along, without the need to explain anything to anybody.

"Finished my deposition early, so I thought I'd come and join the party," he says. "I've missed you."

It has been a week since she told him she was feeling sick and sent him home. She hasn't seen him in all that time. Normally, they spent weeknights together and weekends in his house in the suburbs. She's at a loss for faking normalcy and so she tries her best to avoid him.

"Are you hungry?" she asks as Ciela rejoins her friends. "There's so much pizza on the tables. I think they have a few with peppers for the parents." She leads him toward the boxes and trays.

Will grabs a piece and sits next to Tessa as they watch Ciela pick up where she left off. She twirls around in her little pink tutu, ballet slippers gliding on the floor, trying her best to mimic the dance steps brought forth by the mascots.

"She's really getting into it," Will says proudly.

Tessa pours him some root beer.

Ciela runs toward them carrying an oversized balloon. Will stands abruptly and approaches her before she reaches her mother. He takes the object from her hand.

"No!" Ciela shrieks. "Mama, wook! Owange!"

"Ciely," says Will. "Let's get a blue one instead, okay?"

Tessa turns around to collect herself, straightening her sleeves and then her blouse and repeatedly running her palms against her jeans. There are triggers. And that color continues to be one of them. Will keeps Ciela away from her mother for a good half hour.

Until Ciela decides she's too tired to sit through the opening of the gifts. It's the same routine, refusing to set foot on the ground, her legs curling up as she lifts her arms and asks to be carried, followed by the kicking and whining. Will gathers their things as Tessa bids goodbye to the birthday celebrant.

Later, at the house, Ciel motions for Will to take her upstairs and put her to bed. He steals a glance at Tessa, asking with his eyes if he could spend the night.

Tessa takes his hand and nods.

When the lights are out, and the house is quiet, Tessa and Will remain relaxed on the couch in front of the fire. They talk about their week, about Will's most recent case. Tessa asks if he's had a chance to review the production studio's latest offer, and his thoughts on the indicated terms. He teases her about her choice of fixtures for the renovation and she teases him back about his lack of taste in hardware.

Before Simon's call, Tessa had been slowly giving in to the nesting phase of her life. Will has convinced her it's time to update the look of the house. With the money she made from selling the movie rights, cash is never a problem. But then again, Will would have gladly paid for everything—he is, in his own right, a successful partner in a respected law firm. Who would have thought she would be dating someone in a suit?

The glow of the fire, the silence in the house, their closeness to each other, the laughter they share. It just isn't the right time for Tessa to tell him about Simon. Will holds her face in his hands and pours his love out when he kisses her.

But tonight, she struggles to feel it. She consciously trails her hand downward and touches him, wanting him more than ever. She's developed a habit of doing this, of initiating pain and coupling it with pleasure. Part of her resolve to live and feel in the moment. The force of his body inside her keeps her in the present, gives her something to focus on, even just for a few minutes. She gets what she wants from him. There would be other days or nights that would bring her more courage to tell him about the secrets she's been hiding.

She breaks his kiss, turns around and lifts her skirt up, urging him to enter her from behind. He obliges, pushing her down on the sofa, muffling her cries into the pillow, too involved to hear her utter the name of the man on her mind.

forty-one

And so, here she sits in her therapist's office.

"Did I ever tell you the original Lionel and Carissa weren't star-crossed lovers?"

Tessa crosses her legs before tucking her hands under her thighs. She wiggles her eyebrows at the man sitting directly in front of her, trying her best to lighten the mood in the room.

"No, you didn't. Why bring it up?"

"I originally planned a HEA for those two. Until. Well, until I decided they didn't deserve to end up together."

"HEA?" he asks, confused. Sometimes she forgets not everyone lives in her world.

"Happy Ever After. You know, happy ending."

"Oh." He nods and stares at her. Is he waiting for something?

She matches his head bobbing with her own and digs her fingernails into the leather couch, focused on connecting old scratches with a new one.

"Tessa."

"Owen, I know. I'm sorry about the absence. I thought I was fine. I didn't think we were making any progress, and Ciel was growing so quickly and the days just blended into years, and now she's almost two," she rambles.

"I was just going to ask how you've been," he laughs. "How are things? And what brings you here after two years?"

"Well," she exhales loudly. "Three weeks ago, I got a call from Simon."

"Simon Fremont? The man you were going to marry before the—"

"Yes, yes."

"And what did he want from you? Didn't you tell me you were separated at the hospital? That the doctors advised you to separate from him for the sake of your recovery?"

What was he trying to be so articulate for? It's not like she doesn't know.

"I think it was a temporary thing. But he never came back," she said. "Anyway, long story short—he said he just wanted to hear my voice. But it stirred something inside of me that won't let things go anymore. I can't stop thinking about him. I want to find him, talk to him. I can feel it, Owen. If he stayed away for this long, why now? Something must be wrong."

"Find him?" Owen asks. "How?"

"Well, for starters, I reactivated my Twitter account. Last week, I sent him a message."

She looks at her therapist's face for a reaction. There is none.

She pulls her phone out of her purse and leans forward. "Remember that's how we first started communicating? He followed me on social media. Well, since I don't know where he is, I thought I would just post a message for him. Look."

GIRL IN 7C is searching for her friend, @DISCONNECTED. You called me three weeks ago and now it's my turn to look for you. Please message me back.

Owen leans back, and Tessa does the same. She puts the phone away and twists so she's facing sideways, her cheek resting on the headrest.

"So, it's been a week? Have you heard from him?" Owen asks.

"No."

"Tessa, have you considered how Riley is feeling in all this? The memories you're trying to face are hers too. Have you guys talked about it?"

Tessa pauses. "Not really. I know she's more advanced in her process because she kept with the PTSD sessions and I stopped because I was pregnant shortly after. All she said was that she was supportive of my decision."

Owen nods.

She continues. "Owen? Why do you think I can't remember anything about that night? I mean, it was all over the media outlets. Nineteen people were killed, and it was international news. Jacob was honored one month later and maybe if I wasn't so sick in the hospital, I could've relived what I needed to then, instead of holding on to it all these years."

She shivers when she remembers spending the holidays at *Pitie' Salpetriere'*, a hospital in Paris, heavily sedated and alone. Riley's parents had come from Madrid to take her home.

"You're experiencing one of the main characteristics of PTSD which is avoidance. A person may avoid people, places, thoughts, or situations that may remind him or her of the event. Your feelings of detachment and isolation from family and friends, as well as a loss of interest in activities you once enjoyed, is how you're reacting to the trauma. It's normal, Tessa. This new development may force you to face things sooner rather than later."

"Yes," she agrees. Although she doesn't know if she would have avoided this forever if Simon hadn't contacted her.

"Okay," Owen begins again. "I think we need to break this down in a few parts. What is your major concern at the moment?"

"It's Riley. I'm afraid she may resent knowing that Simon is still here. First Ciel and now Simon. It's like my life never suffered, but hers did. At least they are living, here in this world. Jacob is gone."

"Riley is married, starting a life of her own. Let's focus on you."

"I know that," she says, her eyes clouding with tears. "But Jake's gone!" She begins to cry. "I'm going to have to relive what happened. And that's why I'm here, Owen. I know. I know I can't search for Simon if I don't accept what's happened."

Owen stands, walks to his desk and grabs a box of Kleenex. He places it on the coffee table in front of them before returning to his seat. Tessa pulls a wad of tissue and blows her nose.

"Assuming you end up finding Simon, which in today's day and age may not be a difficult endeavor, what next? What do you want from him?"

He clicks his pen once, twice. She watches as he begins to scribble furiously. She's running out of time and she can't believe she's here instead of on a plane headed for somewhere to find him.

But she can't break down, can't give in to the chaos in her heart. She has a daughter now, a child who depends on her. She needs to go about this the right way.

Tap. Tap. Tap. The sound of Owen's pen against the clipboard calls her to attention.

"Oh, sorry. You were waiting for me to say something." She giggles nervously. "What was the question again?"

"Your plans, Tessa. And what you'd do once you find him."

"Well, aside from sending him messages, I may go to London to see his family. Right now, I don't know what his situation is, but all I want to do is remember. I want to tell him what's happened in the past three years. I want to see for myself that he's okay. It's been so long—the last time I saw him was that day in the hospital. No, wait. Did I see him at the funeral? Was he there, Owen? Did I see him? I don't remember." She giggles again.

Owen looks worried. She can tell he thinks she's having a breakdown.

Is she? She sits up, back straight, hands on her lap. She needs to pull herself together.

"As you go through your plans of searching for him, there are things that will just naturally come back to you. It's important for you to keep in touch with me. If you end up traveling," he says with a smile, "and I expect you'll be traveling—we can Skype."

At first, she reacts by nodding. And then she lifts up her finger, stopping him, reminding him they're not done. "Owen. What about Will?"

"You tell me. What about him?" Owen asks.

"I...I don't think I can be with him anymore. How do I tell him I can't divide my heart into two? That he never had it, really."

"Is that how you've been feeling for the past year you've been dating?"

"He's so good to me, to Ciela. I thought I could learn to love him one day. But hearing Simon's voice makes me realize I'm not over him. Nor am I over losing Jake either."

She scoots forward, intent on grabbing another Kleenex. "I want to tell him about Ciela. I want another chance with him."

"What if Simon doesn't want a chance with you?"

Tessa is taken aback by the question. It's the ugly truth that never crossed her mind. How presumptuous of her to think he'd still want her. After everything she had put him through.

She turns to the side and places her purse on her lap. Her right hand goes in, swirling and digging for something she's trying to find. Owen watches calmly, expressionless.

"I'm sorry," Tessa mutters, as she removes each item from her purse. One by one, she lays them on the couch next to her, a pen, her wallet, her glasses, a pair of sunglasses, two lip balms, her face spray, some hand sanitizer. And then his card. She remembers this was the purse she wore the first time they met. She hasn't carried this purse in almost three years. "I have his card. See here, I still have it."

"Do you think that's still relevant? Three years later? Does he still work there?"

She laughs. And then she tries not to blink her eyes because she knows what's coming.

"I'm not okay, am I?" she whispers, drop after drop cascading down her cheeks.

"No. You're not. But you'll get there. There's nothing to heal if you don't admit you've been hurt. You may not have been ready to remember before, but I think you are now. When you recall the trauma of that night, you will find yourself. You will get yourself back."

forty-two

Spring is finally in the air. The warm sun streams in through the open windows, the crisp smell of blooming flowers filling the house. She sits cross-legged on the floor, photographs of the past few years all around her. It's time to face them, to remember how she got here. Two bestsellers, two movies. One of them still in production. The second book brought even more success, finished one year after the tragedy and published shortly thereafter.

After that book, she had no more words. She wonders what it would be like to start writing all over again. The long hours, the sleepless nights, the words that seemed to flow so easily are nowhere to be found. They were in her veins, in her heart, but now she's completely drained of them.

Life just passes you by when you're busy, when you're sad, when you're lonely. You fill your days with contentment. Tasks, goals and bouts of staring, sitting, contemplating. And then before you know it, your daughter is two years old and you've wasted two years in a blur. You're still walking the same road with the same blinders on. You stop questioning yourself. Being alone feels right more and more. Until you've completely fooled yourself into thinking there's nothing else you can do, your life is just...

This.

This complacency consumes you, eats you up, dwindles your hours into days into months. And then you look up and you've forgotten why you were sad in the first place. It stays in your heart like a lump, a stone, a heavy mourning. Sometimes, you awaken from this dirge, you try to escape into song. But then complacency comes back to help you drift through life.

Complacency is your friend. It is also your biggest foe. This enemy kills you, snuffs the life out of you. Fools you into thinking you're living, when all you're doing is scraping by.

Around her living room are reminders of who she used to be. Not bad for someone who started out without a plan. Nowadays, it seems like that's all she has—plans, timetables, schedules.

She's caught off guard by a familiar voice at the front door.

"Yoohoo! Where are you?"

"In here!" she shouts.

The sound of heels clicking and clacking on the wood floor is all she hears until Riley stands in front of her. "Fulton Market had so many beautiful tulips," she says as she lays them on the table. "What's all this?"

"Spring cleaning," Tessa responds, her eyes fixated on the scattered mess. "I took them out of storage. Never got to sort them out."

Riley kicks off her shoes before she sits on the floor. "Look!" she says, holding one of the pictures. "I can't believe your hair has grown out so much."

"Holy shit, I looked like such a dork. It was so short then." Tessa smiles.

"Do you ever think you'll start writing again?" her friend asks.

Tessa shakes her head. "Nah. That person doesn't exist anymore. That was another time, in another universe."

"That universe was your world. It's what got you here," Riley counters.

"Many things got us here, my friend," Tessa says, her eyes wetting with tears.

She heads toward the kitchen to grab a vase, fills it up with water and unwraps the flowers. Riley follows suit and settles on a leather stool facing the counter.

"Why are you doing this to yourself, Tess?"

Tessa avoids the real question. "What? You mean consulting? It's structured, it's safe. This is how life has to be with Ciel."

She turns the question back at Riley. There are things that can no longer be ignored. She knows they'll both have to face it. Tessa doesn't know how just yet.

"Do you…" She pauses. "Still think about him?"

"Of course I do. Every day," Riley says, clutching the edges of the chair. "But it's different now. When I think of him, I think of a place so far away from where we are. Like a trip we took, a vacation that had to end. That's how I cope. And Liam, he's there to hold me whenever the dreams get ugly."

Tessa nods. Will is her present, her lifesaver, her island in the middle of the sea. But if she had a choice, she would tumble back into the water. This safe place, this refuge feels more like death to her. Who would ever think acceptance could be so suffocating?

She turns towards the refrigerator, pulls out a tray of cupcakes and takes two plates from the shelf.

"My sad attempt at baking for my daughter. Okay, before you say anything, they're supposed to be Cookie Monster, but they turned out more like Grover."

"Well, I've never seen so many blue Grovers before."

Riley takes a ravenous bite. Tessa pours two cups of coffee before taking her place next to her friend.

They never feared the silence. It was good for them. Their many moments throughout the years were quiet ones, sitting side by side doing their own thing. It was as if they were comforted by their proximity to each other, nothing more, nothing less.

"How do we start?" Riley finally asks. "How do we find him, Tess?"

"I don't know," Tessa whispers. "All I know is that I want to see him again. Most likely, he's married. He was probably just being reminiscent that day."

"You know you're risking everything at this point, don't you? For the past. We've both learned dredging up the past can be dangerous. What happened that night killed us—you'll die all over again."

"We're already dead," Tessa says, tears falling freely this time.

Riley spreads her arms open and Tessa sinks right in. They've become quite adept at blending their tears. Different hearts, same pain.

"Okay." Riley lets out a deep breath. "No more crying. We're not going to get anywhere by sitting here and crying. We must have a plan.

Go get a piece of paper and a pen," she orders.

Minutes later, they're back on the floor, in the midst of all their memories. Tessa quickly draws a map, scribbling circles for continents and placing dots in strategic places. Riley picks up a pile of pictures and turns through it.

"Vegas. Do you think he's in Vegas?"

Tessa shakes her head. "Maybe New York or Boston."

She scrolls through her phone and hands it to Riley. "It was a Boston number. He was staying there for a few months when we met."

"Yes, but he returned to London," Riley argues. "It's been three years—who knows where he's ended up?"

"He said he was visiting our places."

"What does that mean?"

"I don't know." Tessa is lost in wistfulness. They had seen the world through the eyes of love. To choose one place over the other would be like trying to pick a favorite child. Each one was special, it had brought them together in very different ways.

"Visit our places?" she says with a lighthearted chuckle.

Riley shakes her head. "What?"

"Visit them." Tessa reiterates. "I know he's had a head start but maybe I can catch up."

Gently, she takes the pen from Riley's fingers and spreads herself across the floor on her elbows. "I'll start here." She draws an X right on the state of Nevada. "And then, from here, to there." She crosses over through the ocean and makes a circle back to North America. "And end up back here."

Riley grabs the pen back. "No, that won't work. Too much time has passed since his call." She crosses out the arrows Tessa has drawn and instead, traces a circle around only two places.

"Go find him there. And if you don't, then…" She drew another line across the ocean. "Head over…" The line comes to a stop. "Here."

Tessa heaves a sigh of relief and leans against Riley. Silence once again is their only recourse. There's too much to remember. They both know it's time to face the music.

"I'm coming with you," Riley whispers.

"No, it won't be fair to you, to drag you through this."

"It wasn't fair to you. To. You." Riley emphasizes. "You walked away from Simon for me. We have to talk about this, Tess. You and I, we've got to come to terms with it. It's been three years. I couldn't give my heart to Liam unless I let Jacob go. And Liam knows. I will never love anyone like I loved your brother. But he's willing to come in second, because he's not going to compete with a dead man."

The subject of death is her defeat. Tessa recoils, pushing both shoulders back. "I'm not ready yet. I know I have to be. And I will be. I promise you, we will talk about everything soon."

"All right, then. But leave Ciel with me. We'll take good care of her."

"Rye, all I know is that I have to try. My life will never be the same after that call."

"Then do what you have to do."

It's going to be the longest journey she's ever taken. Nothing about this could compare to anything she's ever done before.

But first things first. She must tie up the loose ends of her life— letting Will know and letting Jacob go. When she woke up in the hospital two days after the tragedy, her mind had managed to eliminate all recollection of their last night together. To let her brother go, she must do her best to remember that night. And then she has to face the most difficult task of telling the man she still loves he had missed two years of his daughter's life.

forty-three

"Ciel! Ask your mom if we can swing by Dairy Queen on the way to my house," Riley says while walking around the living room to gather Ciela's toys. "Is it just Glowy you want me to bring tonight?"

Ciela skips alongside Tessa. "Ya, ya, ya!"

Tessa kneels down and embraces her daughter. "Sure. Say thank you to Auntie Rye for taking you tonight."

"Ta-tu," Ciela says happily, clutching her glow worm. "Wowy."

"Hold on a minute," Tessa says, standing up and leading Riley away from her daughter.

"Thank you for taking her," she says to her friend.

"Of course, anytime." Riley answers, taking Tessa in her arms. The two friends remain locked in an embrace. "By the way, I started seeing Dr. D'Antonio again. I'm sure you know."

"I'm so sorry," Tessa whispers before pulling away.

Riley shrugs, turns around and heads toward the front door. "Ceee-ye-leeey!" Ciela comes running straight into Tessa's arms.

"Be good, baby. Mommy loves you."

"O-lo-tu, mama. Set doe." Riley and Ciel walk hand in hand, out the door, down the driveway.

Tessa chases after them, almost knocking Riley down, who's just strapped Ciel into the car seat.

"What's wrong, honey?" Riley asks, concerned.

"Rye, do you remember? Was Simon at Jake's funeral?"

Riley tries to smile, but her eyes won't cooperate. She rubs Tessa's shoulder. "Yes. Yes, he was."

"Wow, you look. Wow."

Tessa self-consciously pulls the hem of her dress down with both hands as Will greets her with a kiss. She's ten minutes late for his work function, a dinner in honor of some foreign partners who are in Chicago for a meeting.

"Sorry, I had to park a couple of blocks off Adams Street. Traffic was insane," she said, still out of breath from running across the never-ending lobby. The Metropolitan, a private club whose members are mostly the professional elite, is in the Willis Tower, the tallest building in Chicago.

Will leads her into the elevator. It's an awkward, silent ride to the sixty-seventh floor. Tessa refuses to let another night go by without telling him.

"Thanks for coming," Will says, inching slowly toward her, his gaze fixed on the top of her dress.

Slowly, she moves away from him. "Will, I've been wanting to talk to you about something, but you've been out of town all week. Do you think we can do that tonight? After this dinner?"

"Yes, of course. Is anything wrong?"

"Just stuff," she answers, avoiding his eyes.

Finally, they're at their destination. She loops her arm in his and allows him to lead her to the table.

There are twenty guests in the longest table she's ever seen. Around her, the view of the city is resplendent. In the old days, she would think nothing of being so high above the ground. It's the first time in years she's done this, and tonight, the walls are closing in and there's not enough air.

Will senses her discomfort and immediately tries to put her at ease, his hand firmly planted on the small of her back, holding her up in a way. As he makes the introductions, he stands tall and proud. There are partners and vice presidents and two of Chicago's top politicians.

Will introduces her to a woman with long blond hair and bright green eyes. She's wearing a low cut black dress made to look professional by a slick fitted leather blazer. She registers a look of recognition as Tessa approaches.

"Tessa, this is Maxine Winters, a partner from BDO, a CPA firm headquartered in London. Maxine is here to work on some due diligence for an acquisition we are coordinating."

Maxine can't be anywhere over thirty. She's that young and that successful.

Could it be? Simon's ex-girlfriend from before? Tessa doesn't have to wonder for very long.

"Tessa Talman!" she exclaims. She's not lacking in personality, that's for sure. "I'm so glad to finally meet you. I'm wondering whether you remember who I am?"

Does she lie? Does she pretend this woman is crazy? Tessa extends her hand and Maxine shakes it briskly.

"Yes! Hello, Maxine, likewise. It's a pleasure to meet you."

"Small world, isn't it?" she adds, her low, hoarse voice a complete contradiction to Tessa's high-pitched tone.

"Indeed!" Tessa says with a smile. She can see why Simon had been attracted to her. She exudes confidence and spunk. A strong, beautiful woman in a man's world.

Will gently pushes her along until they end up by their seats. He's a big deal, she is reminded. He sits at the head of the table and all attention shifts towards him. While exchanging pleasantries and commentaries about some recently concluded meeting, Tessa hides her phone on her lap and checks for messages. There are none. Her fingers deftly sweep through the keys.

GIRL IN 7C: @*Disconnected, I'm sorry.*

"Tess?" Will nudges her gently.

Everyone is looking at her as she jerks her head up. "Oh, sorry."

"Did you want a drink?" Will asked.

"Moscato, please," she addresses the server.

The phone rests on her lap next to Will's hand. Every so often—no, every minute—she pauses to check for a response. Pretty soon, dinner is over, everyone knows about everyone's business. Will is frisky, and his colleagues have become way too comfortable with each other; the aftermath of their drunken revelations.

Tessa begins to calculate the time differences in her head: 4 a.m. London, 11 p.m. New York and 8 p.m. San Francisco. She's been doing this ever since she heard from him. Imagining where in the world he would be and why he may be ignoring her messages.

Thank god, someone is brave enough to break this party up. And of course, it has to be Maxine. She makes her round of the table, shaking everyone's hand before giving them a peck on the cheek. Until she gets to Tessa. With a sweep of her hand and a flick of her wrist, the unlucky guest gets up and moves to her vacated seat. She pulls it up until she's close enough to kiss Tessa's ear.

"Tessa, I just wanted to say how glad I am to have met you. I must admit I was upset when Simon broke up with me but everything's good now. You see! I'm engaged to be married!"

This is what Tessa's been trying to avoid all night. Eventually, he was bound to come up.

"Congratulations!" Tessa responds. "And I'm so sorry, Maxine, for what happened."

"Don't be. That was ages ago. And more importantly, it was Simon's choice, not yours. But as you can see, it always works out. I wish you all the best."

She responds with a nod.

"Speaking of Simon, have you seen him lately?"

"No, no, I haven't. Where is he, Maxine?"

"Well, I haven't seen him for quite some time but the last time we met about two years ago, he was setting up a business in the U.S. He asked me for tax advice. Pharmaceuticals, I think. Plan was to IPO in six months, doing extremely well then."

Useless. This exchange is just useless. There is nothing Maxine could offer except to prolong Will's annoyance with her.

Tessa cuts it short. She stands up. "Sorry, I do need to run to the washroom. Once again, it was so wonderful meeting you, Maxine. I wish you the best. Congratulations again!"

C H R I S T I N E   B R A E

"Let me get this straight. He calls you almost a month ago, and you've kept this from me since?" Will asks, his dolor highlighted by the stoop of his shoulders and the lines on his forehead.

Tessa stands facing him in the parking garage, one hand clutching her purse, the other gripping his hand. She wrestles with her line of vision—orange lines all over. They make her twitch uncontrollably. Will tries to hold her shoulders down and then grabs her hands.

"Did you know I had very short hair once? And I was so disorganized I didn't even know if I was coming or going, didn't even know where I'd be the next week, the next month."

"What?" Will cocks his head, before shaking it in disbelief. "Tessa, you're not making any sense. Answer my question, please."

"I was trying to process it all."

He tries to turn around and head toward her car. "Let's talk about this at my place. I'll meet you there."

"No, please. We can't."

He tilts his head to the side and releases her hand. The devastation on his face moves her to tears. His right cheek twinges. He begins to bite his lip. She'd never really looked closely at him before. Never noticed he had a tiny scar on the left side of his eye. She hasn't really seen much these past two years. She'd been too involved in her sorrow to indulge in anything meaningful.

What a pity. She would have loved to know where that scar came from. But it's too late for that now.

"All I'm suggesting is to talk at the house instead of here, in this garage."

"I know, Will. I know. Please forgive me," she cries. "I can't come over anymore. I don't want to be dishonest about this. It's time."

Maybe he can't help himself. Or maybe he's seen it all along. How lost she's been. How broken. He leans on the solid white column in the middle of aisles E and F and takes her in his arms. She sobs into his chest. She cries for him, for what they never had.

"I need to find him because he will help me remember." She can

224

hardly get any words out. "I'm sorry. I'm so sorry, Will. You've been my lifeline for these two years; I couldn't have survived without you. And now, here I am, telling you I'm still in love with someone else."

"Tessa," he says, his hand firmly pressing her back. "I knew what I was getting into. All the triggers, the anxiety, the nightmares and panic attacks. The thing is, I thought my love would one day be able to help you move on, that in a matter of time, we would get through it. I guess I was wrong."

She looks up at him, tears still rolling down her face. "I can't see you anymore, Will."

"I know," he answers. "But tell me this. Is it this easy for you? To say goodbye?"

"When I met you, I threw away my past and didn't look back. Simon once told me, the past matters. It matters because I lost the most important person in my life. It matters because I never said goodbye to him. Because I have the chance now to make it right. No, it's not easy at all. But I don't have a choice."

Tessa knew a large part of his pain would be that of missing Ciela. She's become like a daughter to him. "Listen," she sniffs. "I know this isn't much, but you can always come and visit Ciel. I'll be traveling for a few weeks and she'll be with Riley. And even after I get back, you are always welcome to see her."

"What are you going to do, Tess? What if he's no longer available?"

"I need to close this of my life, regardless of his situation. Ciel and I need to move on. Maybe I'll move away, start writing. Who knows?"

"Yeah," he says, his tone low and quiet. "Who knows?"

His voice is flat, his chin trembles.

With a step back, she releases him. "I'm going to let you go now, Will. Thank you for everything."

"I love you, Tessa. Whatever these two years were to you or to me. I love you."

forty-four

GIRL IN 7C: *@Disconnected, where are you?*
GIRL IN 7C: *@Disconnected, please, please, send me a message.*
GIRL IN 7C: *Not giving up, @Disconnected!*
GIRL IN 7C: *@Disconnected - help me to find myself. I'll be waiting where it all began.*

Four messages over the past week, and still no response. Yet she goes, thinking that if anything, she could take a break, clear her head and try to move forward.

The park looks much smaller, the giant Ferris wheel no longer daunting. She wonders why she never even noticed its name. The High Roller. While she stands in line waiting to board, she discerns every single detail. The tulips lining the sidewalks, faded red and pink and yellow, the palm trees that seem to tower above the rooftops blowing in the wind, brightly lit neon signs announcing each store, each shop, each stand. And the people. Were there that many people before?

She realizes she had been lost in him way before she even recognized it. There was no one else, nothing else, but her and him even way back then. This time, she is standing, hands on the rails, eyes on the clouds in front of her. She remembers every detail of that day, the pictures, their conversation.

The older lady next to her isn't impressed by the view from the top. "Hmmph." She turns to Tessa. "I suppose it would be better if our view wasn't just of buildings and empty parking lots."

Tessa smiles back. "There are mountains too."

"Have you been on this before?" the lady asks. "What a waste of money. There's nothing to see!"

Tessa nods her head. She begins to wonder, what is she doing here alone?

"I was here a few years back. It brings back good memories for me," Tessa says. "And what brings you here?"

"Well, my son and daughter in law are taking me on a trip of the west coast. My husband passed away six months ago, and they don't know what to do with me," she says, laughing. "I decided to give them both a break today and am spending the day by myself."

"Oh."

"My name is Millie. Millie Olson."

"I'm Tessa. How's your day going?"

"It's going pretty darn well. I haven't been able to spend any time alone since Peter died. It's quite nice just having some time to remember. Peter loved Vegas. Between his horses and dollar slot machines. We were here at least twice a year. Before he passed away, he had finally purchased the RV he'd always wanted, and so we were taking many cross-country trips."

Millie has the kindest eyes Tessa has ever seen. They remind her of Jacob's. Transparent and expressive. She used to be able to see Jacob's every emotion through his eyes.

"Sounds like you both lived life the way we all should," Tessa says.

"We did. He died suddenly. He slipped and fell in the yard one day and just never recovered."

"I'm so sorry," Tessa says, reaching out to touch Millie's shoulder. There's just too much loss of love in this world. She doesn't understand why everything good always has to come to an end. *Is this the universal plan? Are we not meant to hold on to happiness?*

"Oh, no, don't be. After he died, I tried to go back to see what he had left behind. And there was not one thing we said we'd do that we didn't. Whether it be the simple joy of raising two children, bathing in the Dead Sea, walking through the Roman ruins, even betting on the winning horse. We had done everything."

Millie says this with the biggest grin on her face.

It feels meant to be. That Tessa would meet this woman and receive this message. There is still so much living to do. With or without Jacob. Or Simon.

Their pod comes to a stop, and people begin to disembark. Tessa loops her arm in Millie's and helps her to step down from the ride. They walk a few steps in silence, arms still looped around each other.

"Millie," says Tessa. "I know a really cool place that serves the best banana splits. How 'bout we walk down memory lane together? My treat!"

"I truly enjoyed our time today," Tessa says, as they stroll down the area of the strip called the Promenade. "Where did you say your son was going to meet you?"

"Right over there." Millie points to a billboard with a giant bowling pin. "Can you see the fountain by Brooklyn Bowl?"

The two women deliberately take their time. Tessa relishes her time with her new friend; she's sad to see her go.

"Remember you're always welcome to stay with me in Chicago. I went ahead and keyed in all my contact information into your phone. I would love for you to meet Ciela someday soon."

"And I, as well," Millie says as they face the giant fountain. A large gushing spray of water surrounded by many metal spigots of different heights changes color every few seconds. It releases water in perfect rhythm with the music. "It would be such an honor to visit the home of a well renowned author."

Tessa throws her head back in surprise. Millie responds by winking at her.

"You knew the whole time?"

Millie opens her arms and allows Tessa to step in. This is what it must feel like to be in the arms of your mother. Safe. Secure. Protected from all harm. She will always be this for Ciel.

"Thank you," Tessa whispers. "For sharing so much with a stranger."

"You're no stranger, my dear. You're a wonderful woman just at the beginning of the greatest adventure of her life. Remember, Tessa, have faith in love. Whether or not you find him, it's the journey that will mold you, build your character. Never regret anything you do from the heart. Never fear, never doubt you will find love again."

"His love is all I want," Tessa whispers.

"I know, honey." Millie lightly rubs her back. "Unfortunately, time is temporary. It passes. You have to live with what you have here and now. Contentment, acceptance, these things are hard to come by. But if you spend your life living in the past, you'll never be able to truly appreciate the present. And by the looks of it, you have so many people here and now who want to be a part of this new of your story."

And with that she turns around and walks towards a handsome man with silver hair. Her son.

Tessa takes a seat along the stone wall of the fountain, feeling lost and alone. In front of her is a store displaying colorful cupcakes, lined up neatly on many shelves. She watches as the people sitting under brightly lit patio umbrellas engage in lively conversation. She tries to lose herself in the flurry of activity in front of her. *It is only a matter of time,* she tells herself, *I'm going to have to accept the fact that I'm all alone.*

For the next few minutes, she opens the airline app on her phone and saves some information on direct flights to Paris. And then she sends another message. This time, she wants to let him know it's okay. That she understands.

GIRL IN 7C: *@Disconnected, yes, it was love at first sight. And I will write our story.*

Slowly, she gathers her purse and hops off the ledge. She fixes her eyes on the ground, making sure that she doesn't stumble along the uneven brick stones.

"Tess."

She looks up, her eyes are so clouded with tears, she can hardly see. But there's no mistaking that voice.

It's him.

She hurriedly wipes her eyes. His hair is still thick and unruly, but his face is clean and shaven. There's something different about his stance, although he still looms over her. He looks leaner. And save for

229

a few tiny lines around his eyes, he's as beautiful as ever.

"Simon!" She strains to lift herself up on her toes and throws her arms around his neck. "Oh Simon!"

He wraps his arms around her and crushes her to him. And when she lifts her head up to look into his eyes, he caresses the back of her head and runs his fingers through her hair.

"Your hair," he says, smiling. "It's so long."

She nods her head, still in shock, closing her eyes and savoring the feel of him.

"You came," she says.

"I couldn't stay away anymore. I tried to avoid you, after you sent that first message, but I had to see you. Had to know that you were all right."

He tilts her chin up and gently wipes away her tears with the pads of his thumbs. "Can we talk, Tess? Coffee or something?"

"Yes," she says. "Coffee is good."

forty-five

With the strip coming alive at this time of the night, noise is everywhere. Hand in hand, they walk in silence until they reach her hotel. The touch of his skin feels familiar, yet the way he holds her fingers feels forced. They find a cabana suite, one of ten lined up along the pool, completely empty and dark. It's art deco in an overstated sort of way, bamboo screens separating each area, metal chaise in white, pillows in blue, pink and black. The walls as well as the upholstery are highlighted with prints of different shapes and sizes—hearts, circles, squares and diamonds. It's a psychedelic outburst, loud and in true Las Vegas style, not far from the clashing of emotions elicited by their encounter.

Simon leads her to the closest set of chairs, eager to cut the silence between them. Tessa stands frozen in place, shaking her head. It's the orange cabana.

"Let's find another one," she says.

"Yes, sure," he answers. "I'm sorry."

Tessa finds it odd that he sits at one end of the L-shaped couch while she sits on the other. They both lean forward, she with her legs crossed and her hands to her sides, Simon with his hands clasped resting on his knees.

She starts out by making small talk, afraid to dredge up anything that might push him away. "How are your parents? Adrian and Ashleigh?"

"Everyone is well. Henry now has two more little brothers. Twins. Evan and Angus."

"Oh my!" she exclaims. "Ashleigh has her hands full!"

He nods His eyes bear into her and she looks away. "And you? Do you still live in Chicago? Are you—"

"No, no."

His face registers nothing. This feels more like a job interview.

"Who do you live with?" he asks.

She hesitates, makes sure she gives nothing away. It's not the right time—they need to get over the niceties first. "No one, just me. But I see Riley quite often."

"Riley. Yes. How is she?"

Where are you, Simon? I can't find you.

She squints for a moment, wishes she could see past the thick film of nothingness in his eyes. "She's doing as well as expected. She married Liam."

She sees a slight smile break through. "Liam? The guy in Athens?" he asks.

"Yes!" She laughs. "He was Jake's best friend from med school. So, she's still living with a doctor. She's also in advertising. An executive with a firm called Amazon Turner."

"And you? Are you still writing?"

"I've gone into consulting. For a publisher based in Chicago. I don't like to move around these days."

He shakes his head. "I find that hard to fathom! You loved to travel!"

"Well, I have responsibilities now." She drowns her own words with a fake cough. Too close.

"And how is that different from obligations?" he asks.

She wonders if this is the point of no return. She doesn't even know how much time they have.

"It just is." Years ago, her obligations impeded her ability to love him. Ciel is a welcome presence in her life. To her, that is the difference.

Simon rubs both hands together. He tilts his head to the side, and then looks at her again. "You dropped out of sight."

"So, did you," she counters.

"You don't...?"

"What? I don't what?"

"Nothing," he cuts her off.

"I want to explain it to you," she begins.

He nods again.

"I disappeared on purpose. I didn't want Jake to get lost in the story. They kept referring to him as my brother. And he was the hero in all this—he needed to be honored and named along with everyone else who died that night. The never-ending coverage became unbearable for me. I couldn't turn on the TV without reliving the incident."

"Tess."

"The news had a blow-by-blow account of the event. But I couldn't recount those final few seconds. I couldn't even remember his touch, his words, what he did, what he looked like. Was he scared? Did he suffer? What occurred next? Were you there?"

Her voice cracks. She notices Simon pull back his instinct to reach out for her. She sees him dip closer and then retract all in a single movement.

There's an acceptable silence for what seems like five minutes. Permitted. It's needed. Neither one is panicking, trying to find words to say. Both know that it's their thoughts that matter. That each word must be carefully chosen.

Simon breaks the silence. "So here we are."

"Here we are," she says, her voice inaudible.

"What made you want to find me?" he asks.

"Your call. After that, I couldn't take not knowing how you were."

"I have to share something with you," he says, looking up and then down and then staring straight ahead.

She sits up and tucks her hands under her thighs. This is it. He's going to tell her he's married. He has a family, and everything is too late.

"I had open heart surgery. As a matter of fact, when I called you, I was about to enter the operating room."

She closes her eyes and shakes her head. This is worse than she expected. "Open heart?"

"The hole in my heart never healed, obviously. I finally had a heart attack while on a climb in Kilimanjaro."

He climbs mountains now?

She throws all caution to the wind and moves closer to him. Sliding all the way down the L shape until she's only inches away.

"Oh, Simon! I'm so sorry! How are you now? Are you okay?"

"Still recovering. I have my own business. It's based in Minnesota. We completed our IPO six months ago, which is just as well since my doctor said I should probably take it easy. I'm transitioning out, staying on the board but leaving the management in more capable hands."

To lighten the moment, she taps his arm and gives him a warm smile. "Look at you. Retired at age thirty-three. But how come I never—"

"You never saw me sick? I hid it well, didn't I? I was already under medication then. But we only saw each other for days every few weeks and so it wasn't like we lived together constantly. And it really didn't bother me then. I felt fine, had regular check-ups, did sports and lived normally."

"I thought they were your jet lag pills," she laughed softly.

"Right next to your hairspray."

"I still feel like I should've noticed it. I'm sorry I didn't," she says, wistful and regretful.

"Don't be. You are probably the reason why I felt great."

He pauses to take her hand in his. She looks up at him and smiles. "Okay, your turn. The writing?" he inquires.

"I don't know. Just haven't been able to do it. After Lionel and Carissa," she says, chuckling under her breath. "I gave them a bad ending by the way."

He laughs.

She goes all in. She feels great about doing it. Like the old her coming up to the surface. "Do you remember," she starts, her mouth curved up in a half smile, her voice coarse, sly, seductive. She taps the back of his hand.

"I remember a lot of things," he says.

"This is where we first made love."

Boom. Simon pulls away, and it's like someone pulled a lever on the imaginary gate and it falls right on her head. Or on her hand.

"Tessa. No." It's a side of him she hadn't seen since that day she'd barged into his room. The day he put his walls up after she'd stood him up.

She rounds up the courage to try again. "Simon?"

The canvas awning begins to flap in the wind. She refuses to hear anything else but his voice. And yet, the breeze is all she hears.

"Please stay the night. With me."

"I can't. I have my plane ready and waiting at McCarran. We take off in an hour. I had to do it this way, knowing I can't stay."

"What then, Simon? What's next?" she asks softly. Tessa sees the point of no return, yet she can't help but wish she could still change things.

"Oh Tess. I don't want to hurt you, and I don't want to hurt anymore. I called you because I didn't know whether or not I was going to make it. I wanted to hear your voice, tell you how much I loved you."

"And that love? It's gone?"

"That's not the point."

"Yes! Yes! That is the point. Love is the first step. All this can follow."

"Love doesn't erase the memories of the past. Love doesn't change the reality that I'm a part of your loss. And I can't compete with what happened," he says, voice raised, his eyes darkening. Ominous, a foreboding of the pain to come.

To her, he is Greece. He is the sea and the sky.

He is Ciel's father. How does she tell him?

She tries, but all she can see is his pain. She tries to ease it with her words. "But—I want to move on. I just don't know how," she insists. "How can I leave it behind if I don't know what happened?"

He hugs himself as his face goes slack. "Do you remember the first time I met you? Here? I feel that way today. I couldn't wait to hold you. And yet, I'm unsure. Unsure of the path we should be taking. After what happened, to you, to me, I don't know if that's even reparable."

"I think it is." She says this with conviction. She doesn't turn away from him—she returns his stare, his gaze. She doesn't retreat or cower even though he is leaving her.

Once he leaves, he's never coming back.

"My girl with her head in the clouds," he says with a sad smile. His eyes don't change their shape; they take a stand against displaying any emotion despite his upturned lips.

"Am I still your girl, Simon?"

"My god Tessa, do you know what you did to me? You turned me from someone who'd taken love for granted to someone who was hopelessly in it. My actions, my words, never have I ever been that way with another person. You showed me what it was like to truly live."

"But I—"

He stops her by shaking his head. "I miss that. But at the same time, it's no longer the kind of life I can have."

"I've changed. I don't float around anymore."

"I loved the floating you," he teases. "You brought me along to coast right next to you."

Tears fill her eyes. She wonders whether he notices because he looks away. "I missed you so much."

"That's hard to believe, Tessa."

"I did, Simon. I did. But I had other things in my life requiring my time and attention."

"Like what? Enlighten me." She hears the undeniable resentment in his tone.

"Just life. I shut off completely and tried my best to live in the moment. It wasn't until the day you called that I felt strong enough to try to remember."

She watches as he slowly inches forward, and then backward. How he holds his hands firmly on his lap, how he refuses to blink, how his lips begin to quiver.

"It's funny, you know. When we were together, I hated saying goodbye. And you promised me once it would never happen. In Paris." His voice cracks. He squeezes his eyes shut. She sees the lines on his face. They do nothing to diminish its majesty.

"Simon."

He rubs his chest. "In Paris. They transferred you and refused to tell me where you were. It felt like death to me. You see, Tessa. I had a loss too."

She doesn't understand why he says this. But his pain is indisputable. And she can't take it. "Simon!" she cries freely, allowing her tears to flow. "Simon, please!"

She stands up and moves toward him, settling in his lap, her arms tight around his shoulders. He pulls her in like a barrier coming up, protecting her from all the pain she's ever felt.

"I'm sorry," she cries. "I'm sorry for everything."

"I'm sorry too," he says, crying. They are suffocated by hopelessness; there is no redemption. Too much time has passed, too many things have come between them. Tragedy has a way of tearing the human heart apart. It's the people left behind who really die.

They swim in their emotion, leaving the silence to save them from drowning. Minutes pass until the sobbing subsides and all they can hear is a sniffle or two, and lots of deep breaths.

He exhales loudly before gently lifting her and settling her on the cushion next to him.

She swipes her face with her hands and looks up at him. "No."

"I have to go, Tess."

"No, please, Simon. Please hear me out." She clings to his arm, grips it tightly, digging into his skin. "Even if I'd lived with loss since I was fourteen years old, I always had Jacob. He handled the loss of our parents so differently. He loved more, while I loved less. When he died, I realized I wasted so much time regretting what I'd lost instead of appreciating what I had. And now I'm asking for another chance. I'll take a second. A minute. An hour. A day. With you, I'll take anything you're willing to give me."

He shakes his head and pulls his arm away and holds it close to his body. His shoulders hike up, he folds into himself. Like he's repulsed by her touch.

"You'll be fine. We'll be fine. It's time to move on. You are right. Life is short, we have to make the most out of it."

He disappears into the night without that familiar goodbye.

Like fog, like smoke, like a snowflake so beautiful and soft and light, it melts away after you touch it.

She'd touched him, he was there. But now he's gone.

forty-six

"Jesus! You're the only one I've ever known to run and talk at the same time! I don't know how you do it," Riley says.

In the background, Tessa can hear laughter and the banging of pots and pans.

"Practice," she answers, each stride hitting the pavement, her pace steady, her breathing in check "How's my baby?"

"Can you hear them? Liam is making pancakes and she's banging the rolling pin on the strainer. My husband is doing a monkey dance. He's lost it."

Change of venue. Today she's running along the Hudson, starting out at the West Village, intent on ending at Battery Park.

She had made a conscious effort to stay as far away from Midtown as possible. Owen had warned her about certain triggers. Best to avoid them as he didn't want her to regress.

"Are you there, Tess?"

"Sorry, so many cyclists, I need to pay extra attention. It got busy all of a sudden," she breathes into the mouthpiece. "I'm slowing down, hold on."

She hits the stop button on her watch and looks for a bench to take a break. "Okay, can you hear me?"

"Yes, I can," Riley answers. "How was it? The run?"

"Great. It's a pretty clear day. You know I love this route. It's beautiful. Although there was a boatload of people by Chelsea Piers this morning. Maybe a tour of some sort."

Tessa takes a gulp from her water bottle and wipes her face with her shirt.

"That place is like your second home. Oh hey, wait, Ciel, say hi to Mama!"

"Hi Ciely!"

Riley is back on the phone. "Oops, she just walked away."

Tessa laughs. "That's my daughter. Always on the go." She catches her breath when she hears herself say that. "So, she's good?"

"Yeah, she's been sleeping really well too. And you, how are you holding up?"

"Well, the good news is I don't think about him every hour anymore. The bad news is I still think about him at least once a day." She stretches out and does a number four, knees folded, hips on the ground.

She still sees him every day in the eyes of her daughter.

"That's normal. It's still fresh. You're grieving. It will get easier, Tess."

"I suppose. I did start to write again, though. The other night, I just whipped out my notebook and wrote his last words to me. I want to build a story around it," she says.

What she doesn't dare to say is she wants to write about how love can evaporate in an instant. How loss can overshadow every happy memory, how it cripples, how it kills.

Riley doesn't need to hear this. She's lived it.

"I have to let him go," she sobbed as Riley held her the night she arrived from Las Vegas three weeks earlier. She's determined to remain strong despite the days when the tears still come, and the pain feels oppressive and punishing.

You think it's the end of the world, but really, it's just the end.

"That's good! So how long do you have to be there?"

"I'll be home in two days. The meeting with Harper Collins is this afternoon," Tessa says.

"The Lionel and Carissa Part Two meeting?" Riley teases.

"Yeah, they want me to make things right between them," she says. "Anyway, tomorrow night we have a little get together at Nobu and then I'll be flying out at 8 a.m. the next day. Should be in Chicago by 11 a.m."

"Okay, take your time. And be safe."

"Thanks, Rye, for always being here for me. For taking Ciely, too. I love you. I'm going to make myself better, I promise."

She walks around in circles, trying to avoid the birds that have settled next to her.

"Love you too, babe! Go get 'em! You're writing again. Best news ever."

Tessa ends the call just as a giant pigeon perches right next to her, its scrawny little feet clinging to the rusty arm rail. She swears his head is bigger than her hand.

She springs up and walks away, back in the direction of her hotel. She's got a few hours to stay by the pool before having to get ready for her meeting.

The signs of summer are all around her. Joggers, bikers, swimmers, worshiping the heat and the humid air. She thinks about the winter months, when she'd heard from Simon for the first time after three years. And how far she's come since then. And although she doesn't regret searching for him, finding him, telling him how much she loves him, she's thankful for the warmth of the sun and signs of life blossoming all around her.

forty-seven

Summertime at any of New York's rooftop bars is the season to see and be seen. When Tessa and Revete decide to celebrate with a drink at 230 5th, little do they know everyone else has the same idea. Luckily, or unluckily, they are able to squeeze into an Adirondack bench with Adam, Jerry and Marco—three investment bankers from Blackstone.

"I still can't believe how you pulled it off," Tessa raises her glass to Revete. "Cheers."

"Don't thank me. They wanted you so badly they knew they had to make concessions. Where are you going, by the way?"

Tessa takes a sip of her Moscato. "Next week, Paris, and then I just want to stay home in Chicago to tie up loose ends." She turns away from Adam, who's been trying to get her attention. "I figured it would probably take me another six months to finish the draft. Stamping takes a few more months and then the first round of edits. Signing the agreement for a period of eighteen months should be plenty of time for me."

"This is good for you, the break, the writing," Revete says, taking Tessa's hand and squeezing it. Everyone's been too benignant lately. She could embezzle, cheat and steal all in the name of a broken heart and they would look the other way. Revete drops her hand hastily just as her phone buzzes with a message.

"Who is it?" Tessa asks, leaning sideways, curious.

"Oh, it's Roman. He's checking in from school," Revete says, without directly addressing her, speed typing first and then immediately throwing her phone back into her purse.

"At this time? Did he go somewhere after school?"

"Don't know. I'll ask him later," Revete says, reaching out for her glass and then turning to Marco. "So, Marco, tell us, are you a native New Yorker?"

Leave it to her agent to indulge everyone in conversation. The guys begin to weigh in about New York, their jobs, where they live, where they go to hang out. All three are NYU alumni, enjoying the single life, sharing a penthouse in Manhattan. They flaunt that fact a few times.

Adam has taken an interest in her. She knows this because he doesn't pay attention to what the others are saying. His head is constantly moving as he turns to her and unleashes a litany of pick-up lines.

"So, what brings you guys to New York?"

"You are definitely the prettiest girl here tonight."

"What do you say we go for a cigarette? We can ditch these guys for a few minutes."

Tessa is bored. She looks around and notices how beautiful the flower boxes are, violets, peonies and hydrangeas. How fake the palm trees look. She wonders how the shrubs have grown so thick in just a matter of weeks. Did they transplant those to line the barriers? Are peonies perennials? She should ask Riley when she gets home.

She cranes her neck to see what the people next to her are eating, thinks about ordering some chicken nuggets and tempura vegetables. And then a few feet in front of her, a dark-haired woman is dancing in the arms of a tall, blond haired man. They remind her of Jake and Riley, professional, stoic doctor by day and big ball of mush by night. Next to them, looking lost and alone, is a man with sandy brown hair and the saddest blue eyes. His hair looks just like Simon's except it hasn't been cut in a while. His beard is scruffy, thick and unkempt, and he is wearing jeans and sneakers. Nothing like the business types trolling the place tonight. But his presence draws her to him. He is stunning.

"Adam," Tessa says, patting him on the shoulder. "I think I'm ready for that cigarette now."

Revete looks up at her and shakes her head. "Tessa."

"Don't worry. I'll be back in a few minutes. I also want to call Ciely to say goodnight."

Tessa stands, squeezes her way between the maze of outdoor chairs and walks toward the outer part of the bar. Adam smiles at his friends and follows behind.

They meet in a secluded corner facing the view of the Empire State building. It's strangely dark and empty. She chalks it up to the diminishing number of smokers in the city. Adam gives her a cigarette and a lighter and cups her hand to shelter the fire from the wind. They talk about the view from where they stand. He tells her some interesting facts about the Empire State Building, standing tall and illuminating the sky. That it was built in a year and forty-five days. That it cost forty million dollars to construct. That it briefly regained its "Tallest Building in New York" status after the downing of the Twin Towers in 2001. That since 2012, the One World Trade Center has eclipsed its designation. And then they venture into movie trivia and talk about the three movies filmed in that location.

"Name your favorite movie," Adam challenges.

Doesn't he know she's the queen of pop culture? Her brother had a thing for board games. While in Paris, they'd lost a game of Trivial Pursuit to Jake and Riley. At least the happy, insignificant memories managed to stay in her mind.

"*An Affair to Remember*," she declares without missing a beat.

"Nice. I'm impressed," whispers Adam, taking one step, two steps, three steps, toward her. "Tessa, I'm so attracted to you."

Tessa ducks as he tips his head to try to kiss her. "I think we should be heading back. Revete wants to leave soon."

She doesn't wait for an answer. Tessa plods away and resurfaces back where she left the rest of the group. Except there's that same man standing next to her friend.

"Simon?" The inexplicable pull deciphered.

"Tess. Hi." He steps forward and extends his arms to her. She steps back. Immediately, he runs his hand through his hair and draws a deep breath.

"How did you—" Tessa glances at Revete and then at him.

Revete throws her arms in the air. "What can I say? I told him where we were. He's been trying to reach you since this afternoon."

By this time, the three men have scampered away, moving on to more accessible conquests.

"Please, Tess. Can we talk?"

"I don't understand. I. You—"

Tessa covers her mouth and shakes her head. What did he intend to do? Engage in useless talk, make her beg again, like she had just weeks ago?

"Please. Can we talk?" he repeats.

Revete steps in between them. "I'm going to leave you two alone. It's getting late and we have an early flight tomorrow. Tessa, I'll meet you in the lobby at six. We have to be at La Guardia by seven."

Before Tessa could argue, Revete is gone. Simon gently steers her by her elbow toward a table for two underneath the fake looking palm trees.

"Would you like a drink?" he asks, just as soon as he pulls the chair for her.

Tessa nods. He leaves to go to the bar. She sends Riley a text message.

TESSA: *Can't call yet, sorry. We were at 230 5th and Simon shows up!*
RILEY: *Simon? What's he doing there? From Minnesota?*
TESSA: *Don't know. Says he wants to talk.*
RILEY: *Are you okay?*
TESSA: *He went to get me a drink. I need it LOL. Don't worry. All cried out.*
RILEY: *:(*
TESSA: *Please kiss my baby for me. Tell her I love her, and I'll be home tomorrow.*
RILEY: *I already did. Love you. Be strong.*
TESSA: *xoxo*

She slips her phone back in her purse just as he lays the drinks on the table. "They're out of Moscato so I hope a Bellini is okay."

She nods.

"Cheers," he says, raising his whiskey glass up to her.

She doesn't return the gesture. Instead, she stares at him, hands on lap, expressionless. "What is it you want to talk to me about, Simon?"

He places both hands on the round mesh table. "Tess, I'm sorry for what I did, what I said to you in Vegas. These past few weeks, I've been trying so hard to forget you. To live up to my words and walk away. But I can't. Not at this moment, at least. I'm not ready to stay away. I can't stay away. Nothing has changed. Not my feelings, not the way I see you, not even after..." He pauses. "After what you did to me."

"What did I do, Simon? What happened?" Tessa pushes her drink to the side and crosses her arms on the table. She rubs her forehead, furrows her brows and bites her lip. Her hands begin to shake.

Simon takes the opportunity to lay his hand on hers.

"You really don't remember?"

"No. I don't. The last thing I remember is that you left us to go to the pharmacy two doors down. I remember you asking me to marry you. What happened, Simon? What did I do to you?"

He sighs deeply, like he's out of air. She can see the pain in his eyes. He lets go of her hand, covers his face and starts to sob. She is so overwhelmed by his pain, she begins to cry too. "Tell me," she begs, pulling his hands away from his face. "Oh god, please tell me."

"I was with you at Pitie'. At the hospital. You were recovering from a broken collarbone, from the force of your fall. You were also under observation, spending three days in the psych ward. You told the doctor to keep me away from you. You told them I was the cause of your nervous breakdown. That you never wanted to see me ever again."

"And you never tried to see me again."

"It's not like that, Tess. I blamed myself. If I were there with you, maybe things would have been different. I left you with your brother to buy a silly ring at the drugstore."

His voice squeaks while delivering that final line. His pain is so evident, she can't bear to watch the destruction in his movements. His head, his shoulders, his body bent over, cowering. Spineless. Those moments broke him. He's a broken man. And they're both about to die all over again. She decides he's had enough.

"Oh no! No. No," Tessa repeats in a toneless drone, pushing on the table, desperate to free her legs so she can run away. She flees from him. Through the outdoor lounge, into the nightclub, down the red, dark hallway and into the first elevator she sees. It's packed full of people, but she doesn't care. Her tears just won't stop. She has to get away. Has to leave him be.

"Taxi!" she yells at the top of her lungs as she flies out the door.

Before she knows it, she's in his arms. He grabs her from behind and lifts her up, kicking and screaming. "No! Let me go! Please Simon! I have to go!"

"No, no, no," he says, his arms locked around her shoulders. "I'm not letting you go. I'm here, I'm here for you. It's okay."

"Put me down now!" She's not sure whether she's scared him into releasing her or whether he's run out of strength. She hears his breathing. It's uneven and shallow. And he's wheezing. There's a bunch of watchers now. Some people come and go, others remain standing to the side, watching their spectacle.

"I've done enough damage to you," she says. "I don't want to hurt you anymore. You're better off without me."

The pain she's experiencing is physical. It causes her to double up, her knees hit the ground.

"Please, please. Just go!" she says this calmly, trying to regain her composure. "I'm fractured. I'm shattered. Nothing can put me back together."

He kneels on the ground and with both hands, gently pulls in her head, nestles it against his neck. "Shh, shh. That's not true. We can fix each other. I love you, Tess. What happened to us was beyond our control. But you were right. We have love. Nothing can take that away from us."

"You'll leave. Just like the rest of them. You'll leave," she mutters.

"No, baby. I'm here to stay. I'm here. Let me fix you. If you love me, that's all we need."

His heart is failing physically.

But tonight, it's thriving, screaming with life, gloriously beating, ferociously fighting.

Because of her.

He holds her like this until her shaking subsides, stroking her back, planting kisses on her head. "Of all the places you've taken me to around the world, the only place I want is with you. This is the best place," he cries. "Here. With you."

The feel of his skin, his smell, the steady beating of his heart against hers, they all manage to reel her back in. To quiet her down. He tips her chin up and looks into her eyes. She's back in Greece. On top of the world. He holds her face in his hands and puts his lips to her ear.

"Did you hear me? I love you."

Her head bounces up and down until he finds her mouth and kisses her. "I love you too," she mumbles into his lips. "Please take me home."

forty-eight

Simon's doubts about the way she felt disappeared completely that night when she undressed him for the first time. Tessa fell back at the sight of the flaming red incision spanning from his collarbone down to his stomach. She sank to her knees and wailed loudly, overtaken by the gravity of Simon's sickness. "I'm sorry, I'm sorry, I'm sorry," she mumbled over and over again. Until she quickly composed herself and lovingly trailed her finger along his jagged skin. She followed it up with tiny kisses up and down his great big scar. "I love you," she whispered, undressing herself completely and holding her arms up in offering. "Take me. I'm yours. My love will fix your heart."

"I think you'd better put on something decent," Tessa tells him as she sets the laptop up for a Skype session. "I don't think we'd want to shock Owen. At least not yet."

There they were in his hotel room at the Standard, drunk and hungover from an emotional night together. He saddles up to her, presses himself against her back and turns the laptop in the opposite direction. "Position it this way, you'll be fine."

She laughs. "Yeah, smartass. You're in this session with me in five minutes. Please put on a shirt. You can keep your bottom part the way it is, if that's what you want. I like looking at it anyway."

She takes the computer and places it on the coffee table instead.

"Fine," he grumbles. Tessa dials in. Simon takes a seat next to her on the sofa, fully clothed. He hooks his arm around her and kisses her head. "Are you okay?"

"I will be," she assures him. She can see the worried look on his face when she gently pulls back and sits up straight.

"Okay, it's ringing."

"Hello, Tessa." Owen's face comes on just as the computer bleeps.

"Hi, Owen! Thank you for making it today. I was delayed in New York this morning but wanted to keep our appointment. I think it's important for me to fill you in on what's happened since we last spoke."

All this time, she's pushing Simon away, signaling for him not to show himself just yet. She pushes the camera with her feet until it's far enough to capture them both on screen.

"I'm here with Simon. In New York."

"Oh?" Owen leans back and his chair creaks. "Tell me what happened."

Tessa glances at Simon and clasps her hands together. "I was here to attend a meeting and Simon came to see me."

Simon bobs his head. First a squeak, and then a croak. "Hello, Owen. Dr. Allen. It's a pleasure to meet you."

"Likewise," Owen says. "Simon, didn't you tell Tessa a few weeks earlier that it was over? That it would never work between the two of you? She was quite devastated about this. What made you change your mind?"

"Uh." Simon clears his throat. "Well."

Tessa is nervous. They had talked for hours last night. Why does it seem like he has something new to share? He brings his hand to his face and begins to rub his cheek with the tip of his thumb.

"Well," he begins. "I'm not in the best shape, health-wise. Tessa is a free spirit, you know? That's the beauty of this woman. She never stays in one place for too long. I was worried that my limitations could hamper her ability to do what she likes to do."

Tessa looks at him, surprised, her eyes pinched, her mouth slightly open. Gently, she caresses his face. "No, Simon, that's not important to me."

He smiles at her and continues. "And then when I saw her, and she asked me to stay with her that night, I realized I would give her the choice. That I just couldn't walk away. And that she would have to be the one to decide."

"Okay," Owen says. "And Tessa? What do you think?"

"I have a lot of work to do, Owen," Tessa says.

Simon pulls her to him and keeps his arm around her shoulder. Their knees are touching and she's leaning on his chest.

"Simon told me about my recovery at the hospital after Jake—" Slight pause. "After we lost Jake. And I felt so horrible, so mad at myself for hurting him that way. I don't feel I deserve this love, I don't feel he should love me after what I said and did."

"Do you realize you weren't in your right mind? That the trauma of the tragedy you went through made you say those words, do those things? That it wasn't you?" Owen asks. He disappears from the screen for a few seconds and comes back with a coffee cup. He starts to drop sugar cubes in it—one, two, three—and then stirs through the vapors steaming out toward the computer screen. *He probably thinks it's going to be a while.*

"I still find it hard to accept the things I did to Simon. How could I hurt him like that?"

"What do you think happened that you didn't even try to contact him or look for him when you got home to the States?" Owen asks.

Simon leans forward, interested in her answer.

"Two months had passed." She addresses Simon, facing him with her hand on his knee. "And I focused on rebuilding what had been left behind. There were matters related to Jake, his things, Riley and her grief. Time just slipped by and I…"

Tessa stares straight at Owen, who nods ever so slightly. She knows he's trying to get her to reveal her secret.

Simon notices it. "And you what?" he asks.

"I had to work hard on accepting Jake's absence in my life."

The answer appeases him. Both men nod in unison. Owen's chair creaks again. He leans forward. "The two of you have so much more to discuss. You will need to catch each other up on the three years you've been apart. Communication is key. And love. You have the love, you have the commitment. What's next?"

"I'd like to take her to Paris as soon as early next week," Simon says.

Tessa smiles at him. "I'm not in a rush."

"It's better that we go soon, try to help you put the missing pieces of the puzzle together. So we can move forward."

She pulls his hand, lays its palm on her cheek and kisses it. "Okay."

"Listen Simon, Tessa—Paris may not be the be all end all to your story. Don't expect too much from that trip. Trauma like this can take years to unravel, and most times, there is damage. Tessa won't be complete without Jacob. Ever. But you're not alone now, Tessa. You have Simon. And Simon, make Tessa tell you everything you want to know about the years you missed. Don't allow any resentment to fester. Get it all out in the open. I can see the love between the two of you. I heard about it, but now I see it."

Tessa and Simon turn to look at each other. She smiles first, he smiles back.

Owen looks to address Tessa. "Listen, I've known you since you were in your teens. You've suffered so much loss, all inexplicable, all tragic. I truly believe everything happens for a reason. Don't quote me on this, as this observation is more personal than professional. But philosophically, I think Simon went to the store at that exact moment for a reason. I think Jacob knows you're in good hands. Call me, Tessa, when you get back. And if you need to speak to me while you're there, you have my home number and my cell phone. Dr. Mathieu is also there, I'm sure he'll be happy to see how well you're doing! Bye for now!"

"Bye, Owen!" Tessa clicks *end* with the mouse and exits out of Skype.

Simon takes it from her hand and double clicks it twice.

"What are you doing?" she asks, laughing.

He kneels in front of her and spreads her legs. "Making sure he doesn't see what I'm going to do to you."

forty-nine

This time, they travel together. She meets him at the gate in O'Hare and they board the American Airlines flight to Charles De Gaulle. "Our first plane ride," she says as they settle side by side in two pods.

"No, it isn't," Simon counters. "Tess! Have you forgotten where we met?"

She pinches his arm playfully and giggles. "Chill! I was teasing. Do I need to keep the boarding passes too?"

7C and 7D. Serendipity. "Of course."

She leans in to kiss him. "You are such a romantic. I love it."

Nine hours later, they're in their hotel at the Place Vendome. It's the same place that held such happy memories—a two-bedroom suite with three balconies, all with a view of the Eiffel Tower and the Tuileries Gardens. Laying in each other's arms with the French doors wide open, the bright sun and the comfortable wind sweeping through the room, they catch up on the week they spent apart since their reunion in New York.

"Are you going to be okay?" Simon asks, turned to his side, his legs entwined with hers, arm across her waist.

"So far, so good. Do you think I'll just remember things as we visit the place where it happened?" Tessa wove her fingers in between his.

251

"I don't know, babe. But I think we should just make this like a vacation. If you remember, you remember. And if you don't, then we have new memories to add to the old ones."

"Sounds like a plan," Tessa agreed. "Although I really was in no hurry to come here. We could have waited—"

"No!" Simon said emphatically. "We needed to do this as soon as possible. Thank you, by the way."

"For what?" She rests her head on her elbow.

"For taking good care of me. Constantly checking on me and making sure I took my meds. For waking me up every hour to check if I was still breathing," he says, smiling.

She giggles in response, although her mind is elsewhere. She wants to tell him before they leave the hotel. If they're going to put together the missing parts of her past, she needs to connect the missing parts of his. She wonders briefly whether he already knows, and then she decides it's unlikely. She dropped out of the limelight after the tragedy and there hadn't been any photographs taken of her since Paris. Slowly, she sits up, scoots her body back so she's leaning on the headboard. Simon remains prostate on the bed.

"Simon?"

He looks at her and smiles.

"I need to tell you something."

"Okay, what is it? Are you remembering something?"

"No, no. But I need to fill you in on what's happened since I arrived back in the States."

He props his head up, leans on one hand. "Okay."

Tessa slides off the opposite side of the bed and walks toward one of the larger suitcases. She returns to his side with a large, leather bound book.

"Sheesh. That's what made your luggage so heavy!" he teases.

She doesn't smile back. He sees the terror in her face through the tight line of her lips and the constant blinking of her eyes. She lets out a deep sigh and then her eyes fill up with tears.

"Simon, please listen before you say anything. You wanted to know why I never tried to contact you as soon as I returned home to the states. I don't remember much about Paris, but I do remember arriving back in Chicago. I stayed with Riley and her parents. They moved back to Chicago at that point, intent on nursing their daughter back to health. I was so sick for weeks—we all thought it was the exhaustion and the shock that had simply taken a toll on my health. Besides, I thought it was impossible. I mean, I only had one ovary. They said it would be hard to—"

Simon hears the last sentence and knows. He reaches out for her, but she moves back, afraid his touch would mean anything more than sympathy.

Instead, she hands him the book. "We have a daughter."

He gets up from the bed and circles around it. Repeatedly. He grabs his chest with his hand before covering his mouth to stifle a sob, his eyes upturned, his body shaking.

Simon returns to where she is. He takes the book, holds it and sits in silence. She waits. Her heart has dropped down to her feet. All the noise around them has dissipated. The window panes bang noiselessly against the walls, the curtains twirl and twist around each other. The wind becomes a muted breeze, blowing silently through their hair, their room, their things. In her mind, she begs for the explosion to happen. Anything. Anything but this silence.

"This is what you meant," he mumbles. "How time just ran away."

"Yes!" she cried. "Oh Simon. Please understand. I had such a difficult pregnancy. I had to be on bed rest from three months until she was born. And then I spent—"

He finishes her sentence. "You spent the last two years with our child. Alone."

"Yes."

He nods and turns to her, still clutching tightly to the unopened book. He turns pale, his cheeks hollow. And when she doesn't hear anything, she pushes her luck.

"Simon, please. One truth. Tell me."

She's given him permission to unleash. And so, he does. The book drops on the bed and he whips around, driving his fist through the wooden slats on the headboard.

"Simon!" Her hand flies to her mouth.

"Fuck!" he yells. "I'm bloody pissed, okay? That's my one truth!"

She covers her face knees tucked under her body, rocking back and forth. She doesn't dare lift her head up. She feels the bed shift. He's getting up.

"Don't follow me." He grabs the book in one swoop, swings his legs sideways and walks to the balcony. He then takes a seat on one of the chairs facing the gardens. Tessa watches as he slowly opens it. He lingers for minutes on each page, stopping sometimes to raise his head toward the sky.

She waits. And waits. And waits. At first, she sits motionless on the bed and watches him from behind. And then she decides to occupy herself by unpacking his things and putting his clothes away. Still, there's no change. She turns on her laptop and downloads her manuscript. Before she knows it, two hours have passed. There he is, still sitting outside with the open book on his lap.

She turns to him in time to see him shaking violently, his shoulders shivering, his head thrown back as he takes deep breaths.

His pain. She needs to take away his pain. If only by leaving him, she will do it. The moment she always knew would happen is at hand. Who in their right mind would forgive such a thing? He had missed two years of his child's life. That, to her, is irreconcilable.

Gently, she pushes open the French doors and walks outside, her bare feet on the artificial turf covering the ground.

"Simon?" she says. "Simon. I know I've done a very selfish thing. But please believe me, I wasn't well. I could only focus on one thing at a time, and I chose to immerse myself in the only thing I had left. I know you won't be able to forgive me. I'm okay with leaving. Let me take my stuff and leave."

"I'm straddling the line between gratitude and irrational fury," he starts out. "We have made a life, Tess! It fills me with such joy. But I'm angry about the years that have gone by, wasted by pride and false assumptions."

Without another word, he places the book on the small round table, extends his arm and offers her his hand. His knuckles are swollen, there's a small cut right above one of them. She cradles his hand in hers and kisses every knuckle, each bump, each groove. She wants her tears to wash away the blood, the anguish.

He pulls her to him, lifts her by the waist and places her on top of his lap. She's straddling him. They are face to face.

"I should have come for you. I wasted time. I wasted three years."

"I don't think I would've been ready," she whispers. "Jacob had overtaken everything."

"What's her name?" he asks. She tenderly wipes the tears from his eyes, sweeps her thumbs over his cheeks.

"Ciela Aurora Fremont."

"Heaven. You didn't forget." His face is a confluence of tears and smiles. "She has my last name?"

"Yes."

"She's beautiful."

"She looks just like you," Tessa says proudly, tracing her fingers along his chin. "She has this dimple right here, like yours. And guess what her favorite thing to do is?"

"Follow her mother around?" he smiles weakly.

"Jigsaw puzzles. She can do thousand-piece puzzles by herself."

"Wow."

"But she still can't talk very much. The therapist says she's so intelligent, her brain moves faster than her mouth."

"What?" he says, chuckling. "When is her birthday?"

"August 2nd." Tessa doesn't know where this is going. "Simon. Please, tell me what you're thinking. Please forgive me."

"There's nothing to forgive," he says with a sniff. "We have a daughter. You needed time away from the past to focus on the future."

"Don't make it too easy," she begs. "I know I was wrong. Listen, Riley is ready to bring her here, if you would like her to come and see you or your family. Or we can check out tomorrow and go to Chicago." She is desperate to please him. Whatever he wants to do after this news, she will comply.

He keeps his hands on her waist and rubs his nose against hers. "No, not yet. I'd like us to fly straight to Rochester, if we could. I need to tie up loose ends and then I'm coming with you to Chicago."

Loose ends? Does he mean the business? She makes the choice not to question it for now.

"Okay."

"I also have to call my mum."

"Okay."

She holds his face in her hands and kisses him. "I love you, Simon. You see, even when you thought I'd left you behind, I'd taken a part of you everywhere with me."

He slides his hands under her blouse and feels her skin, with eyes closed, he touches her, teases her, until she arches her back while he trails his lips down her neck. She holds his hands in place, and cups them tighter.

She's a woman now, with a child, with wounds that may never heal. Time might have passed between them, but her heart has been his since she was twenty-six years old. She senses his need to know that. He lifts her skirt up and caresses her. She breaks from him, planting both toes on the ground so he can unzip himself. "Show me, Tess. Take me deep inside you and show me how much you love me."

fifty

"**B**aby, let's try tomorrow," Simon says, his arm around Tessa who's been standing across the street from the restaurant on Rue Destin for twenty minutes. They had just come from a visit to the hospital where she'd stayed for two months.

"No. I have to do this." She exhales loudly and steps forward.

"But you're shaking." Simon rubs her shoulders and dips his head, so his lips are grazing her ear.

She takes his right hand from her shoulder and holds it tightly, pulling him toward the entrance. They ask to be seated outside. She has no point of comparison. She doesn't remember the place, what it looked like, or whether it has changed since. Simon has helped her to relax considerably. They order some red wine and speak casually. He tries hard to keep the conversation at an even keel, but then he realizes she's back to normal.

"Does it look the same? The place?" she asks, as the server brings them an order of carpaccio. She feels ashamed. She asks herself why she's taken so long to yearn for healing. She wonders how long it was until they reopened. How the restaurant owner who lost his wife could miss her every single day. Like she did Jacob.

You see? Everyone must find a way to move on. The thing is, Ciel may have been brought to life the night before this. This place has brought her sorrow, but also joy.

He nods his head. "As I remember." He doesn't tell her everything has been redesigned. The bar takes on a new look, lots of chrome, no tiles. It's also been moved to a completely different area. The blood spatters and bullet holes are gone, but they're still all he can see.

"Dr. Mathieu said you lost your job because you stayed at the hospital with me."

He shrugs. "I'd been wanting to branch out anyway. Start my own thing. It wasn't like I didn't have a plan. It was the right time."

"Thank you, Simon. For everything."

He places his hand on hers and keeps it there. They work through their food with one hand, anchored together to this place, this moment, the past, the future. Simon's phone begins to beep.

"It's my family," he says, smiling. She giggles as he tries to maneuver the phone with his free hand. Tessa tries to pull the other hand away.

"No," he orders.

Tessa laughs. "You're on Facetime now too? Wow! You techie."

His mom's face appears. She looks radiant. Prettier than Tessa remembers. Beside her is Adrian, who's holding the phone and panning it from side to side.

"Hello, lovely couple!" Adrian greets them.

"Hi, Mum, Adrian."

"Tessa! So nice to see you!" their mom exclaims.

"Hi, Mrs. Fremont! Hi Adrian," Tessa says, her grin sheepish, unsure.

"I am being told I have a new granddaughter! My first one! Adrian, here, has three boys now."

"Yes, yes, you do!" Tessa answers. "Would you like to see her?" She fishes into her purse and pulls out her wallet. She places a picture of Ciel, dressed as a ballerina in all pink, in front of the camera.

Mrs. Fremont's hand flies to her mouth and she begins to cry. "Oh, my! Oh, my! She's beautiful! She looks just like Simon when he was that age."

"Except she has more hair," Simon jokes.

"When can we meet her?" Mrs. Fremont asks.

"As soon as you want." Tessa loops her arm around Simon's.

"We have to go now, Mum, I'll call later. Back in St. Paul tomorrow evening."

"Simon! Dad and I will come visit soon. Adrian will help make the arrangements."

"Brill!" Simon says. "See you bro. Talk soon. Love you both."

Tessa waves at them before the screen goes black.

It was the best sleep he's had in years. Granted, they were exhausted after walking around Paris all afternoon. In the evening, they stayed in. Ordered dinner for two at the hotel, drank some champagne and enjoyed each other for hours until they both fell asleep.

Simon squints his eyes as they open to a golden streak of sunshine filtering in through the windows. He turns around, missing her face, craving her touch, and is shocked when she's not there. He flicks his head up and looks around the room.

Their suitcases are all packed up, Ciela's toys still on the floor as they'd left them. She didn't leave him.

Relieved but worried, he searches the suite for her, walks quickly down the narrow hallway from the bedroom to the sitting room, and then turns toward the bathroom. When he doesn't find her, he steps out onto the balcony and looks out into the street. He knows where she's gone.

Before we leave, I'd like to check those gardens out. It looks like a maze from here, doesn't it? I wonder if people actually get lost in those trees.

Simon is dressed and out the door in ten minutes. He makes his way across the *Place de Vendome* to *Rue de Rivoli*. Tessa's maze is the *Terrasse de Feuillants*—a long pathway lined with groves of Chestnut, Elm and Lime trees, neatly manicured and shaped. Simon walks along the road until he reaches *Place de la Concorde*. As he enters the park, he is met by a grand big wheel. Since it's the middle of the day, no one's there.

He sees her immediately. Seated on a green park chair facing a large pond named the *Fontaine des Fleuves*.

He breathes a sigh of relief as he approaches and kneels on the ground next to her. "You're not going to get me to go on that again," he says quietly.

She doesn't acknowledge his presence, keeping her eyes on the Ferris wheel in front of them. He's struck with fear as he sees she's been crying. Her eyes are swollen, her nose is red. She's hugging her purse to her chest.

But before he can do anything, she starts to speak. "It was because you fainted, the reason I said all that. The stress of what happened was too much for you. Sleepless nights, I guess. All the time you spent taking care of me at *Pitie'*. I couldn't bear to think about losing you, too. So, I sent you away. I think I knew." She turns to look at him. "I think I knew that you were sick. It was a different kind of bullet, but it would take you away too."

"Tessa." He reaches out for her, but she leans back, avoiding his touch.

"That night, you were asking him about the wine. 2006 Bourgogne Pinot Noir. The owner. He stayed at our table and gave us an education on wine. You told him you would retire in Paris and work for him. You enjoyed his company so much," she says, her tone flat, emotionless. She sniffs. "His wife, she asked us three times whether we were enjoying ourselves. She looked at a picture of Henry. He was Jewish, you know. And she was Algerian. She died in his arms during the attack. There were three birthday parties going on that night. Everyone was laughing, celebrating. You asked me to marry you. I said yes without thinking. I loved you more than I ever imagined I could love anyone. I was thinking that night, that my love for you combined my love for my parents and Jake. That you were the world to me and nothing else mattered."

Simon begins to sob. He, too, is awash in the torment of their past.

She reaches for his arm, without removing her gaze from the sky. She doesn't console him. "Jake looked so handsome. He was wearing another button-down shirt. Green, this time. The afternoon before, I'd convinced him to buy a pair of expensive jeans from *Saint Honore'.*" She giggles maniacally. "He wore them that night. I remember his laugh most of all. He was so happy because Riley was missing her period and so they thought she might be pregnant. And then you left with her to go to the store. He talked to me then, told me how happy he was for us. I was trying to get him to promise to go to London often. He told me he knew we would be fine, that I'd found the one for me."

"Tess," he whispers, at a loss for words.

She releases his hand and rummages through her purse. Her actions are wooden, urgent. Mechanical, like she's a machine on a mission.

"I need to call Riley. Where's my phone?" She finds it shortly after, hidden in the side pocket. She dials Riley's number and puts the phone to her ear. The volume is loud enough for Simon to hear voices, but he can't make out the words.

"Riley!" Tessa squeals. "He held me down, wrapped his body around me. I begged him to let me go, I couldn't see anything." There is silence on the other line. Tessa goes on. "He told me to tell you he loved you so much. That you were his home. I never gave you that message. I'm so sorry, Riley. I'm so sorry!"

She knows the high-pitched wail through the speaker is loud enough for Simon to hear. Riley sounds inconsolable. And Tessa sits in silence and listens. She doesn't mute Riley's screams. As if she needs to hear them. She closes her eyes and keeps the phone on her ear. The howling continues. There she sits, absorbing the sounds, wishing they would cleanse her, run through her veins.

And then he hears Riley's voice. "I'm sorry, Tessa. I'm sorry I left you in the hospital. My parents came to take me away after my miscarriage!"

"I know, I know, Rye. Please don't apologize. Simon was there. He was with me all that time," Tessa cries. "And I told you once that I was already dead. But I'm not! I'm alive because of Jake. Because of Simon. Because of you!"

Riley's voice rises a pitch and she's hysterical once again. "What do I do, Tess? It hurts so much! I miss him every single day. He was my air! He was my everything!"

"Shh, shh," Tessa says. This time she turns to Simon and smiles. "I'm okay," she mouths to him. "See you at the hotel."

Simon knows that Tessa will be fine. She wants to spend time alone with Riley. She wants to be there for her friend like the way her friend was there for her. Simon stands up and kisses Tessa on the mouth. She allows him to taste her, caressing his face in silent assurance that she is present. And then he gives her the space she needs. He leaves her to herself at the park.

PART III:

When They Believe

fifty-one

Simon's private plane lands at the St. Paul downtown airport exactly ten hours after the couple leaves Paris.

Tessa immediately senses a change in him upon deplaning. He's turned all business, providing instructions to the copilot to have their bags brought directly to his apartment and addressing his limo driver in a very formal manner. It makes her wonder about a number of things, but she knows she'll find out soon.

When she returned to the hotel after her phone call with Riley, Tessa was full of memories. Her recollection of what transpired before and after the tragedy had come back and she was slowly finding her peace. As far as she's concerned, Simon could call all the shots going forward. It's going to be a long process, getting from here, adjusting to the fact that he has a family. She wants to give him all the space he needs.

"You didn't tell me you lived at the Lowry," she says as they buckle themselves into the backseat of the car.

"You know it?"

"Jake wanted to buy a place there when he was interning at Mayo. Of all places, a historic building!" she exclaims.

"It's been redone quite nicely." He takes her hand and places it on his lap. "Speaking of Mayo, that's where we're going. I have someone you need to meet."

"Oh?" she asks. He turns to look out the window and says nothing.

The hour drive to Rochester is light and easy. Simon watches the news in the car and she falls into a deep sleep. When they arrive, he leads her down a long and endless hallway toward a bed of elevators ensconced in large white columns. They get off on the 11th floor. Tessa halts abruptly as she sees the sign—*Pulmonary and Critical Care.*

"No."

Simon takes her into his arms.

"No, Simon. What is this?"

He keeps her in his arms and whispers in her ear. "It's all right, baby. I just want you to meet with my doctor so you're well informed and whatever decision you—"

"I've made my decision," she says, turning around and running back to the elevators. "I don't need to know this today. There'll be time. I promise, I'll learn all about this later. I've made my decision. I'm staying with you. Nothing will change. Please, take me home."

"I'm going to die." He chases after her.

"We're all going to die," she says, refusing to look at him. There's a knife in her heart, twisting, turning, digging itself in.

She slaps the down arrow repeatedly, making sure its clicking sound drowns out the rest of his words.

"Come on, Tess. You know what I mean."

She whips around to face him. "Then I'll take a minute, an hour, a day, whatever I can. We're going home, and we'll deal with this later."

There has been no end to these tears. How long has it been without a day of tears? Why is this happening? She wants to go home to Ciel; she wants to see Riley and Liam. And she wants Simon to see her home. The home she built with their story.

And then it all begins to make sense. "You were always in a hurry. Everything you accomplished. Me. You. Us."

"Yes. When I look back to those wasted years, there is so much I could have done. I was healthier then. All I had to do then was pack a suitcase and be on my way. Things are different now. I love you, Tess. But I'm running out of time."

"No. Stop it. Don't say that." She covers her ears while looking away.

"You have to know," he says, all the while trying to pull her into him.

She succumbs. They stand in the hall wrapped around each other. "And now, this is why you didn't want to proceed directly to see your daughter."

"Yes," Simon admits again. "I want to tell you all about my illness, make you aware that..." He stops. "Make you aware so that if you don't want me in her life—"

"Of course, I want you in her life! In my life! Simon, please, please, don't do this to me."

She cries in his arms while he strokes her hair, rubs her back. And then she pulls away, her view so blurred by her distress, she just wants to break free. Slowly, she paces on autopilot, unaware of her surroundings.

She sees herself moving but she's nowhere near. She's out somewhere flying through the sky in a hot air balloon.

The sound of a shutting door interrupts her reverie. She comes crashing down into a pile of leaves. Simon is there to hold her, laughing as he shakes the dirt off her face.

An elderly man with silver hair enters the room. "Hi there, Simon," he says as they shake hands.

"Dr. Butterfield, this is Tessa Talman."

"Excuse me," she says, turning around to swipe the tears from her face with the back of her hands. She clears her throat, straightens up her blouse and faces both men with an outreached arm. "Hi, doctor, nice to meet you."

Simon is amazed at the transformation. What luck! To be loved by this incredible woman.

"Talman. The esteemed Richard Talman?" Dr. Butterfield tilts his head and stares at her. "I should have known. You're his daughter and Jacob was your brother."

"Yes, sir."

"I am honored to meet you. Your father was a pioneer, an innovator in the field of medicine. And your brother, I was blessed to have him as a student."

She turns to Simon and smiles. He squeezes her hand, filled with pride. "Thank you, doctor."

A brief second of silence follows. And then Dr. Butterfield sets his clasped hands on the table in front of him. He crosses his eyes, looking stern and tough, the lines on his face more pronounced. "Simon, where's your portable oxygen?"

"I…" Simon looks down at the floor, like a child being chastised.

"And you took a flight to Paris against doctor's orders. Do you know what the air pressure could have done to you and your heart? You took a big risk, young man."

Simon sees the look of surprise on Tessa's face. "It's that bad?" Tessa asks.

"Simon has early stages of Pulmonary Hypertension. His heart and lungs are working extra hard to keep pumping oxygen into his body. There's no cure for this disease. Unfortunately, he has to live with it and make significant changes in his lifestyle."

Simon remains quiet. He knows Tessa will step in.

And she does. "Such as?"

"Well, he's had a heart attack. Heart failure is inevitable. But with proper management, there's no telling how long we can keep it at bay. He can no longer do any strenuous exercises, so climbing mountains"—he pauses and looks at Simon—"is out of the question. He's currently a Class II, which means he has started experiencing symptoms—shortness of breath, chest pain, fatigue—with normal activity. He's always been a healthy guy, so this is by no means a death sentence."

Tessa's chest twinges with pain at the mention of that word. She rapidly composes herself. There's no room for weakness at this point. She needs to take care of him. He is her heart. "Is this why you moved here? To Minnesota?" she asks Simon.

"Yes. I'd been having check-ups so often, it was getting difficult for me to fly back and forth."

"Airplanes, airports, public places that can weaken his immunity are a no-no," Dr. Butterfield stresses. "Regular exercise, which I know he has no problem with, oxygen therapy and medication will be his maintenance regimen. What Simon wants me to make clear to you, however, is that there is no cure for this. Some people die in two years, others live for more."

Tessa pushes the bile that has risen in her throat back down where it belongs. *I just found him.* "Nothing you've told me, nothing I will ever find out about this disease, will make me change my mind. I am committed to Simon, to our family, to our life together. I'm not going anywhere. I'll be moving here as soon as I can. In a few days at the most. I just have to leave to pick up our daughter."

"Congratulations, Simon!" Dr. Butterfield exclaims.

Simon says nothing. He wants her to have the time to absorb this information. There is time to change her mind. She doesn't know what it's like to take care of a sick man.

"Is there anything else I can help you with? Any questions I can answer?" Dr. Butterfield asks.

Tessa shakes her head. "No, not for now, I don't think so. Thank you for the time you took to meet with us today."

Simon looks at the doctor and mutters. "Sex."

"What is it, Simon?" the doctor asks.

"You forgot to explain about the sex," Simon says, turning beet red.

"Oh yes," he says in agreement. "Tessa, Simon wanted me to make sure I explained things to you. You have no need to worry, no need to cut down on sexual activity. If it doesn't cause him to have shortness of breath or chest pains, then he should be fine. I always tell my patients to just remember to take it slow and to listen to their body. And PPH doesn't limit his ability to father another child, although his medication may reduce sperm count. Oh, and the head is never good below the heart. Just keep it in mind when you guys choose your positions."

"That's my guy," Tessa squeaks, trying with all her might to stop the tears from cascading down her face. "Priorities."

fifty-two

It's chaos back in Chicago. Tessa can't bear to be away from Simon for more than a few days. She hires the big guns to accomplish the world's fastest move. There are packing boxes everywhere, workers and movers are in every part of her home.

"Honey, are we marking the boxes correctly? The blue ones are for storage and the white ones go to St. Paul," Riley shouts from the kitchen at Liam, who's busy figuring the cable wires out.

"Yup."

Ciela sits next to him on the floor, playing with her new Les Coquettes rag dolls, a gift from her father, along with many other toys from Paris. She's busy trying to push Manon, the baby boy, toward Liam.

"What, baby?" Liam asks.

"Bed!" Ciela answers.

"Okay, you want me to put him to bed. Let's do this." He places the doll on the wooden bed and pulls the blanket over him. Simon had gone overboard. A dollhouse.

"Hey, hey!" Tessa walks into the living room, scoops Ciela into her arms and showers her with kisses. "Where's Auntie Rye?"

"Hello! How was it?" Riley saunters in and sits down on the couch. Tessa follows suit.

"It was good. I listed the house and also called the manager of Jake's condo to let him know the boxes will be stored there for now. Until we know where we're going to be. How many did we end up with?"

"Six boxes to St. Paul. The rest will stay until you let us know," Riley answered.

"Sweet."

"How is Will?"

"Great, I think. He's dating someone from his office." Tessa smiles.

Liam takes a seat next to the women. Riley leans over to give him a kiss. Ciela pulls on his hand and motions for him to take her to the kitchen. "Dwink."

Riley stands. "Oh, I'll get it, Ciely. Let's go."

"No!" Ciela squeaks, pointing at Liam.

The two leave for the kitchen while Tessa takes Riley in her arms. "I'll miss you, Rye. We should probably be getting ready. We leave for O'Hare in an hour."

Riley nods. "Tess, thank you for everything. You didn't have to do that. And all the paintings you gave us—they're worth so much!"

"Jake would have wanted you to have that money. He was saving that for you. I'm glad the trust was able to change it to your name before I left."

"It's a million dollars."

"Keep him in your heart. In your memories. Tell your children about him someday. About how wonderful your life was with him. Give them a taste of that with this money. As for the paintings, I'll have many more after these books are written."

Liam is back. This time, Ciela has a bottle in her mouth. Her eyelids are heavy; she's trying to keep them open. Tessa gently lays her on the couch and kisses each eyelid closed. "Okay, baby, stay here and drink your bottle while Mommy gets our things together, okay? We're going to be seeing Daddy today!"

The three friends stand together, arms locked around each other.

"Thank you, Liam. For taking care of my friend," Tessa whispers. "And for taking care of my child as if she were your own."

"It's been my pleasure," Liam says. "We'll see you soon, okay? The Uber's here. I'm going to start loading the car." He leaves the two women alone.

"As always, there are no words," Riley says. "And I'm crying because I'll miss you. But I'm happy for you, Tess. You deserve this. I'll see you in two weeks, okay? We'll come visit when you're settled."

"I love you, Rye. And congratulations again on your pregnancy. Take it easy, okay? Try to get as much rest as possible. I can't wait to spoil another little Riley."

"I will. I love you too."

Tessa walks over to Ciela and carries her sleeping daughter in her arms. The two friends walk out the front door. Tessa turns to her with an afterthought.

"You're my home too, Riley."

"Thank you," Tessa tells the driver as he unlocks the door to Simon's apartment and deposits their luggage near the front entrance. Somehow, Simon had neglected to tell her he occupied the two-story penthouse atop the Lowry building in downtown St. Paul. Opulent isn't quite the word she thinks of to describe this place, but it sure is close to it. She sets Ciel down on the floor and remains holding her hand.

"Now to find Daddy," she says as they both walk slowly across the checkered black and white Italian marble floor leading from the passageway to the living area. The transition to aged wood floors makes their footsteps a little louder. For sure, he would hear them. She can't contain her excitement. "Okay, Ciely. Let's practice. What are you going to call your daddy?"

"Wiw?" Ciela says with a big smile. Smart girl, already getting her father's wisecracking abilities at such a young age.

"Yes of course, sweetie. He will always be your Uncle Will. But you have a daddy."

"Dada."

"Perfect." They walk around some more. Here's the kitchen. Wood floors, white marble counter tops.

On the far right, by the large vase of fresh flowers stands a flask of Cristal, two glasses, and a cup of apple juice.

Tessa skims her finger along the side of the bottle, raises her eyes toward the sky and gives thanks.

Oh, and this must be the family room. Need to do something about those sharp stone fixtures. And these stairs? Ciel can crack her head open on one of these. And the railing? Metal and wood, very chic. Very unsafe. Lots of childproofing to do here. Where is the bedroom?

"Simon?" Tessa calls out to him. "We're here!"

The atmosphere changes significantly. What started out as a warm and cozy feeling upon entering the home has turned into an eerie stillness. It's peculiarly quiet. She wonders whether he's left to go to the store to pick up some things. He had called her every fifteen minutes at the airport. He spoke to Ciela as they boarded the plane and he called again as they landed. Where can he be?

Tessa leads Ciela back into the front room. She didn't feel right about checking his things out in his absence. He'll be here soon. She's sure he's left to get some last-minute items, maybe take a walk around the block to calm his excitement.

"Let's sit here for a while, baby," she rests on the white suede couch with chrome borders and legs. *This won't work,* she thinks. *Too many potential dangers.* Although Simon did mention converting a part of the second floor into a suite and play area for their baby.

More time passes and before she knows it, Ciel has toys spread all over the floor. The door swings open just as Tessa decides to call the doorman downstairs.

"Hi!" Tessa begins to run toward him. She stops momentarily to grab Ciel's hand. "Come, Ciela, let's go to Daddy!"

Something is off. His face is ghastly—white as a sheet.

"Dada?"

Simon stands motionless, a slight smile crosses his lips.

He sways back and forth.

And his eyes roll back.

He clutches his chest and falls to the ground.

"Simon! Simon!" Tessa runs to him. "Oh God, please help us! Simon!" she screams at the top of her lungs.

fifty-three

What feels like an eternity is really only fifteen minutes. That's how long it takes for the ambulance to arrive at the penthouse. By dusk, Riley and Liam are at the hospital to take Ciela to the Marriott across the street. Tessa sits in a metal chair next to his bed, her hand gripping his, eyes closed, her forehead resting on his arm. The sounds made by the machines are deafening. They're shrill and thin and sharp. Every second, something goes off. The numbers on the monitor change continuously and she has no clue what they mean. She wants to pray but she doesn't know how. She tries to talk to Jacob. To her parents. But she finds no process, no cohesion in her thoughts. There's discordance and anger and confusion. But since she doesn't believe in anything, she doesn't even know who's to blame.

She looks up just as someone enters the room.

"Tessa," the kind old gentleman says.

"Hi, Doctor B."

"Would you like to step outside so we can talk?"

She follows him out the door. They stand to the side; her arms are crossed tight and he's pulling out the green shower cap on his head. At least that's what it looks like. He's still wearing those same green shower caps on his feet.

"That was quite a scare, wasn't it?" he starts out.

Nodding has been her favorite thing to do lately.

"Well, at first I was worried about his liver. I thought maybe it would be inflamed. That's one of the effects of the extra effort the heart needs to make to produce oxygen. But his liver is fine. What I think happened, and we won't find out until he wakes up, is that he exercised too much. That boy overestimates his fitness. He needs to slow down."

She breathes a sigh of relief. "So, he'll be okay?"

"You need to make sure he slows down, Tessa. Yes, he's okay now. But lifestyle changes really have to be made. These are warning signs. Remember, it's a progressive disease. I've given him a sedative and we'll keep him on oxygen while he sleeps. He can be discharged when he wakes up."

"Oh, Dr. B!" She runs into his arms.

She catches him by surprise. He stiffly pats her head. Once. Twice. "The medical van will take two oxygen tanks over to your home. He will need to use it every night when he sleeps."

"For good?"

"For good."

"Dr. B, I'll defer to Simon's decision at the end of the day, but I'm going to suggest to him that we move back to London to be close to his family." She'd been thinking about it all afternoon.

"What about yours?" he asks. His glasses slide down to the tip of his nose and he pushes it up with his finger. "Won't they object to that?" As soon as he utters those words, he catches himself. "Oh Lord. I'm sorry. I'd forgotten your situation."

"He's all I have," she answers.

"Well, I have a wonderful colleague at St. Thomas Hospital who will gladly take his case. Simon has a great reputation back home in the field of scientific medicine. He has done so much for the community, I'm sure they will be happy to take good care of him."

"Thank you, Doctor B," she says, smiling. She sees bits and pieces of her father in him. When she was growing up, everyone she met, people in the street, in the stores, would tell her what a kind and generous man her father was. He held free clinics on the south side of Chicago, in the projects every weekend. They loved him. She could tell that Dr. B was that kind of a man.

When she reenters the room, he's still unconscious. She sits on the side of his bed, her legs dangling to the side, hands on either side of his body. The oxygen mask has shifted slightly. She leans over and gently repositions it on his face. Lovingly, she touches his forehead, his eyebrows, his eyelids. She follows each touch with a kiss. And then she allows her lips to linger on his cheek. "Mom, Dad. Jake," she whispers. "If you can hear me now, please give us the gift of a few years. Give me a chance to fill his heart with so much love, it will transcend time and space and everything we've missed. Make him stay long enough to see what a beautiful, strong and intelligent daughter we have made. This is the love you've always wanted for me. This is it, I finally have it. And I'm begging you to intercede with the heavens for me."

With those words, she wraps her arms and legs around him, closes her eyes and falls asleep.

They are dancing. She's laughing in his arms as he sweeps her across the floor, his bright blue eyes glimmering with delight.

"I still can't believe I made it all the way to this day!" he says happily, while mouthing the words to their favorite song.

She glances around the room, curious to see where they are and who is with them. A striking young woman with long brown hair and bright blue eyes, walks toward them on the arm of a handsome young man. She realizes it's Ciela; they are at their daughter's wedding.

Tessa's overpowering joy makes her cry. Simon reaches out to console her, his touch light at first, right before she hears his voice.

"Don't cry."

She lifts her head as she opens her eyes. He's awake! He's pushed the mask away from his mouth so he could speak.

She springs upward and turns to him. "Oh, Simon!" she fixes the mask on his face, keeps it on his nose only enough to expose his lips so she could kiss him.

"I'm sorry," he mumbles, his voice hoarse and weak.

"No, no. Don't be. I'm here now. I'm here, you'll be okay."

"No," he says turning red. "I'm really sorry. It was such a stupid thing for me to do."

"What? What did you do?"

"The elevator was taking forever, and I knew you were waiting at the apartment. So, I walked the ten flights of stairs."

"You what?" She gasped. "Oh, baby. We really need to make some changes, okay? I know you want to do all the things you're used to doing, but you must stay well. For me. For Ciela. For our family." She leans in and brushes her lips against his ear. "For our sex life."

He lets out a squeak. He's still too weak to laugh. "Sold."

"Simon, I was thinking. Do you think we could talk about moving back to London? I think it would be better if we were close to your family. They could spend time with Ciel. It can be a new adventure for us. You know, starting a new life in a new place."

"I've thought about that. What do you think about my business?"

"We can try to sell it?" Tessa's tone was shy and timid. She didn't want to overstep her bounds. She wanted him to make his own decision. Come to terms with what he had successfully built on his own. She knew his net worth, and he knew hers. They had discussed it in London, even before their trip to Paris. Back then, they were already considering the consolidation of their investments.

"Let's keep it. Who knows? Ciel may want to study in the Midwest at some point."

"So, we're doing it? We're moving to London?" Tessa asks, thankful for his concurrence.

"If that's okay with you, yes, I would like to spend as much time with my family. With you and Ciel."

"I have the perfect idea," Tessa purrs, her eyes fixed solidly on him. "You just lay around all day looking hot, and I'll write books. You'll be my muse."

Another squeaky, wheezy laugh.

Tessa hops off the bed and takes something out of her purse. She walks back to the other side but remains standing in front of him. "Simon?"

"Yes babe?"

"Are you there yet?"

"I've been there since you stepped on my seat with your boots," he says with a wide grin. At that moment, he's the man she met forever and a day ago, the one with the sparkling blue eyes, the one who just couldn't say goodbye.

"Then, marry me," she says, placing a bright orange object in his hand. He cups his fingers around it, holding it tightly as if it is the most precious thing he's ever held. And then his tears begin to fall as he shakes his head in surprise. He unwraps it to find a half-eaten chocolate egg with a gold-plated ring on the bottom. "It was in one of the eggs you sent for Ciela."

Nothing is coincidence.

He can't help himself. He laughs out loud. Loud enough that the nurse comes running in just as he begins to cough.

"Don't mind us," he says to the nurse, waving her back out of the room. And then he whips away the mask completely, pulls her to him and kisses her. "Yes," he mumbles against her lips. "Yes, right away."

"Look who's heeeeeerrree!" He would know that voice anywhere. "Sayyy-moonnnn! Look who's here!"

Riley and Liam enter the room with the most beautiful little girl he has ever seen. Ciel wiggles in her arms and reaches out toward Simon. "Da?"

Tessa adjusts the bed so Simon can sit up. She places the mask on his nose once again. Simon opens his arms, his eyes filled with tears. "Come here, my beautiful little baby."

Tessa, Riley and Liam watch as father and daughter cuddle and hug and kiss and coo at each other. He holds out his arm to Tessa and beckons her to join them.

"You see," she says, clasping his hand and bringing it to her lips. "We don't have to travel to see the world. We have everything we need, right here."

"Thank you, Tessa," he whispers, holding his daughter close to his heart. "Thank you for giving me my life back."

One hour later, Dr. Butterfield comes to check on Simon and signs the permission for discharge. Two hours later, Tessa and Ciela are walking hand in hand as a lovely nurse named Rachel pushes Simon in a wheelchair. They walk down a long white hallway, past the emergency department and on to the emergency entrance. A little stoop about two steps high separates the hospital from the street. Between them is a big, bold orange line marking the end of the hospital property.

"Wait, stop!" Tessa shrieks. She looks at Rachel and then at Simon. The nurse signals for Simon to stand up. It's the end of the line for her and she expects their car to drive up so Simon can get into it. But Tessa has other ideas. She takes Simon's hand in her right and Ciela's hand on her left. Together, they stand with their feet right on the orange line.

"Simon!" She turns to him with a glint in her eye.

He looks back at her with the same expression. He knows where she's going with this and he's up for it. She watches him pull his shoulders back and hold his head up high before taking a deep breath.

"Let's do it, let's just do it, Simon!" she screeches. "When I say three, we go for it, okay? Just like we did before. Here we go: ONE. TWO. THREE! JUMP Simon! Ciela! Let's JUMP!"

And together, they rise with the wind and soar across the sky.

acknowledgements

For the past few years, the city of Paris and its remarkable people have welcomed me as a second home. And although the names and places have been fictionalized in this book, the tragedy that took place two years ago at various points in the city (Stade, Bataclan, Petite Cambodge, Le Carillon, Belle Equipe, Boulevard Voltaire) was very real. I worked in Saint Denis, knew people who went to the concert, received calls from friends late that November afternoon in 2015, and cried for those whose lives were lost. This book honors the brave men and women who perished in that massacre, as well as the loved ones that were left behind.

They are the true heroes.

This book is also a testament to the brevity of life and the importance of living it to the fullest. See the world, learn about other cultures. When you open your eyes up to others, you begin to see yourself clearly.

This list gets shorter with every new book, but the same people have stayed through the years, and that means the world to me. So, THANK YOU:

Italia Gandolfo, for always believing in me no matter what.

Vesuvian Books, Vesuvian Media and **Liana Gardner** for your faith in this story.

Spark Books, Anvil Publishing, Xandra Ramos and **Andrea**

Flores for the honor of publishing in my home country.

Sarah Hansen of **Okay Creations** for this amazing book cover.

Jim Thomas, my editor – who continually teaches me how to be a better writer.

Holly Atkinson, for your impeccable line editing.

Meryl Moss of **Meryl Moss Media**, for your friendship and tireless efforts to get this book out in the world.

Angela McLaurin of Fictional Formats for taking care of all my books and making them look beautiful.

Stuart Reardon for your image, **Golden Czermak** and **Reggie Denching** for your help and collaboration in getting Stuart's image.

Ashley Baker, you are the best PA ever.

To all the **BLOGGERS** who have supported me through the years. **Giselle of Espresso Tours** for organizing our blog tours. Everything you do for us, the small authors – your actions, your kindness and your generosity have changed our lives. **Nelly Martinez Aguilar**, who got stuck reading this book. Again. And who just stays, no matter what. **Michelle Kannan** for your love. You don't love many people, so I feel honored. **Leylah Attar**, in sickness and in health, for running to the pharmacy for me every time we're together. **All the wonderful authors and colleagues, who have supported me through the years. Thank you for continuing to inspire me every day.**

My Butterflies – there are more than one hundred of us now, and so I can't name you all. But you know who you are and what you stand for. You are all amazing human beings, and I am honored to be one among all of you. I love you so much.

Mi familia (B.R.A.E.) for allowing me to live my dreams. Living two lives isn't easy. And I get to live both sides of my life to the fullest because of you.

And to all of you who have read, will read, will review, will recommend and talk about the story of Simon and Tessa – from the bottom of my heart, I THANK YOU. Your love and constant encouragement have kept me afloat.